The Candy Capers

KATY BERRITT

Black Rose Writing | Texas

ISBN: 978-1-68433-947-1
PUBLISHED BY BLACK ROSE WRITING
www.blackrosewriting.com

Printed in the United States of America
Suggested Retail Price (SRP) $20.95

The Candy Capers is printed in Calluna

*As a planet-friendly publisher, Black Rose Writing does its best to eliminate unnecessary waste to reduce paper usage and energy costs, while never compromising the reading experience. As a result, the final word count vs. page count may not meet common expectations.

Dedicated to:

My sister Sherry, who edits way better than I do.
Thank you for your expertise.

My daughter Beret, who runs her own business, takes care of a husband
and two children under the age of three, and yet still found the time to
put up with endless inane questions about how to get set up on
Facebook, Instagram, Twitter, my web page, my blog etc, etc, etc,
And yet I still can't manage to do it myself.
I'm going to have to hire someone.

To my critique group, who told me I could do it,
and cheered when I did.

Cast

Our Heroine Candace McCready
Our Hero Gabe Jones
Our Murder Victim Fred Jones

Fred's Wife #1 Susan Jones
Mother of Gabe - our hero

Fred's Wife #2 Wendy
Mother of Candace - our heroine.

Fred's Wife #3 Vanessa Luckless - Society bitch
Mother of Twins -
Lance Luckless - Icky Tattoo guy
Lucy Luckless - Scary Goth Chick

Fred's Wife #4 Tiffany Tempest - Gorgeous Las Vegas dancer
Julian Romano - her Boyfriend aka the Greaseball

Fred's Wife #5 Hillary Hickok - Aspiring country western-singer
Gone to Nashville but not forgotten

Others
Murray Jones – Mister Toad - Brother of Fred
Junior Jones – The Tadpole - Murray's son
Floyd Daniels - Pseudo butler and all-round mooch

The Candy Capers

Pro

He looked so natural lying there in his ratty green Barca-Lounger, a box of Contessa Bourbon Cherry Chocolates sitting opened in his lap and a streak of dark chocolate smeared across his chubby cheeks.

It wasn't until Candace McCready picked several dozen candy wrappers up off the ten-thousand-dollar Aubusson rug and tugged the mostly empty box of chocolates out of his slack hands that she realized the small scarlet splotch in the middle of her stepfather's chest wasn't one of the trademark red foil wrappers from his candy company.

Oh shit! What would Contessa Chocolates and Confectionery do without the Contessa?

1 Gummi Bears and Greedy Heirs

The Sweet Tooth
New York City

The store was a carousel of eye-popping colors. Barney purple, neon green, and Day-Glo orange candies filled clear Lucite bins standing sentinel on the red, white, and blue polka-dotted linoleum floor. Ribbon-tied bouquets of all-day suckers in swirls of red, yellow, and green adorned the corners of the counters while clear plastic bags of pink and baby-blue cotton candy hung from wires strung across the ceiling. Colorful metal buckets nailed to the wall held bags filled with a hundred different exotic sweets. The smell of sugar was enough to send a diabetic to intensive care.

But as far as Candace was concerned, even intensive care was preferable to listening to the greedy heirs who had gathered to "mourn" the Contessa, aka poor Fred Jones.

Still, she'd almost rather listen to their complaints than worry if Fred had kept the promise he'd made to her several years ago. If he hadn't, the alternative was ending up in the unemployment line. Not that being in the unemployment line was shameful or anything. Heck, half her friends were currently unemployed.

However, this wasn't about her; she'd survive just fine, or at least she thought so, but Contessa's five hundred employees might not. She bit off the thumbnail she had been nibbling. If only the attorneys would hurry.

Just then a dark shadow appeared at her side, making her jump a foot.

"How nice to see you again," the shadow said, but the tone of his voice implied differently.

Just what she needed, more grief. "Dolan," she responded, glancing down to find him giving her a narrow-eyed look in return. According to Law and Order, and every other TV cop show she had ever watched, police detectives were supposed to be tall, dark, and handsome. Dolan was short, fat and, well...ugly.

He smirked. "That's Sergeant Dolan to you." He rocked back and forth on his heels, hands on his chubby hips as he casually surveyed the gathering. "So, how's my favorite suspect?"

Candace gritted her teeth, wishing he would just disappear. She'd already seen more of him than she wanted during the three hours he interrogated her yesterday right after the murder.

"I wonder what your superiors will think," she told him. "When they find out you've made a big fat booboo?"

His smirk grew. "Oh, but I haven't."

"For God's sake. Why are you picking on me?" Yeah, weren't there a million other suspects he could chase?

He chuckled. Oddly, he seemed genuinely amused by her comment. Probably imagining how she would look in prison orange. With her blond hair, orange was *so* not her color.

"Let's see." He tapped his chin. "First of all, you have the most to gain by his death."

Geez, she could learn to hate this guy. Correction, she already hated him. "For the hundredth time...not necessarily. Only if Fred left me the business, but there's no guarantee he did." Yes, okay, so he promised he would, but she certainly wouldn't murder Fred to get it.

"He has a son, you know," she reluctantly added.

"Gabe Jones. Yes, so you said. But I learned he was disinherited so not much to gain."

She slapped a hand over her face.

"Secondly, you found the body," he continued. "About fifty percent of the time, the killer is the one who 'finds the body'."

"Seriously? Fifty percent?" She snorted. "You just made that up."

He had an expression on his face like a cat in cream. Yep, he'd made it up. "Give me a break, Dolan. Since my mom and I practically live in Fred's apartment, who else is going to find him?"

He gave her a look that said, *and yeah, how weird is that.* Okay, yeah, it was weird but then Fred was weird. Who else would take an eight-bedroom apartment and partition off two bedrooms and add a kitchen, all so his ex-wife, and her daughter Candace, could continue to live next door even though he'd remarried?

They both looked over to where the afore-mentioned ex-wife sat, waiting for the proceedings to begin. As if sensing their attention, Wendy turned away from the conversation she was having and lifted a hand to wave but somehow knocked her glasses off instead. They skidded across the room and ended up underneath one of the glass display cabinets. Ignoring the fact that she wore heels and a skirt, Wendy dropped to her knees and scrambled to retrieve them.

Oh boy. She loved her mother to death, but the woman had a mind like cotton candy. It seemed as if it had substance, but it was all air and spun sugar.

"Hmmm," Dolan murmured. "Personally, I think the culprit is you, but you said you had a few possible suspects you could point out, so go ahead, I'm open to suggestions."

Yeah, sure you are. Candace could tell just by the expression in his beady little eyes, she was, and would always be, his number one suspect. The man needed to get a brain. "Fine. How about her?" She pointed at an elegantly slim woman in her late forties on the other side of the room, looking down her long nose with a sneer on her face. Slouching at her side were two sullen twenty-somethings, Lance with his green hair, and Lucy with her black lipstick.

"Wife number three. Vanessa Luckless and the Goth Twins."

He cocked a brow at her description but made a note in his notebook. "Right. You mentioned her yesterday. I suppose it's possible but why?"

"She's obsessed with owning Fred's apartment and thinks he'll leave it to her."

"Hmm. What about the others you mentioned?"

"Number Four. Stage name, Tiffany Tempest." She pointed across the room at a gorgeous blond woman with enough curves for an Alpine road.

The detective's jaw dropped as he took in the woman's exquisite face, the mass of golden hair and a bosom that would make the gods weep. "And he divorced her? Good lord, why?"

"Turns out she had him on the side." Candace nodded toward the greaseball standing next to Tiffany. "Julian Romanzo, aka Julie, only don't call him that, you might lose something you want to keep." Candace loved a lot of things about Fred, but his taste in women, not so much.

"Mob?"

She wiggled a hand. Maybe, maybe not.

Dolan looked thoughtful. "Motive?"

"Revenge. When they divorced, Fred promised her he would buy her a gym then he reneged."

"All the more reason to let him live in hopes he would change his mind."

"No, he told her he left her enough in his will so she could buy her own gym. He's worth more to her dead than alive."

Dolan rolled his eyes but jotted something else in his notebook. "All right, anyone else?" he asked.

Candace felt a certain satisfaction at his response. Seemed the good detective wasn't so cock-sure anymore. "Oh, there's more although you can probably eliminate wife number five, Hillary Hickok, since she's been in Nashville for over a month."

"Good God. Okay, remind me again; how many wives did this guy have?" Dolan asked, sounding exasperated.

"Only five," she answered aloud, but inside she knew if he hadn't died, Hillary wouldn't have been the last. Fred had hit that midlife crisis thing where suddenly one woman wasn't enough. His problem was he wasn't satisfied just having them; he wanted to marry them.

"Only five." Dolan shook his head in disgust. "Fine. Keep going."

"Well, there's—"

At that moment, two men, dressed in black suits and white shirts, their dark hair slicked back in shiny helmets, climbed the stairs up to the tall podium and looked down on the crowd like two sleek ravens on a telephone wire overlooking their uglier vulture cousins. Candace breathed a sigh of relief. Finally, she would have some resolution to all her anxiety.

"Ahem," the first raven, Mister Mott, said. "Please, if everyone would take a seat. I'm about to read the will."

A mad dash for the chairs followed. Through sheer force of will, and a little judicious toe-stomping, Candace managed to wangle a spot next to the wall in front. She desperately wanted to know what the will said but inside her stomach threatened vile things at the possibilities. Everything, her life, and so many others, depended on what happened in the next few minutes.

Dolan followed. "Who else were you going to say?" he asked in a low voice.

Candace looked around. She started to tell Dolan about Fred's brother who sat in the front row, his buggy eyes intent on the podium but at that moment the door of the candy store erupted open, and a six-foot tall, dark-haired woman charged in. With a wide sweep of one arm she tossed her coat to the side as if she expected someone to catch it and hang it up. Amazingly, someone did.

"Her," Candace said grimly. "Susan Jones. Fred's first wife." And Gabe's mother.

"All right," Susan announced. "I'm here now. Let's get this show on the road." With a determined stride, she went to the front row and found a chair even though two seconds ago there wasn't an empty seat in sight. Once settled she held a hand out and a cup of coffee was placed there. The woman was magic, there was no other explanation.

Mister Mott cleared his throat. "Fred's instructions state that the will must be read within forty-eight hours of his death to insure the smooth continuation of the business, so we will now proceed." The attorney turned to the picture on an easel behind him. With a grand gesture, he drew back the black satin drape and revealed the enormous photo.

A hush fell over the room.

"Good God," the detective said, his eyes widening.

Candace glanced at him from the corner of her eye. She totally got his shock. Who would have thought that a picture of Fred Jones dressed in a nineteenth century gown, complete with lace collar and cameo, wearing a curly blond wig and the biggest, ugliest tiara in the Western hemisphere, would be unveiled? She had loved helping him pick out that outfit for the photoshoot.

"And there you have it," she whispered. "The Contessa."

"Good God," Dolan said again. "No wonder he was murdered."

"Hey! That was his favorite picture. It's the one he used on the Bourbon Cherry Chocolate box."

The attorney picked up a sheaf of papers and began reading. And reading. And reading. There were the usual gifts to this foundation and that foundation, blah, blah, blah. She tried not to worry, but it was taking the attorneys forever to get to the point, and every minute that passed was another minute when her life could take a left turn into hell.

"Yo," Julian Romanzo yelled. "Get to the good stuff."

Yeah, get to the good stuff. She needed to know what was going to happen to Contessa.

Mister Mott's beady black eyes got beadier. "And to Floyd Daniels, my assistant and general factotum," he continued doggedly. "I leave the sum of five hundred thousand dollars for his long-standing service and loyalty."

Everyone in the room turned to stare at the man, but Candace noticed Floyd looked pretty darned happy. As well he should. All that service and loyalty? It amounted to a minimal amount of obsequious kowtowing when Fred was in the same room and an enormous amount of whiskey tippling behind Fred's back.

A number of smaller bequests to a few loyal workers at the factory followed. Finally the attorney got to the end of the pages. He set them aside. "Fred asked me to play this for the rest of the will." He popped a video tape—geez, who the hell used video tape anymore?—into a VCR and hit *Play*.

Fred's face appeared on the TV screen hanging on the wall. "Okay, you greedy bastards," he said, looking larger than life and twice as cunning as when he was alive. Her eyes teared up at the sight. His death left a big hole in her life, and her heart.

The video continued. "I know you're all sitting there salivating over my goodies but don't worry, 'cause you're all going to get what you deserve."

He looked down at the paper in his lap. "Vanessa, I know you've always lusted after the Park Avenue apartment."

So true, Candace thought. From the minute she moved in, Vanessa coveted the place and had done everything in her power to get Candace and Wendy to move out.

"Sorry, kiddo," Video Fred continued. "I've got other plans for the place. But I *am* leaving you the parking spot I bought in the underground garage. Now you can truthfully say you have a Park Avenue address. Lance. Lucy. Sorry, kids, I paid for a year of private school, even though I'm not your father, thank God, so I don't owe the two of you anything else."

A loud bang resounded through the room as several tall towers of candy fell to the floor, courtesy of Lucy's steel-toed black brogues.

"That asshole!" she yelled, her black-lined eyes shooting fire. "I'll—"

"—kill the bastard," Lance whined. "Yeah, I know. But Lucy, like, he's already dead so—"

Lucy slapped him. His silver lip stud flew across the room and landed in the cotton candy maker. He rushed over to rescue it while Lucy and Vanessa stormed out of the store.

Candace shared a smile with her mother, who wasn't a fan of the twins either.

The video continued with a lifetime membership for Tiffany to Gold's Gym. She looked murderous while her boyfriend looked stunned. To his brother he left nothing, saying Murray already got his share when Fred bought him out in '05.

Video Fred paused. "Okay. That takes care of them. Now, let's get serious here." Another pause. "Susan," he said, looking directly into the camera. "You may think you deserve something for giving me Gabe, and for putting up with me for fifteen years but, sweetheart, I think the forty-five million in cash and the million a year you got in the divorce settlement was plenty for any woman."

Susan gasped. "But—" she said loudly then stopped, her mouth ajar as she looked around at the remaining heirs and heiresses who stared at her, avidly waiting to hear what she said next. Something in her eyes shifted. She stood, coolly surveyed the room, then turned and walked calmly to the door. Her magic being what it was, her coat was handed to her as she walked by, and the door held open. A cab pulled up to the curb before she even lifted her hand and she climbed in. See—magic.

Video Fred continued. "Okay. Now Wendy, I've got some serious things to say to you."

Candace turned toward her mother and was dismayed to see tears in her eyes. Damn it, she was still in love with the old reprobate, although it was probably hard to get over someone when you lived practically under the same roof.

"Wendy, I don't know what I was thinking, divorcing you. I'm not sure what I was looking for with all those wives, but thinking back on it, I came closest with you. Divorcing you? Biggest mistake of my life."

A grimace crossed his face. "Yeah, I realize I act like an idiot sometimes, but what are you gonna do, right?"

Candace shook her head. She loved her stepfather but like so many men, he was totally clueless about women's emotions, however, her mother was kind of clueless as well since she had been perfectly happy with the arrangement.

"Anyway, I told you when I made you stop working at Contessa so you could marry me, that I'd always make sure you had a home, even if I remarried. So I'm leaving you the apartment and a bunch of money so you never have to worry." He grinned into the camera, apparently satisfied. "Love ya, and stay off ladders and away from electrical outlets."

A sickly smile then slid across Video Fred's face. "Lastly, to my stepdaughter Candy..."

"Don't call me Candy," Candace growled under her breath.

"Sweetheart, you're the daughter I never had. Heck, you're the son I never had. You've worked harder than anyone I know to learn this business. You know I love you, and I know I promised but I just can't do it, at least not exactly what I promised."

Candace felt her stomach sink into her shoes.

Video Fred took a deep breath. "Candy, baby, I'm leaving the business to Gabe."

Candace heard a squeak of distress come out of her mouth. Her legs got weak and she fumbled for a chair so she could sit down. Fortunately, there was one since people had fled like rats off a sinking ship as soon as they realized they got nothing.

"But..." he continued. "I'm leaving you *The Recipe*. Take care of it 'cause it's worth a fortune." His video image held up a small red box. "When the time comes, Mott knows where this is." He snickered. "But if you're watching this tape, I guess the time is now. So go ahead, you can give it to her now."

The other attorney, nearly identical to Mister Mott in his raveness, leaned under the podium and pulled out the same red box.

On the screen, Fred said, "Oh, and Candy, there's just one more important thing you need to know. About the business—"

Scraaawck!

Fred's image on the screen froze, then a tiny black hole appeared in the middle of his forehead which rapidly spread until it ate his whole face. In seconds, his entire body had disappeared. All that was left on the screen were the frayed black edges of the hole.

Candace gasped. "What, Fred? What about the business! What was so important!"

The ravens stared at the machine, stunned. One of them leaned over and fiddled with the knobs of the VCR. All he got for his efforts was a beep, a hiss, then the screen went black.

They both turned to look at Candace. Mister Mott shrugged.

No! No, no, no, no, no. What about the business? "Oh, my God, don't you have a backup?"

Another shrug.

"Nooooooo!" she screamed.

"We do have this," the other attorney said and held out the box.

Tears of anger and frustration filled her eyes. Her hands trembling, Candace took the box because it was better than nothing. Yes, she was now the owner of *The Recipe* and yes, it was worth a fortune, but what good was it if she didn't have the factory filled with thousands of feet of conveyer belts and wrapping machines, never mind the roasters, the conching machines, and the molds, much of which must be ordered from Belgium. She got depressed just thinking about it. And that ratfink Gabe Jones? Saltwater taffy-making Gabe Jones, who had no respect for chocolate? He got it all.

Wait. Actually, no, maybe not. Gabe already owned a patootie full of machinery, but it was all taffy-making machinery. What did he need with a bunch of useless chocolate making equipment? All that machinery was worthless without *The Recipe.*

The wheels started to turn. She could work a deal. She had always been good at working deals. It could work. It *would* work. She just needed to figure out how to bamboozle Gabe, although long experience taught her he could be devious. What she needed was a plan. Lucky for her, planning was her strong suit. Feeling more positive, she opened the box.

And screamed for the second time in two minutes.

The box, that vessel of all things valuable, the receptacle of *The Recipe*, the font of her entire future, was empty.

2 Recipe for Disaster

Sweet Remembrances Inc.
Brooklyn, NY

Gabe Jones was born into chocolate. Chocolate paid for the enormous Park Avenue apartment he grew up in, purchased by his grandmother, the original Contessa, a poor immigrant from Belgium who'd made a fortune with her old-world recipe.

Chocolate ensured he went to the best private schools in Manhattan, had nannies after school and gained him entrance to an Ivy League college even with his not-so-Ivy League grades.

In the early days, chocolate supported Gabe's mother in the style she had always aspired to, then ultimately paid for her divorce when Gabe's father, Fred, decided he would rather be married to his secretary, Candace's ditzy mother. Eventually the ditz was set aside for the socialite, who was dumped for the Las Vegas showgirl, who was then replaced with his most recent ex-wife, an aspiring country and western singer with a heavy twang.

Being born into chocolate had shaped Gabe's earlier attitude toward life, but time, and aging being what they were, eventually he'd wised up and learned there was no such thing as a free lunch—or, in this case, free chocolate.

Anyway, who needed chocolate when there was saltwater taffy? From his place on the factory floor, Gabe surveyed his taffy-making domain.

"You!"

Hearing the shout, he turned and looked down the length of the long, narrow building and took a hasty step back, but it was too late to stop the crazy blond heading his way.

A finger jabbed into his chest.

Ouch.

"You..." Jab.

"Miserable..." Jab.

"Greedy..." *Really ouch.*

"Face sucking..." Both words were punctuated with another jab.

"Stop!" Gabe grabbed the offending finger and moved it to the side. Her hand came up again, this time in a fist. He ducked. "What are you talking about?"

More steam erupted. "You, you, you..."

"Me, me, me what?" He stopped, squinting as a sudden thought hit him. "Oh, wait. Wow, was the will read today? That must be it. So what happened? He left it all to Susan?" He chuckled. Not that any of this was funny.

The fist slammed into the middle of his chest. "Shit, Candy. What the heck is the matter with you?"

"Don't call me Candy," she yelled.

Okay, so she was upset. Who could blame her? He inhaled a breath and held it until he was sure he could speak without his voice shaking. "Hey, I'm really sorry. I know you loved him. I loved—"

"Of course, I loved him. And now he's dead, and you don't even care! You didn't even come to the will reading."

A muscle in his jaw twitched. "No one told me it was today. Anyway, why bother? It's not like he left me anything."

"Why bother? He was your father." She punched him in the shoulder.

A fireplug of a guy rounded the corner of one of the machines just in time to see the punch. The man grabbed Candace's arm. "None of that," he said. "There's already been one murder too many in this family."

Candace swung around. "What are you doing here?" she demanded. "I thought I left you in the city. Go away."

The fireplug smirked. "I don't think so. I have business with Mister Jones so I thought I'd take care of it now." He held his hand out. "Mister

Jones, I'm Sergeant Joe Dolan from the NYPD. Someone from my office called you yesterday about your father's murder."

The reminder sobered Gabe. He hadn't spoken to his father in far too long. The last time they talked, they had fought like a couple of wolverines in heat, but the realization his father was lost forever had created a deep ache in his chest that refused to go away. Who would have thought he loved the old bastard so much?

With a sigh, he pushed the pain aside. "Why don't you both come into my office so we can talk," he said grimly, and led the way to the back of the warehouse, past his employees, who, having heard all the screeching, turned their heads to watch as they all climbed up a flight of wooden stairs to his lofted office. The whole way he could feel Candace's eyes drilling holes in his back. Crap, would she ever forgive him?

Keeping his thoughts—and hands—to himself, he opened the door and waved them in. His office wasn't much. Real success had only come in the last four years when he expanded into other candies such as licorice and gummi candies. Even then, he'd never upgraded it from its cheap Office Depot furniture. It certainly didn't resemble his father's office with its five-thousand-dollar Oriental rug.

His heart clenched inside his chest. He spent hours playing GI Joe on that rug as a kid, but then he grew too old for GI Joe and things between him and his father changed.

Dolan took a stance beside the door. Candace threw herself into a steel-framed chair, her short black skirt riding up to expose lots of long tanned legs. A sudden memory of those legs wrapped around his waist popped into his head. He gulped and transferred his gaze upward, which didn't help since she had crossed her arms over her chest, making her breasts swell over the edge of her black tank top. Feeling his blood heat, he forced himself to focus on her face. Her blue eyes blazed back at him and any desire he felt wilted.

He took a deep breath before he said, "Okay, explain what's going on."

More steam. "There's nothing to explain. You stole *The Recipe.*"

"What? You're nuts. Why would I steal *The Recipe?*"

Candace bolted out of her chair and started toward him. Gabe jumped up. He held out a hand, keeping her away from his chest. It wasn't as if he was afraid of her or anything but his chest still smarted from the multiple jabs and he wasn't taking any chances. "Whoa! Hold on. I swear to you, I didn't steal anything. Come on, gimme a break here. Sit down and let's talk about it."

She hesitated.

He nodded, smiling encouragingly, and waggled a hand toward her chair. "Come on. Sit down. Please?" Outside he was all Mister Man-in-Control, inside he cringed at the thought she would freak out on him again.

She backed off a step. Thank God. He moved forward, one hand over his heart, protecting his sore chest as he made her back up. "That's a good girl," he said when she hesitantly sat down.

"Okay." He gazed at her for a few seconds, wanting to make sure she wasn't going to attack him again. "Listen, I don't know what's going on but I promise I didn't steal *The Recipe*. Are you sure it's gone?"

"Of course I'm sure it's gone. It was always in the box Fred kept in that lock box he had hidden behind his bookshelf."

Dolan chose that moment to add his thoughts. "Here's how I see it, Mister Jones. Your father was murdered then conveniently, at the same time, someone stole that secret recipe worth millions." His pale blue eyes speared Gabe.

"Son of a bitch. So just because it's missing, you think I took it? That's crazy."

A glare from Candace greeted his question. "Well, once upon a time, you did have the key to the safe."

"But I don't have it anymore. Dad only ever had two copies. I had one but when he kicked me out of the house, he took mine back and gave it to the attorneys. The other one he always kept on his key ring so if I was after the key, I would have had to kill him in order to steal it."

Candace leveled a narrow-eyed look on him.

He caught his breath. "Holy crap. You think I murdered my father."

"Well," Dolan replied then paused before saying, "Did you?"

What was this, a fucking police interrogation? "My dad and I didn't get along, but that doesn't mean I would kill him. I have my own successful business, and it isn't making chocolate. Besides, he's left me out of his will, therefore, I had no reason to either steal *The Recipe* or murder my dad." Asshole.

"Au contraire. I'd say there's several hundred million reasons to kill the man."

At first it made no sense. Then it did. No, his father wouldn't have done that, would he? Nausea gripped Gabe's stomach. "What are you saying?"

"Fred changed his mind and left you Contessa, you no-good, double-dealing, teen-age seducing ratfink," Candace said, her voice shaking. "He left me *The Recipe,* but you stole it," she finished.

* * * *

Gabe pushed open the door of the police station and stalked down the stairs, disregarding the woman who trailed in his wake. He reached the curb and waved a hand for a cab.

"I'm sorry," Candace mumbled.

Gabe stepped into the street and waved harder but the cabs all ignored him. It was peak rush hour and yet every single cab in New York City had their off-duty light on. How did that happen? Why didn't the Mayor fix this situation?

Oh, yeah, the guy rode around in a private limo, so what did he care?

Candace sidled up to his side again. "Really, Gabe, I'm sorry. I'm just upset."

Gabe grunted. Like he wasn't upset. His father had just been murdered, and all he wanted was go back to Brooklyn and sink into a well-deserved depression. He wasn't normally the type to get depressed, but the longer he contemplated the years when he and his father hadn't spoken, the more he realized how stupid he was. He'd always thought, if his father really loved him, the man would pick up the phone and apologize. Now that it was too late, Gabe realized it went both ways. Why hadn't he picked up the phone instead? Stupid. Just effing stupid.

He watched the sea of cars as they drove by, trying to forget the constant ache in his chest. Still no cabs. Looking downtown, he could see six other guys lined up along the street with their hands raised, also trying to hail a cab. Conceding defeat, he turned and walked north on Third Avenue toward 68th Street, weaving in and out among the other pedestrians, all of whom seem to be going the opposite direction, making his progress slow.

Candace followed, like a small Chihuahua nipping at the heels of a larger dog, her sandaled feet slapping on the hot sidewalk.

"I made a mistake. How was I to know you couldn't possibly have stolen *The Recipe* because you were in Atlanta the one time it could have been stolen?" She shrugged, grinning sheepishly, sounding truly contrite. "My bad."

Gabe stopped so abruptly Candace ran into him. He grabbed her arms and set her at arm's length. "Stop."

His fingers tingled where they touched Candace's bare skin, and he forced himself to let her go. If it weren't for the fact she would knock his block off, he would have crossed his fingers and held them up in the form of a cross, warding off her evil. Desire and resentment created a hard knot in his chest. He resented the desire. He resented the resentment even more because he always thought he was a better man, but apparently he wasn't.

Backing up a step, he pointed a single finger at her. "Stay."

She looked up at him, lower lip thrust out as puppy-dog eyes gazed soulfully up at him. If she thought he would fall for that old trick. Been there, done that, not doing it again. Even the breeze wafting past her, causing her blond curls to caress her rosy cheeks, wasn't enough to soften his attitude although it did make his fingers twitch. Along with something else.

Turning on his heel, he stalked away and made a left at the next street toward Lexington Avenue.

She didn't stay. "Aw, come on, Gabe, don't be like that. I told you, I made a mistake. Everyone makes mistakes, right?" Her sandals click-clacked on the hard sidewalk.

He stopped again. "Right. A mistake. Just like it was a mistake to accuse me of murdering my father?" Just like it was a mistake to wheedle her way into his father's affections.

Red flooded her face. "I never said that. That was Detective Dolan." She bit her plump lip with her perfect front teeth.

"Hmm," was all he could manage.

Her hands went to her hips, making her knit T-top stretch tight over her high, round breasts. God damn it. Hoping to escape, he set off again.

"But you have to admit you deserve it," she panted as she ran to catch up. "After what you did..."

He screeched to a halt. "After what I did! What about what you did?" Son of a B, the woman had some nerve.

"What! What did I do?" she huffed. Her hands went to her hips again, pulling everything tight.

God, she was even more gorgeous now than she was at eighteen, if that was possible. Not that he was still attracted to her. Because he wasn't. No way. "You ratted me out to Fred. He accused me of being a child molester." Giving her the evil eye, he muttered, "Like you were actually a child."

Her eyes dropped. She scuffed a sandaled foot against the pavement. "Well, you dumped me," she mumbled.

"I didn't dump you. I went back to college. I was failing a bunch of classes and needed to take make-up exams." Yet another failure in the eyes of his father. And he just barely passed them the second time around. It was too bad they didn't give diplomas for playing football. Oh, wait, they did, but those guys only had a few good years in them before they sank into obscurity. He had bigger plans than football for his life.

"How was I supposed to know that?" Indignantly. "I mean, what the heck did I know about college and stuff? I was eighteen and still in high school."

Gritting his teeth, he resumed walking, dodging around the mobs of people on their way home from work, his eyes on the subway entrance just ahead. "Well, I was only twenty-one."

"You should have said something," she panted. "Instead, you took advantage of my youth, my innocence, my naivety. You used me."

Oh, brother. He jerked to a stop, then sidestepped when she nearly ran him over again. "I did not," he told her. "You wanted it just as much as I did." And God bless America, he still wanted it, even after not seeing her for all these years.

Her nostrils flared. Her eyes looked up, then down, then sideways before coming back to meet his. "Okay, you're right."

"Gee, thanks," Gabe said. "Now we've settled that: Good-bye." He turned and headed down the dirt-encrusted subway stairs, leaving Candace behind on the sidewalk. Taking out his iPhone, he tapped it on the OMNY system to let him through the turnstile and prayed a train would come quick. He could see one as it approached and for a minute, he thought he'd escaped, but no such luck. Next thing he knew Candace showed up at his side. He glowered at her. She smiled back. The hair on the back of his neck stood on end. So did another obviously functioning part of his body.

The train pulled into the station with a roar and a blast of hot air, and the doors slid open. Passengers pushed past as they exited the train. Taking his hand, Candace pulled him on board. He shook his hand free and made his way to a seat. She followed and crammed in her skinny little butt— okay, not skinny but certainly slim enough to fit into the narrow space next to him—nearly pushing an older lady off the seat. Scrunching her shoulders together, Candace sat on the edge of the seat and made herself as small as possible. The old lady threw her a dirty look.

"We need to talk," Candace told him.

"No, we don't," he answered, crossing his arms over his chest and grimly staring at the subway map on the opposite wall as if it was a map to the lost treasure of El Dorado. He would be happy if they never talked again. The roar of the train filled his ears. He wished it would block out the sound of Candace's voice.

"Sure we do."

He growled and turned his head to look at her. That smile still graced her face. Fucking scary. "I don't want to talk to you. I'm still mad at you."

"Well, I'm still mad at you too."

What! "What the hell for?"

"You took my virginity. I had plans for it, you know." The woman on her left squawked then got up and moved to another spot at the far end of the subway car where she sat and scowled at Candace. Good for her, she was smart enough to know she didn't want to sit next to two crazy people. The space now wider, Candace relaxed against the hard plastic seat. "Oh, good. Now we can talk comfortably."

Gabe put a hand to his forehead. She made him crazy. She had always done that to him, even when she was eighteen. The fact that he hadn't seen her since the day his father kicked him out of the apartment meant nothing. He remembered when he came home from college right after Fred married Wendy. Completely unaware of the seismic changes that had occurred while he was away, Gabe walked to his bedroom, lugging his tote bag filled with dirty laundry, and kicked open the door only to be greeted by a shriek and the sight of long slim legs, pink panties and pink-tipped nipples. The long legs bounded over to the bed and all that pinkness dove under the covers.

Gabe tried to get his lungs to function again.

Eventually the top of a blond head and big blue eyes peeked up over the edge of the covers. "What are you doing in my bedroom?" the girl (yes, it was definitely a girl) squeaked.

"Your bedroom? This is my bedroom."

"Nuh uh," she answered. "Fred told me I could have it." The blanket came down so that he could see the rest of her face.

Wow! *Deep breaths, Jones, deep breaths.* "Um. Sorry to disagree," he said, untangling his tongue. "But this is my bedroom. It's always been my bedroom."

"Right. So who the heck are you?"

"Gabe Jones. Fred's son."

The blanket dropped into her lap, exposing all her luscious pinkness. She smiled. His lungs went on strike again. Seeing his face turn red from lack of oxygen, she slowly pulled the blanket back up to cover her chest.

"Really," she said, drawing the word out. She eyed him up and down. "Cute. Very cute." Pause. "But you still can't have this bedroom."

He knew right then his goose was cooked.

Yanking his thoughts out of the past Gabe said, "You're giving me a headache." Along with another ache afflicting him whenever Candace was within ten feet.

"Well, you're giving me a pain in my ass but I'm willing to deal."

He scowled. "Hey, don't do it on my account."

She beamed a smile. "Oh, I'm not."

"Jesus Christ, Candace, what do you want from me?" This whole conversation made his back teeth hurt, like he'd eaten too much sugar...or more precisely, too much Candy.

"I want you to help me find *The Recipe*," she said, still beaming that smile at him. He didn't trust that smile. Bad things always happened when Candace smiled like that.

"Not interested."

"Even if it means we'll also find out who killed Fred?"

Okay, that was different. Sort of. Maybe. It would depend on the circumstances. All right, damn it, definitely, as long as he could control the circumstances. "Okay, I'm in but I'm in charge." She opened her mouth to protest. He held a hand up. "My way or no way. Deal?" No way would he tell her he planned on searching for Fred's killer anyway, with or without her.

After a brief hesitation she reluctantly took it.

And for the second time in his life, Gabe knew he had made a terrible mistake.

3 Kisses and Killers

Candace followed Gabe into his apartment. *Wow.* Big and airy, fabulous wall-to-wall windows, and a great view of the Brooklyn Bridge crossing the East River, as well as all the other bridges, plus the skyline of Lower Manhattan. A totally early-thirties bachelor pad, meaning lots of expensive brown leather furniture, chrome tables and a view to die for, versus just-graduated-from-college thrift store décor, the kind with a lumpy futon, cinderblock shelves, and a three-by-five view of a brick wall.

It seemed Gabe was doing pretty well for himself even without Fred's help, unlike Candace whose ambitions had been supported and encouraged by Fred for the last ten years.

Was that why Fred had changed his mind? Had she done something wrong? Something squeezed in her chest at the thought she hadn't lived up to Fred's expectations. Swiping a hand across her brow she forced her mind away from the unpleasant feeling. There was no time for self-pity. She needed to remember she was here because Gabe had something she wanted.

Gabe made his way into his spacious kitchen. Opening the refrigerator door, he stuck his head inside. "Okay, so let's talk about our suspects," he said, his voice echoing from the depths of the fridge.

Yeah, Candace thought, because doing something to find the murderer and *The Recipe* would take her mind off her sadness, and hopefully help her figure out how to recover Contessa. She threw her purse onto the modern brown leather sofa then went back to the kitchen and hiked herself up onto a barstool at the island.

"Number one on my list—Mister Toad."

Gabe pulled his head out of the refrigerator. "Who?"

"Geez, Jones, get with the program. Your Uncle Murray. You know. Short. Squat. Bulging eyes."

It took a second before Gabe got it, then, "Ribbit."

Candace laughed. Damn him, he was always able to make her laugh. It was why she had fallen into bed with him so quickly, that and the fact that he had mile-wide shoulders, killer buns, a Hollywood smile, and was follicly gifted. She'd loved running her hands through all his dark, silky hair.

He gave her a speculative look as if he could read her mind. She hated when he was right.

"Stop it," she said.

"Stop what?"

"Stop, stop, stop...oh, you know. Just stop."

"Right." Grinning, he leaned back against a kitchen counter and crossed his arms over his broad chest, stretching tight the knit fabric of his navy polo shirt. A few muscles bulged.

Was it hot in here? "I need a coke."

His grin widened as he stared at her, torturing her with his out-of-control maleness, but eventually he turned and stuck his head back in the fridge, retrieved several icy cans of soda and plunked one in front of her.

"Okay, so why do you think Murray is a suspect?" he asked, popping open the top of his Dr. Pepper and tipping it back to take a big gulp.

Candace stared, mesmerized as she watched the tendons in his neck tighten and his Adam's apple move up and down. She hastily took a sip of her own soda. Hey, it wasn't like watching him made her hot or anything, it was simply that her throat was dry. Really. She cleared her throat just to prove the point.

"Uh, what was the question?"

His lips quirked. "Why do you think Murray is a suspect?"

"Right! Well, duh. He sold his share to Fred for a measly twenty mil and Fred told me Murray's never gotten over the belief he was cheated."

"Yeah. Somehow he's conveniently forgotten my father worked his ass off and built the company up from a business worth forty million to a billion dollar enterprise while Murray mostly gambled and chased women." Opening a drawer, he pulled out paper and pen then rounded the corner of the island so he could perch himself on the stool next to Candace. She took another big gulp of coke.

"Okay, who else and why?" Instead of taking notes, he doodled little squares and circles on the pad.

Candace tapped the pad. "Write it down."

He nodded then slowly printed "Mr. Toad".

"Okay, next suspect."

"The Stiff."

He blinked. "Who?"

"You know, Vanessa Luckless—stiff-necked, stiff-rumped, and rigor mortis in bed."

Gabe snorted coke from his nose. After wiping the coke off his shirt, he said, "I can't see her killing Fred."

"Maybe not but she's deluded enough to think, if she had *The Recipe*, she could exchange it for the apartment, and her kids are greedy enough—and stupid enough—to help her."

"Why would she do that? Why doesn't she just buy a Park Avenue apartment?"

Candace huffed. "Can't afford it. Her dad lost the family fortune back in the Eighties when he invested everything in Enron stock. Somehow, she thinks having a Park Avenue address will restore her to New York City society."

"Huh. So then, was there an opportunity?"

"Oh, yeah. The kids particularly. Fred gave them keys to the apartment when he was married to Vanessa and they never gave them back. Claimed they lost them and Fred refused to change the locks, so they still walk in any time they damned well please. I have to tell you, I've gotten real tired of finding them sitting on the couch, playing video games, picking their noses and wiping it on the furniture. Ick."

Gabe stared at the pad of paper in front of him, seemingly enthralled by the little circles and squares he had doodled, but one corner of his mouth twitched upward.

Candace's whole body twitched in response. "Knock it off."

He looked up, his dark eyes wide. Then he blinked those long, dark lashes. Rapidly. Like a flirty girl. "What?" he said innocently.

Sheesh, what do you do with a guy like that? "Don't give me that crap."

He shook his head and sighed loudly. "I don't know why you always assume I'm out to get you."

Candace narrowed her eyes at him. "Because you have?" Yeah, at least fifty times that summer. Okay, exaggeration. But not about the last time, when he made love to her then left the next morning without a word.

This time his mouth did more than twitch. It curled into a lascivious smile and his nostrils flared. The memory of what they did together was on his face, in his suddenly smoky eyes, and in the slow deep breath he took.

Heat flared all over her body. It was over twelve years but it felt like yesterday. She crossed her legs, hoping to suppress the tingle.

His gaze darted down to look at her legs then slowly rose. He stared at her. She stared back, afraid the simmering heat between them would burst into flames, perversely afraid it wouldn't. Oh boy, she was in so much trouble, because he was the enemy, right? She got up and paced. A finger automatically went to her mouth as she paced. With a grimace, she yanked it out. Damn it, that was her last long nail.

"Then there's Tiffany," she said quickly, and stuffed her hands into her skirt pockets to keep from biting off the pathetic remnants of her nails. "She can't find her way out of a paper bag with a pair of scissors but that greaseball boyfriend of hers, that's a different story. I wouldn't put it past him to steal *The Recipe* and try to sell it back to me." She stopped. Her eyes narrowed as she glared at him. "Okay, it should have been me but now he'll probably try to sell it to you." Which just reminded her, while she was here with Gabe, Contessa languished with no leadership. She should probably do something to fix this dire situation.

She opened her mouth with the intention of changing course, but he interrupted her with, "Same thing applies, did they have opportunity?"

Okay, it should be Gabe out there trying to salvage the situation. At some point, they would need to discuss this.

She jerked her mind back to the more pressing matter. Fred was dead, and she truly wanted the murderer to be caught, but right now, finding

The Recipe took precedence. Without *The Recipe*, there was no way to make chocolate, and without that, there was no Contessa and ultimately, no jobs. So, as much as Gabe got her all hot and bothered, now was not the time. And he definitely wasn't the person. "Our building super is the Grease Ball's cousin." At his quirked eyebrow, she added, "Tiffany's current boyfriend. It's how they met."

"Good grief." He sighed, trying to remember where Tiffany fit on the ex-wife list. Third? Fourth? "Okay, anyone else we should add?" He scrubbed his hand through his hair, his thick, dark, silky, sexy...

Agghhh. Stop! She took a deep breath. "Susan Jones."

"What?" he yelped. "That's my mother you're accusing of stealing and murder." His dark eyes smoldered.

Yow! "She's just as capable as anyone else on our list."

"She is not!" He slammed his notebook onto the desk.

"Is too."

He thrust his hands onto his hips and glared. "What about your mother, huh, Miss Smarty Pants?"

"My mother," Candace yelled. "No way. She wouldn't hurt a fly." That assumed Wendy could even catch a fly.

"Neither would my mother," Gabe yelled back, red-faced.

"Sure she would. Your mother pulls the wings off flies just for the fun of it. You told me she flushed your pet goldfish down the toilet when you were seven."

"It was already dead..."

Excuses, excuses. "She gave away your hamster because it fell asleep in one of her Jimmy Choos."

"It scared the crap out of her when she tried to put her foot in. And anyway, I was away at college and—"

"Bullshit. It was still your pet. Admit it, she's sneaky and greedy and a—"

"Don't say it," Gabe warned, standing.

"Or what, huh?" Candace responded, thrusting out her chin and planting her fists on her hips.

"Just don't." He faced her, legs spread, shoulders bunched, jaw jutting out with his hands flexed at his side. He looked like a linebacker, ready to take her down. It was a well-known fact Candace had a big weakness for football players.

She bared her teeth in a smile. "Admit it. Susan Jones is a regular Cruella DeV—"

He rushed her. His momentum back-peddled her across the room until her back thumped up against a wall then, grabbing her under the arms, he hiked her up the wall so they were face to face. One arm swooped down and cradled her ass.

His dark eyes narrowed menacingly.

Candace blinked back. *Well, this was interesting.* The deep brown of his eyes made her think of rich chocolate which made her think of melting which made her think of sex.

Obviously, his eyes weren't the only thing that made her think of sex. There was the hard bulge pressed low against her stomach, the hard wall of his chest pressed against hers, and the heavy breathing of said chest. Oh, and wait, there was also his tongue, which was slowly licking his lush lower lip. If that didn't make a girl's motor rev, what would?

"Uh, Jones," she whispered then winced. Even to her own ears she sounded scarily like Marilyn Monroe. Whoa. She never sounded like Marilyn Monroe. Marilyn was *so* not her thing.

"Candace," he murmured back, his eyes intent on hers then he slowly tipped his head forward, his lips getting closer and closer, a *tiiiny* little millimeter at a time.

She could feel his breath on her face, could practically taste the cool cherry-cola flavor of his mouth. Her own mouth puckered, seeking the warm moisture of his lips, but he remained tantalizingly out of reach. All kinds of body parts stood up and yelled, *"Kiss me. Kiss me now."* Geez, what the heck was he waiting for?

Suddenly the arm under her ass disappeared and he stepped back. Her kitten-heeled sandals hit the floor with a *thud.*

"What the—" she sputtered.

He dusted his hands off, mission accomplished, the gesture seemed to say then he walked back to his stool and sat. "We'll leave my mother off the list," he said calmly. Picking up his pen, he started doodling again.

Candace glared. That dirty, stinking ratfink bastard. Who did he think he was? George Clooney? Did he think he could just sweep her away with his dark eyes, killer smile and gorgeous hair, never mind all those muscles. Damn, she needed to stop thinking about his irresistible gorgeousness since it just made her forget she wasn't nearly ready to forgive him yet.

Egotistical rat that he was, he believed he'd turned her on, but he hadn't, not even close because she was *so* over him. Ages ago. Like at least ten years. At least. No way would she let him get her all hot and bothered now while he just walked away—again—totally unaffected, cool, calm and collec—

She stopped, taking a closer look. Sweat beaded his forehead, and the hand gripping his pen was white-knuckled.

Okay, wait a minute. She squinted at him, carefully considering before slowly realizing: (A) He wasn't as cool, calm, and collected as he pretended, (B) Having his mother maligned pissed him off, and (C) Pissing him off resulted in his losing his cool, which led to some interesting moments.

Even though it was Gabe who produced the interesting moments, and Candace already decided she was *so* over Gabe, she hadn't had any interesting moments in a really long time and her life could use a few more interesting moments.

Therefore, his mother would stay on the list, however Candace had no intention of telling him that. After all, what would be the fun in letting him know?

But speaking of interesting moments...

Grabbing her purse, she dug around inside until she found what she needed. She pulled the little plastic packet out and lobbed it to him.

He automatically caught it, looked at it. His mouth dropped open. "What the—?" he protested.

Candace smiled, then with a flippant wave of her hand, she walked out the door.

Once on the street, she wavered, trying to decide what she should do next. What she wanted to do was go home and sink into a nice hot bubble bath with a glass of wine and a good book, but what she needed to do was to go to the plant and let everyone know what happened. They all knew the will was read today and they would be worried, and she didn't blame them. She was worried too, but she was the boss, or at least so they thought. Gabe hadn't said anything about taking over and until he did, she was responsible.

Since she was already in Brooklyn and the factory was in Brooklyn, it made sense to take care of it now. She was only a few subway stops away, so she began the walk to the closest station. Her phone rang, and without thinking, she answered.

"OMG!" the caller shrieked. Candace held the phone away from her ear.

"Hi, Phoebe," Candace said as she held the phone at a distance.

"I just heard! Is it true!" Phoebe tended to talk in exclamation points.

Candace sighed. Phoebe was a good friend, but she just wasn't in the mood for her over-the-top enthusiasm, a trait that made sense for the woman since, in addition to being a bank manager, she was a part-time cheerleader for the New York Jets.

"What did you hear?" Candace asked. She stopped and dug around in her purse for her MetroCard.

"Your step-dad was murdered! OMG! That's so awful!

"Yes." The less said the better.

"OMG!" she exclaimed again. "I'm so sorry!" Even her sympathy was expressed in exclamations. "Is there anything I can do to help! Anything at all! Do you need a shoulder to cry on?"

That made Candace smile. Phoebe was a good person—loud—but a good person. "No, I just need time." Yeah, time to find *The Recipe*, and hopefully find the killer.

"Oh. Okay." Her voice came down a decibel or two in her disappointment. "Well, let me know if you do." She was silent for a minute then, "So I guess you aren't in the mood for our Bowling Broads night out, huh?"

Candace felt a bubble of laughter escape. Thursday night was bowling night for her and her three girlfriends: Althea, a lawyer, Fiona, a pediatrician, Phoebe, the bank manager, and Candace, the candy maker. Bowling. So plebian. If people knew, they would laugh themselves sick.

"No, not right now." Seeing the subway entrance just ahead, she kept walking, the phone still held away from her ear.

"Okay! Anyhow, Althea said to say hi, and to let her know if you needed any help! And everyone else sends their best so take care, okay!"

Despite how confused and angry she was, it felt good to know she had friends she could call on if needed, but right now, all she needed was that damned *Recipe*. Oh, and maybe Gabe.

The memory of him in his tight polo shirt popped into her head. Okay, definitely Gabe.

"Thanks, Phoebe," Candace answered and hung up just as she reached the entrance to the subway. Her ears ringing, she descended the stairs and swiped through the turnstile. Once onboard, she selected a two-person seat where she wedged herself into a corner seat to cry a little over Fred's death and his betrayal and thought about what she would say to all the people depending on her.

The minute she walked into the door of the plant, the plant manager, Manuel, rushed up, talking a mile a minute. Candace shook her head, staving him off with an upheld hand. "Come into my office," she directed and led the way upstairs. "Sit."

Manuel sat, his face tight with tension, his eyes pleading. He had a family to support, he had co-workers he cared about.

Candace sat, took a deep breath, blew it out, then told him the facts.

"Miss Candace. What are we going to do?" Lines of confusion and sadness creased his face.

Candace rubbed her temples. The day had given her such a headache. She wished she knew what to do. She wished Fred wasn't murdered. She wished Fred kept his promise. She wished she could figure out why he hadn't. She wished she didn't feel so damned helpless.

If wishes were horses...

But she couldn't let Manuel know so she smiled reassuringly and said, "I'm going to find *The Recipe* and I will find some way to force Gabe to either let me run Contessa or sign it over to me."

He blinked. "I know Mister Gabe is a good guy, but what if he won't?"

She sighed. "Then I'll make sure everyone receives a year's severance and I'll try to help everyone find new jobs."

Manuel nodded and smiled. It was a fake smile, designed to make them both feel better, but it didn't fool either of them. At least he didn't ask any more questions, like *"How will you make sure everyone gets a year's severance"* because Candace didn't know the answer. If she had to, she would borrow it from her mother since it appeared her mother was rich now.

After a few more fake smiles and a lot more head-nodding, Candace stood. "Come on, let's go tell everyone," she told him, and led the way back down to the production floor.

Talk about depressing.

* * * *

She drove him crazy, Gabe thought after Candace left. She always had, and the years away from her hadn't changed anything. He stared at the door, counting the seconds until she returned. Guaranteed she would return as there was no way would she miss a further opportunity to torture him.

Speaking of torture. He glanced at the little plastic packet in his hands. Listerine breath strips? Really?

He held a hand in front of his mouth and blew softly into his palm. It smelled okay. Right? He breathed into his palm again, checking. It was hard to tell. Maybe he should ask someo...

He straightened suddenly then smacked his forehead. See, she'd done it to him again, made him crazy. Well, she wouldn't get away with it. Somehow, someway, he would pay her back but first he needed to fix a few things. He had no desire to own Contessa. By starting his own company and making a success of it, he proved what he set out to prove but running Contessa now his father was dead wouldn't prove anything since the old bastard wasn't alive to see the results.

What was important was Candace wanted the business and Gabe didn't. The best way to make that happen would be to find *The Recipe*. Returning to the kitchen he picked up the short list he and Candace put together then he made some calls.

4 The Frog Prince

Candace answered her ringing cell.

"Where do you live?"

"Who is this?" she demanded even though she knew. How could she not know, she'd heard that velvety voice in her dreams for over a decade.

"Don't give me that crap," he growled. "I know you know who I am."

"I do?" she said sweetly.

The sound of teeth grinding was audible even over the phone. "I'll ask you again, and if you don't give me a straight answer I'll leave you behind when I go talk to Murray."

Damn him. "I live the same place I've always lived ever since Mom and Fred got married. You know that."

"I do?" he answered. Sweetly.

"Goddammit, get your ass over here. I'll meet you in front of the building in half an hour."

"Your wish is my command," he said and hung up.

Right.

* * * *

He was ten minutes late. "You're late," she told him, throwing a quick look up and down his long body. Tight jeans and macho kick-ass boots and a blue T-shirt stretched across his manly chest. *Woof.*

"I am?" he asked. Sweetly.

She wanted to kill him. "Knock it off. And yes, you are late."

Grinning a devilish grin, he snagged her hand then dragged her away, pulling her down the sidewalk and around the corner onto a tree-lined side street. "Couldn't help it. It took me forever to get across the Williamsburg Bridge, and the FDR was wall-to-wall traffic, so now we need to hurry." He stopped a few hundred feet from the corner.

"Which one is your car?"

"No car. We're taking this." He pointed to a beast of a motorcycle parked at the curb. Black with red and orange flames streaming along the side of the gas tank, huge wheels and a front Plexiglas windshield big enough to shield the Chrysler Building. The thing looked capable of consuming large men for dinner then using a leg bone as a toothpick.

"No way. I'm not getting on that thing. I'll die. And I'm afraid to die. Dying will probably hurt." She stared at the thing, horrified.

He laughed. "You're not going to die."

"I might." The fact he was devastatingly gorgeous when he reassured her didn't make her feel any better.

"I'll take care of you."

"That's what I'm afraid of."

Candace was sure she heard a growl. The scary thing was she couldn't tell if it came from Gabe or the motorcycle.

"Either get on the bike or get left behind, your choice." He didn't sound nearly as jovial as a few seconds ago.

"Oh, well, gee, when you put it that way." Taking the bright red helmet he held out, she slammed it onto her head. She buckled the strap then waited while he rocked the bike off its stand and hit the starter. The engine roared to life.

"Get on," he yelled.

Hiking up her skirt, she swung her leg over the seat. Of course she *had* to wear a tight skirt today of all days. And short, really short. "Put your feet on the pedals," he ordered and roared off into the street.

Geez! She grabbed his waist, fingers digging into the blue T-shirt, holding on for dear life. She *was* going to die.

The light on Lexington turned red, and he stopped. Speaking over his shoulder, he told her, "Relax. You're holding me too tight." The light turned green, and he revved the motor so they flew across the avenue.

Candace didn't answer. She couldn't. Her heart had stopped beating, and her body was already starting to decompose as evidenced by the fact her lips were now numb and she could no longer feel her feet.

She had an insane urge to bite a fingernail or two but uncoiling even one finger from Gabe's shirt would surely to lead to death, and they'd already established she was afraid of death. Her purse bobbed wildly in the wind, but she wasn't about to let go of Gabe to secure it. It would just have to survive on its own.

The next two blocks passed in a blur as they somehow managed to hit all green lights going crosstown. Upon reaching Second Avenue, he made a sharp right and headed downtown. The wind whipped past her along with a million yellow cabs and the typical New York landscape consisting of a combination of steel and glass new construction and old brick tenement buildings. Between her legs, the beast whined and snarled and vibrated. After a while, she started to enjoy it. By the time they reached their destination she was enjoying it so much she wanted to jump Gabe's bones.

He turned onto 29th Street then came to an easy stop about halfway down the block. "We're here. Hop off so I can park."

She gave him a look.

"Now what?" As he spoke, he pulled his helmet off. His hair was matted to his head with sweat. Even so, she wanted to run her hands through it. Actually, she wanted to run her hands all over his body. God, he was hot. And so was she.

"Candace?"

"Right. Getting off." Swinging a leg over the seat, she dismounted. Her legs felt like noodles. Worse, so did her brain. She stood while he parked the bike then handed him her helmet. After securing both helmets under the seat of the bike, he dragged her down the block to a small pre-war apartment building with a green awning and a doorman.

"Hey, Frank," he greeted the doorman. Obviously knowing Gabe, the doorman waved them through. They rode the elevator up to the penthouse floor where Murray stood outside his open door, waiting.

"Hey, Uncle Murray," Gabe said.

"Watcha want?" was the answer.

"I told you, we want to talk about my dad's will." He followed Murray into the foyer where he stopped, blocking Candace from proceeding further. She waited for the big oaf to move. When he didn't, she leaned against the wall, tapping her foot impatiently as she looked at the accumulation of crap on the credenza, the only thing to look at other than Gabe's broad back. What a mess. Letters. Coins. Keys. Sunglasses. Envelopes. Pens. Cell phone, keys...

Keys.

KEYS!

Peering around Gabe's broad back to make sure no one was watching her, Candace reached into her enormous tote and rooted around until she located the little egg she'd found under the couch after a friend dropped by with her son. She'd meant to return it but at this point it wasn't likely her little boy would even remember he'd lost it.

She quickly took care of the task.

Finally he and Murray finished talking and moved into the large living room.

She got her first real look. Holy cow. Garish red velvet couches with over-the-top gold rococo trim crouched on two walls. The tall windows were swagged in heavy red and black flocked drapes that blocked out all the sunlight while monstrous gold-leafed tables ate up what floor space the couches hadn't. The floor was covered in red shag carpeting so old the shag had laid down and died. The décor was made worse by the fact it was repeated a million times over in the floor-to-ceiling mirrors facing each other on both long walls. The exception to the garish décor was a tattered black Barca-Lounger (eek, shades of Fred Jones) which Murray fell into with a wheeze and a groan then proceeded to level a bug-eyed stare at Gabe.

Gabe didn't seem bothered. He moved to one of the velvet sofas and sat, pulling Candace down next to him. "So we wanted to know what you know about the missing recipe."

Way to go, Jones. Let him know right off the bat we suspect him.

Murray dipped his head, creating a half dozen double chins. He looked more like a toad than ever. "Nothin'," he croaked.

Candace bit back the *"ribbit"* hovering on the tip of her tongue. "What Gabe meant to ask was have you heard anything—like any rumors or anything—that might give us a clue?"

Gabe gave her a sharp poke in the ribs. *That's not what I meant.*

She poked him back. *Shut up.*

"I didn't hear nothin', and I don't know nothin'."

"Okay. We get it. So let me ask this, if you had to guess who would steal *The Recipe,* who would it be?"

Before Murray could answer, Gabe added his two cents worth (which was about all his addition was worth) with, "More importantly, who would have a good reason to murder my dad?"

Murray chortled. "I can think a lots a people what wanted that SOB dead."

"Including you," Gabe responded. His dark brows lowered over his chocolate eyes. Very distracting.

"Yeah, maybe including me." Murray's bulgy eyes glinted maliciously.

"So did you?" Candace asked, because someone had to.

His mouth widened in a froggy grin. "What do you think?"

Gabe didn't seem to know what to do with that piece of information so Candace grabbed the reins again. "Let's focus on *The Recipe.* Fred stored it in that little red box he kept in his home office safe. The box was still there but *The Recipe* is gone. Can you think of any reason he might have moved it?"

"I don't know and I don't care. It don't do me no good."

This was going nowhere fast. And his grammar was beginning to irritate her.

At that moment the front door opened and Murray's son, Junior, walked in. Mouth hanging open, fat lower lip protruding, he listlessly surveyed the room then meandered across the red shag carpeting and flopped in a chair next to his father.

Candace looked back and forth between the two. Junior was as advertised, a junior version of his father, sort of a tadpole rather than a full-fledged toad, but give him time, turning into a toad was inevitable.

"What about you, Junior? Fred always said you seem to know everything that's going on. Did you ever hear anything about Fred moving *The Recipe* somewhere else?" Again, she stepped in as Gabe seemed to have run out of questions.

"Huh?" Junior answered. "What recipe?"

Candace stood. "Okay, I think we're done here." Grabbing Gabe's arm she yanked him to his feet. "Thanks, Murray," she said, and dragged Gabe out the door and down the hall to the elevator. Even though this meeting was a disaster, after yesterday's announcement to Contessa's employees, she knew it was more important than ever to find *The Recipe*.

She hit the button. Almost immediately the elevator arrived and they got in.

"What the heck?" Gabe said, giving her a scalding look.

"What, what the heck?"

"What was that?" One hand ran furiously though his hair.

Okay, so he was irritated. "What was what?" she responded but instead of waiting for an answer she sailed out of the elevator when the doors opened and out the door of the building.

* * * *

Gabe slapped himself on the forehead. Fuck, she was doing it again. He shook his head, trying to clear it, then watched her tush disappear down the street, the short pink skirt making the most of her long, lithe legs.

Where did she think she was going?

He blinked. Knowing Candace it could be anywhere. He bolted down the sidewalk. "Wait up." She kept walking and he was forced to run to catch up. Grabbing her arm, he made her stop. "Where are you going?"

She shrugged.

Patience. "Okay, never mind. Just tell me what happened back there. I wasn't done so why did we leave?"

"You were done," she said then turned to walk away again.

He grabbed her arm again. "No I wasn't."

"Yes you were." She heaved a sigh.

He slapped his forehead again. It was as sore as his chest. His frustration level had reached epic proportions. "I. Was. Not. Done."

She started walking toward the motorcycle again, so Gabe had no choice but to follow. "Yes. You. Were. You were doing it all wrong, and we needed to get out of there while we could."

Gabe stopped dead. "What?" he yelled after her.

She turned around, fists on her hips. "All you were doing was letting him know you suspect him of something. If he knows anything, he's not going to tell you outright. Your problem is you're not sneaky enough."

Gabe glared. He wasn't sure if he was just complimented or insulted. He wasn't sure if he wanted to find out. "Okay, so if we can't ask him directly, what do we do?"

He cringed when he saw that smile again. "We're going to break into his office, and if we have to, we'll break into his apartment."

His heart skipped a few beats in alarm. "You have got to be fucking kidding me." He was sure his mouth hung open.

"I never kid."

He broke out into a cold sweat. Was she kidding? Oh, wait. She never kidded. Shaking his head, Gabe strode past her in the direction of his motorcycle. At this point he didn't give a damn if she followed him or not. Unfortunately she did.

Retrieving the helmets, he silently handed her the bright red one. She settled it on her head, carefully tucking her soft blond curls inside. His fingers itched to help, but he resisted. She would probably bite them off if he did. He mounted and started the engine. Putting her foot on the pedal, she climbed on board behind him. Pulling out into the street, he headed back uptown.

Her arms went around his waist. They were warm and feminine, and her breasts pushed up against his back, and her legs crooked, hugging the underside of his thighs tightly. Under his ass, the seat of the motorcycle was red hot, and so was he. He sped up. He couldn't get to Park Avenue fast enough.

He tore back uptown, crossed east on 72nd Street, roared north on Park for a few blocks, made a U-turn and headed back south. He screeched to a halt in front of her building. "Get off," he ordered, tipping up his face shield and turning around to glare at her. He didn't know why he was glaring other than the fact he wanted to rip the helmet off her head and attack those lips still red from the wind.

A long pause ensued, then she stood up on the foot pedals, swung one leg over and slid slowly onto the ground. Her skirt rode up and a tiny sliver of lace-edged panty peeped out from under the hem of her skirt. She took her time tugging it back down.

Then she unbuckled her helmet and pulled it off.

Gabe swallowed. It was like watching one of those commercials for hair product. Her hair slowly slid down and hit her shoulders. Next she shook her head, making her hair arc around her head in a glistening blond halo of curls. As if in slow motion. Or maybe it was just his brain that was in slow motion. The curls bounced before settling back down again onto her shoulders. She handed him her helmet then tucked an errant curl behind an ear. Gabe watched, trying to remember why he should hate her.

Juan, the doorman in her building, stood at the front door and watched too. Gabe sent him a hard stare. The man's eyes widened, and he retreated inside.

Gabe turned back to Candace. "I'll talk to you later." Much later, like after he took a cold shower and regained his equilibrium.

"I'm going to search Murray's office tonight."

His heart leaped into his throat. Any second now, he expected to have a heart attack and drop dead right here on Park Avenue. "No you're not!"

"Yes I am."

"No, you're not. If you get caught, you'll get arrested." Although, maybe it would be the best thing that could happen, having her locked up for, oh, say, the next millennium or so.

"I won't get caught." Reaching into the pocket of her blouse she pulled out a long pink box and waggled it at him.

"What's that?"

"Silly Putty."

Grabbing her hand, he took the box and popped open the lid. Inside was an oblong of flesh-colored stuff and in the flesh-colored stuff were imprints of five keys.

His heart did a little stutter, and actually stopped for a second. "What the hell?" No kidding, what the hell, because that was where he was right now. Where did she get Silly Putty? He glanced at the humongous purse still hanging off her shoulder. It looked capable of holding everything but the kitchen sink.

"I have an imprint for all his keys," she said, "and by tonight I'll have the actual keys."

His back teeth ground together. "How did you get that?" he demanded.

"I'll never tell."

No fooling. She was like a clam. Except for the time when she told Fred every little detail about their illicit liaison, then she was like a busted water main in the middle of Lexington Avenue. Waterworks everywhere.

He sighed. "Keys or not, it's too dangerous. We can't take the chance."

She shrugged. "Okay, fine. I know you're not into the danger thing. I'll just go by myself."

Much more of this and he would have heart failure. Lowering his head, he hit it on the handlebars of his bike. Thank God for helmets. "I won't let you."

"You can't stop me."

He opened his mouth then closed it. Damn it, she was right. He would never be able to stop her doing anything she wanted to do. Unless he tied her up or warned the cops ahead of time, she would break into Murray's office.

"I'll pick you up at midnight."

"Make that one o'clock," she replied and swaggered through the doors Juan held open.

His head reeling, Gabe stowed the extra helmet then restarted his bike and took off. He knew he should make plans about how to get rid of his unwanted inheritance but all he could think about was the fact Candace planned to commit a felony and he had just agreed to help her.

5 Death by Dogs

"I'm going to search Murray's office tonight."

Her mother yelped. Candace heard a bang, like something hard hitting metal then a muttered curse before Wendy finally managed to pull her head out of the oven. Rubbing her scalp, her mother checked for blood. With Wendy, there was frequently blood involved.

"Oh, dear," her mother said once she was certain she would survive. "I don't think you should do that." Her fingers delved into her short blond hair, massaging the bump.

"I have to do it, Mom. I need to find *The Recipe*." Why did everyone dismiss her efforts to find it? Didn't they realize without *The Recipe* the business would go up in smoke, along with her job and the jobs of everyone who worked there?

"It's too dangerous. You could get caught. You could get arrested." Her mother looked concerned.

Geez, another pessimist. "I won't get caught."

"You might. And I don't think I'd like visiting you in jail," Wendy said, turning to pull the lasagna dinner out of the oven she had reached for prior to Candace's announcement. She snatched her hand back, shaking her fingers. "Ouch! Shoot. Hot." Picking up a potholder, she tried again.

Without comment, Candace reached inside a drawer, pulled out a tube of ointment and handed it to her mother, then said, "Mom, I won't get caught. I have a key to his office. It'll be easy."

Uncapping the ointment, her mother smeared a dab on her fingers, which could ease the burn but didn't ease her concern about Candace's adventure. "That's what you always say."

Candace gritted her teeth. "Because it usually is."

Her mother pursed her lips, not looking reassured at all. She reached for the aluminum tray of lasagna again and set it on the marble-topped counter. "Murray has dogs. Dobermans." She paused. "I don't think I'd like visiting you in the hospital either."

Okay, Candace hadn't known about the dogs. "I need to do something. It's not like the police are looking for *The Recipe*. They only care about the murder. Not that I don't want Fred's murder solved." Because she did. She missed him so much it was a constant ache, but she needed to stay focused. Too many people's lives depended on it.

Taking a fork from a drawer, Wendy stabbed a hunk of lasagna and blew on it before sticking it in her mouth. "Maybe you could start with someone easier," she mumbled.

"Like who?"

"I don't know." She thought for a minute, frowning, then, "I think maybe I'd start with Susan." Wendy had never liked Susan. To be fair, Susan didn't like Wendy much either. After all, Fred divorced Susan to marry Wendy. Then again, Fred divorced Wendy to marry Vanessa, and Wendy didn't carry a grudge about it the way Susan did, although there was a slight difference. Wendy, along with Candace, continued to live in Fred's apartment even after her divorce, and Susan hadn't. Still, why should Susan care, she owned three different residences and was probably worth in the tens of millions, so it wasn't as if she ended up a loser or anything.

Since her mother raised the issue, Candace thought about it for a moment. It wasn't hard to discount the idea. "I don't think Gabe will go for it."

"Gabe?" her mother said, her face brightening. "What about Gabe?"

"He helped me put together a list of suspects, but he's made his mother off-limits. Not that it's going to stop me."

"Am I on the list?" Wendy asked. Her blue eyes sparkled at the thought.

Oh boy, how to answer that one. "Um, not really."

Wendy took another bite of lasagna. "I don't think that's fair. If Susan's on the list, I should be too."

"Mom, you're not on the list."

Wendy put her fork down so she could cross her arms over her chest. Her dainty chin went out. "Why not? I want to be on the list."

"Mom, you're not on the list and I'm not going to put you on the list, so stop asking." Her mother's face got that stubborn look.

"But it's only fair I'm on the list. At this point everyone should be a suspect."

This was getting ridiculous. "Mom. If you had *The Recipe* you would just give it to me, wouldn't you?"

Her mother frowned then said, "Of course I would. It's not like I would hide something so important from my own daughter."

It took everything she had not to roll her eyes. "Well then, there you are."

Wendy took another bite of lasagna, chewing, the wheels in her head churning so obviously it was scary. "So Gabe's helping you, huh? I always liked that boy. How is he?"

Her mother probably thought Candace was still a virgin so what was not to like. "He's fine. He's going with me to search Murray's offices."

"Really," she said, looking thoughtful. "That's a different story." Turning, she went to the refrigerator, pulled out a clear plastic bag and held it up for Candace to see.

Candace looked at her mother. "Hamburger?"

"For the dogs." Wendy stared at the bag for a minute then turned and abruptly left the kitchen. When she returned she was carrying the same bag but now it was full of meat balls.

Candace cocked a brow.

"I put sleeping pills in the hamburger." She plunked it into Candace's hand then picked up her tray of lasagna. "Give Gabe a big kiss for me," she ordered and left, already lifting a bite of lasagna toward her mouth.

Hah, as if there were kisses on the horizon, but just in case, Candace went to the powder room and brushed her teeth.

* * * *

One o'clock. Other than the taxi cabs driving by, Park Avenue was a ghost town at one o'clock in the morning. Candace stood under the street light on the corner, chewing on the ragged stump of the nail she ripped off earlier this evening. Ten minutes later a big, black SUV pulled up at the curb. Gabe poked his head out of the window.

"You're late. Again," she said, climbing in.

She could hear his teeth grinding. "Knock it off."

Candace smiled and buckled herself into the front seat. Mm, this was more like it. Tan leather seats and lots of leg room. Four solid walls, made of heavy-duty steel. "At least you brought a car."

"Naturally I brought a car," Gabe grumbled. "We're going to be doing some breaking and entering, an activity usually requiring some stealth, and motorcycles aren't exactly quiet." He steered the car downtown until he reached 58th Street where he turned. At this hour there wasn't much traffic so it took him a few minutes to drive across town and onto the 59th Street Bridge (otherwise known as the Queensborough Bridge. Or the Ed Koch Bridge—geez, who the hell knew anymore). From there they crossed over into Queens. The streets were quiet although an occasional MTA bus rumbled by.

He leaned forward and fiddled with the radio, got static, then turned it off. They drove for a few minutes in silence while Candace stared out the window when she wasn't surreptitiously looking at Gabe in his tight jeans, dark T-shirt under a black shirt. It was disgusting how good the man looked in clothes, although, if she remembered correctly, he looked even better out of them. As if he sensed her looking at him, every thirty seconds his eyes would drift over in her direction and rove over her body. She had donned black sneakers, tight black yoga pants and a snug long sleeved black turtleneck for their foray. She could have worn any old black thing but why do that when her current clothes outlined every dip and curve of her body.

"I'm stiff after our motorcycle ride," she murmured and arched her back, stretching. Her jersey top pulled tight across her bust. He muttered something under his breath, and she smiled, satisfied she'd gotten revenge for the motorcycle.

"You did that on purpose," he growled.

"Did what on purpose?"

"That...you know."

Eyes wide, Candace shook her head as if mystified. "No, I don't know."

A muscle in his jaw jumped. "Never mind," he said but his eyes kept drifting in her direction even though he was silent for the next five miles. So far, this was the most fun Candace had had in months.

They continued to drive, slowly traversing the quiet streets of Queens. "Do you know where you're going?" she finally asked. She didn't trust him; he'd always had a crappy sense of direction. One time they went to a basketball game at Madison Square Garden and he got lost returning from the men's room. He had missed the end of the game, and Candace finally took the subway home on her own, figuring he would eventually catch up with her. He did, and Candace made it worth his while to find his way back.

"Of course I know where I'm going," was the grumpy response.

"Don't you need a map or directions or something?"

"No, I don't need a map or something. I told you I'm good."

Looking irritated, he leaned forward and fiddled with the radio again but apparently decided to leave it off since nothing came out of the speakers. He continued to drive for a few miles on Queens Boulevard until they passed Queens Plaza.

The car bonged. *Turn right on Jackson Avenue in...one block.*

Candace turned to stare at him. What a bull-shitter.

He shrugged sheepishly. "GPS." He made the right turn.

Bong, bong, bong. *Make next left.*

They made a few more turns, following the GPS instructions, then Gabe slid into an empty spot at the curb. He pointed at a large dark building down the street surrounded by a chain link fence. "That's his business."

"What does he do?"

"You know those fuzzy animal slippers? He makes those."

"Frogs, I bet."

Gabe chuckled and Candace opened the door and slid out, making sure to grab the fanny pack she'd brought along. Reaching in, she pulled out a plastic bag.

He cocked his head. "What's that?"

"Meat."

"Meat?"

"Yeah, for the dogs."

His eyes widened. "Dogs," he said, swallowing. "You didn't tell me there were dogs."

"I didn't know there were dogs. I've always made it a point to avoid talking to Murray, so how should I know? But my mom seems to like him for some reason. She told me. Anyway, you're his nephew. Seems like you should know if anyone would." Strapping on the fanny pack, Candace walked toward the gate.

Gabe ran to catch up. "I avoid him too."

"Smart man."

"So maybe this isn't such a good idea. I mean the fence has barbed wire. How do you figure we're going to get inside?"

She stopped at the gate. After studying the gate for a minute she took hold of the chain looped through the gate and examined the padlock hanging from it. "Are you afraid of dogs?" she asked, turning the padlock over. Taking out the little ring holding the keys she had made, she inserted the one that seemed most like one that would fit a padlock. The lock snicked open. Opening the gate, she slipped inside.

Gabe followed, although he didn't look thrilled. "No, no, I'm not afraid of dogs. Why would you ask?" His face tensed as he viewed the empty parking lot.

A loud bark answered the question, then two very large Dobermans crept around the corner of the building across the lot. They stalked toward them, growling.

With a shriek, Gabe jumped straight in the air. He locked his hands into the wire mesh of the fence and scrambled up as high as he could where he clung, looking down at Candace. The whites of his eyes shone in the darkness.

They were beautiful dogs, Candace thought as she watched them slink across the concrete, their eyes focused on her. Muscles rippled, their black and tan coats shone under the parking lot lights. As they got closer she could see their long wet tongues lolling from their mouths. Opening the plastic bag, she pulled out a big ball of hamburger and threw it between two cars sitting on the other side of the lot. The dogs slowed, paused for a second, their noses twitching, their eyes shifting back and forth between her and the thrown meat before abruptly turning and racing toward the cars.

"Jump" she told Gabe as she quickly lobbed another meatball to the left of the first one.

He shook his head no.

"Jump down now while they're still busy with the burgers." He hesitated then jumped to the ground. She grabbed his hand and made a dash for the front door of the building. She tried a few keys without success then found the right one and opened the door. Once inside, she pulled it shut.

Gabe seemed slightly out of breath. "What are you going to do when we have to leave?" he asked.

"There are sleeping pills in the hamburger so it shouldn't be a problem by then," she replied. "Come on, let's get to work. Where should we start?"

"His office."

They wound through the narrow hallways toward the back of the building. It was a typical small business building still decorated in worn muddy-colored carpeting, fake-wood paneling, dim florescent lights and lots of Seventies orange.

Eventually Gabe stopped at a door where a sign hung on the wall with the name Murray Jones printed on it. Taking hold of the handle, he jiggled it. Locked. "Do you have the key to this too?" The tone was sarcastic, and hopeful. It sounded like he wanted to leave before they even got started but that couldn't be, not daredevil Gabe, who rode motorcycles, bungee jumped, and who wasn't afraid of anything.

Candace pulled out her ring of keys again. There were five on the ring and she had already used two. She tried two of the remaining three. Neither worked so she tried the last one. The lock turned over, letting them in. She smiled triumphantly over her shoulder at Gabe. He didn't smile back, just glanced nervously over his shoulder.

Heaving a deep sigh, because where was his sense of adventure, she entered the room and stared at it in all its fake-wood paneled glory. A small office, holding a desk, a file cabinet, a trash can and—oh, my God—another beat-up, ratty Barca-lounger. What was it with these people?

"Check the desk drawers. I'll look through the filing cabinet," she ordered.

* * * *

Reluctantly, Gabe made his way to the battered desk. He sat, almost upending when the chair tilted back way further than it was supposed to, a good indication Murray probably spent most of his day leaning back so he could sleep at his desk. After a brief struggle, he righted himself and began searching the drawers. It was a tedious task with nothing to show for it but a cloud of dust (more evidence Murray spent his time at work sleeping) and several paper cuts.

He stuck his finger in his mouth and sucked. "Find anything?" he mumbled.

"This is weird," Candace said. She stopped searching the drawer and held up a folder in her hands, leafing through some papers.

"What?"

"He keeps a log of all his bets. Football games. Baseball. Horse races. Online poker. Even the lottery."

"Murray loves to gamble." Another reason he avoided his uncle; the guy was a total putz.

"Well, he also must love losing because I can't find a single bet he's won. Looks like he's lost thousands."

Gabe snorted. "Nothing weird about that."

"Yeah, but he also has a bunch of deposit slips to his bank account. Ten thousand. Eighteen thousand. Twenty-two, five. Forty-one, nine. Geez, here's one for a hundred thousand. Where did he—" She stopped. "Gabe, did you hear that?" she whispered.

"Wh—"

"Shhhh! Someone's in the building."

He gripped the edge of the desk, tipping his head as he tried to find the sound. In the distance, he heard a scraping noise. *Oh, crap!* "We need to get out of here." His heart leaped. Why in the hell had he let Candace talk him into this?

Candace nodded, her blue eyes wide. She stuck something in her fanny pack then slid the file back into the drawer and pushed it shut. Creeping to the door, she eased it open and put her eye to the crack. "It looks clear. Let's leave while we can."

No shit. Gabe pushed the door open then, grabbing Candace's hand, he pulled her into the hallway and raced toward the front entrance. Her hand felt small and feminine in his, something he'd become intimately familiar with during that unforgettable summer so many years ago. How many times had he laced his fingers with hers as they made love? Just the memory made his breath quicken. At least he assumed it was the memory. Then again, it might be sheer terror.

They reached the front door without meeting anyone. He pulled it open and peered outside. "Looks like the coast is clear."

"Great, good, come on, let's go." She squeezed through the door. "Come on." She started down the short flight of wooden stairs, Gabe stuck to her heels like bubble gum. He glanced around. Other than the distant sound of cars on Queens Boulevard, it was quiet as a tomb. Dark as a tomb too, with the exception of the dim lights in the parking lot casting creepy shadows in far corners. He hated creepy but at least there were no Dobermans. This whole *"adventure"* totally sucked.

"Come on, let's—"

"Arf!"

Gabe swung around. Twin Doberman's appeared from between two parked cars, tongues hanging out, saliva dripping, ears perked up alertly. Nary a sign of sleepy dog.

"Shit! I thought..." he said. The Dobermans trotted in their direction. "Never mind what I thought. Come on." Gabe raced toward the outer gate standing slightly ajar, the padlock still hanging. Candace followed.

The Dobermans' trot increased in speed. He could see the hungry gleam in their eyes. Goddamnitalltohell!

"Run," he shouted and gave Candace a hard shove toward the gate.

"Gabe," she gasped as she hit the chicken wire fence.

He turned to face the dogs. *Crap!* Gabe yanked his shirt off and quickly wrapped the shirt around his forearm. Doberman One latched onto his arm and sank his teeth in. The force knocked him backwards but the shirt protected him so the teeth didn't break the skin. Not yet anyway. He shoved at the snarling dog, trying to push him back, away from Candace. Doberman Two stayed back, growling.

"Run! Get out!" he yelled to Candace, wrestling with the dog.

"Heads up," she yelled back just before something flew over his head and land at the far end of the parking lot.

He saw the dog's eyes swivel as it followed the path of the thrown object, heard a half-hearted *grrr*, then the dog's jaws sagged and he released Gabe's arm. Both dogs spun around and headed for that spot, yipping in excitement, tongues lolling. What the hell? Gabe's eyes rotated toward Candace.

"More hamburger." She threw the gate open. "Quick!"

His heart squeezing in his chest, Gabe dove for the gate Candace held open for him. Once outside, he slammed it shut, snapped the padlock closed, grabbed Candace's hand and ran until he reached his car a block away.

He stopped, panting, wheezing, trembling from the adrenalin rush. Fuck. Fuckfuckfuck fuckfuck.

Candace hiked herself up onto the hood of the car and grinned. "That was fun."

He wanted to kill her. "What the hell happened back there?" he demanded. He peeled his mauled shirt off his arm, shook it out, and checked it for teeth holes. There were a bunch. He shivered. Those holes could have been in his skin.

Candace blinked at him. "What do you mean?"

"Don't give me that crap, you know perfectly well what I mean." His heart still threatened to leap from his chest.

"No, I don't. Are you talking about the fact someone was there? How was I supposed to know the cheapest man in the world would spring for a night guard?" She gave him one of those innocent looks she had perfected. Too bad the look didn't align more with her real self.

Gabe slipped his shirt on, holes and all, wondering why he even bothered. "Yeah, that too, but we'll get to that later. I'm talking about the goddammed dogs."

She turned away. He couldn't see it but he knew she was smiling. "Ooooh, that." A shrug. "I told you, I didn't know about the dogs until my mother told me about them tonight."

Gabe gritted his teeth. "I'm talking about the fact they were supposed to be unconscious. What happened to the unconscious?"

She screwed up her mouth and cast her eyes skyward, thinking, then opening the plastic baggie, she pulled out a ball of hamburger, pulled it apart and inspected it. He heard her swallow then she put the hamburger back in the baggie and moved to drop it into her fanny pack.

Something smelled and it wasn't the hamburger. Gabe grabbed her hand.

She struggled briefly. "Hey."

"Hey yourself. Turn loose." He applied pressure to her wrist and her hand opened, dropping the baggie into his other hand. Pulling the hamburger out of the baggie, he dug through it until he found a little white pill. He held it up to the light.

"Tylenol! You gave the dogs fucking Tylenol!" He glared at her.

She shrugged, her smile a little weak and lopsided, her big blue eyes gazing innocently up at him. "Oops."

Gabe could feel steam come out of his ears. "'Oops?' Are you fucking kidding?"

The lopsided grin straightened out and became the usual Candace smile.

Gabe closed his eyes. "Don't say it. Just get in the car," he ordered.

She did. But she continued to smile.

6 The Cat's Meow

Okay, this wasn't working. Gabe was making her crazy. A little. Sort of. Okay, to be honest, a lot, but only in a good way. Mostly he made her hot. Just looking at him made her hormones fire like tiny Roman candles. It felt fantastic since it had been a long time—a really long time—since her hormones had done anything even close to Roman candles, but still, the Roman candle thing had to stop.

She had a job to do. Actually, she had two. Managing an international confectionary company and finding *The Recipe*. She needed to stay focused, but there was a problem, she couldn't do the first without accomplishing the second. Regardless, work needed to continue as if nothing had changed. The problem was there was only enough chocolate liquor for a few more days. Unless she found *The Recipe*, they would have no way of making any more so the entire production line would shut down. People were not happy.

Neither was she, based on the glower Candace saw reflected in her mirror. Grabbing the mouthwash, she took a swig, swished it around in her mouth, staring at her reflection, wondering what Gabe saw when he looked at her, not that it mattered. She was who she was, and she had no plans to change. Generally, she liked herself. She liked her natural blond hair, her neat little nose and her trim athletic figure.

She spit out the mouthwash. Conversely, she hated her tiny boobs. Mosquito bites. The good news was that her mother had little boobs when she was young but unlike all her middle-aged friends, Wendy still had nice perky ones. She wondered if Gabe liked her mosquito bites. He did when he was twenty-one, but then, tastes changed. He had matured, grown taller, broader, more muscular. Hotter.

Maybe he wanted a woman who had also matured. Translation—had bigger boobs.

She looked down at her chest and sighed. It didn't matter what he thought of her because she couldn't possibly want him. She was over him, right? The fact that just thinking about him got her all warm and gooey inside, and made her think of white picket fences and babies and growing old together, meant nothing. She never wanted those things. The business had always been enough. Yet sometimes she wished she had someone to hold her and tell her everything would be okay. Maybe that same someone would even tell her he loved her.

Instead she had a business she needed to keep running even though it wasn't her business because five hundred people depended on her.

After putting the cap back on the toothpaste, she left her bathroom and walked back to her bedroom, wondering if maybe her life was missing something because of her obsession with Contessa.

She opened the door. And shrieked. Her mother shrieked back. Candace shrieked again. It was a shriek fest.

"Shit, Mom!" Candace yelled. "You scared the crap out of me. What are you doing in my bedroom at three in the morning?" She put her hand to her chest, trying to still her heart.

Wendy's mouth turned down. She wrapped her arms around herself as she seemed to shrink into the depths of her fuzzy robe. "I just wanted to see how your date with Gabe went."

Candace shook off her slippers and crawled into her bed. She was exhausted. Surprisingly, burglaring was hard work. Given how much work it was, you would think all those burglars would get a real job, wouldn't you?

"It wasn't a date, Mom. You know that."

Her mother lay down next to Candace and draped an arm around Candace's waist, just as she when Candace was small. Candace gave her mother a hug back.

"I know but still…" Wendy said. "So, did you find anything?"

Candace sighed. It was hard to stay mad at her mother. Her mom was the best, even though she was a little wacko. "Other than finding out the hard way the pills you put into the hamburger were Tylenol, not sleeping pills, no, I didn't find anything." She decided not to say anything about the suspicious deposit slips until she did a little more digging.

There was a long silence. "Oops," her mother finally said.

"Yeah. Gabe almost got his arm chewed off."

"Oops."

"Hmmm."

"So what are you going to do now?" her mother asked next.

Candace needed to think before answering. "I'm going to keep looking."

Her mother sat up in bed. "Oh, good. Who's next?"

She eyed her mother with suspicion. "Why do you want to know?"

"I just like to keep track, that's all. So, come on, who's next?" She blinked, innocence spread all over her pretty face. Like Candace believed that.

"I'm not done with Murray but I don't think I can break into his apartment right now, not after his business was just broken into. I think I'll do… Susan."

Her mother clapped her hands. "Oh, goody." She snickered. "Can you do something about that nasty Siamese cat while you're there?"

Good lord. First vicious Doberman's, now a nasty Siamese? What next? "I don't think so, Mom. I think she might notice if something happened to the cat."

A sly smile slid across Wendy's face. Candace did a double take. There was something eerily familiar about that smile. She just couldn't put her finger on it.

"Oh, I don't know," Wendy said. "Cats fall out of high rises all the time."

"Mom! That's horrible." Pause. "Anyway, Susan lives right above a terrace. The cat would just end up with the downstairs neighbor."

Wendy sighed. "You're right. Too bad." The long silence dragged out for a while, then she whispered, "I miss him, you know."

Candace felt a pang in the middle of her chest. She rolled over to face her mother. "I know. Me too. But I'm mad at him too." She draped an arm over her mother's waist.

Her mother made a face. "Why?"

"Look what a mess he left me with after he promised Contessa would be mine." She felt a sob catch in her throat. She was trying to be brave about everything, but it was just too much; Fred's death, the broken promise, the missing recipe, the damned attraction she didn't want to feel for Gabe. "Why did he do it?"

There was a long pause before her mother answered. "I don't know. I know he loved you." Her mother could be an airhead at times, but she did have pretty good intuition.

"I know he loved me, but it seems like he didn't trust me."

Wendy sighed. "He did. After all, he left you *The Recipe*."

"Then why?" Candace said, her voice wobbling.

Wendy thought for a moment. "Well, all I can say is he works in mysterious ways," she finally said. Sitting up, she slid off the bed and walked out of the bedroom, leaving Candace to wonder if her mother meant *God* or if she was referring to Fred. With her mom, it was sometimes hard to tell.

* * * *

Candace overslept. She rarely did, even without an alarm clock. Usually there was too much to do, people to see, places to go, but not today. Okay, there were, but not the usual things since the factory would to need to run itself until further notice or at least until Candace found *The Recipe*. Today's people... person?... to see was Susan Jones.

She jumped out of bed. Ransacking her drawers, she found clean underwear then grabbed a pair of jeans and a T-shirt and dressed. She jammed her feet into a pair of rubber flip-flops and flip-flopped through the connecting door to Fred's part of the apartment then down the hall to the small bedroom situated behind the kitchen. She knocked.

"What!"

Geez. How rude. And to think, they paid this guy. She waited until he opened the door then walked in without asking. The guy was still in his bathrobe and held her copy of the Wall Street Journal in one hand and her mother's favorite coffee cup in the other. "Floyd, can you help me out?"

He grunted. Floyd-speak for "Whaddaya want?"

"Susan is going to...um, Chicago today, emergency meeting of PETA, you know?" Candace groaned inwardly. Oh my God. PETA? The woman wore fur even in summer. She rushed to continue, hoping pure speed would confuse Floyd. "Anyway, she's going to be out of town for a day or so, so she asked Gabe to ask me to ask you to give me the key to her apartment, 'cause she said you have a copy from when she and Fred got divorced, so I can feed her cat. And water it. And maybe take it for a walk." She took a deep breath, nearly ready to pass out from lack of oxygen.

He stared at her, dead-faced. "Cats don't go for walks."

Candace frowned, hoping she looked convincingly confused. "Okay, maybe I misunderstood. Maybe she said I should talk to it."

The dead-face didn't change.

Candace batted her eyelashes and dimpled, ala Shirley Temple, only without the tap-shoes. "Hey, you wouldn't want the cat to die of heat prostration because it didn't have water, would you?"

Without a word, he turned, went to a dresser, opened the drawer and pulled out a key ring. He held it out to Candace, still without a word. Candace took it from him and got out of there while the getting was good.

* * * *

Candace opened the door of the cab and got out. Sheesh! Twenty-four dollars and ninety-five cents, plus tip, just to go crosstown then uptown a few blocks. She should have taken the bus. Since Susan's address was an even number, the building would be on the south side so she crossed to the other side and walked until she arrived directly across from Susan's building. She stopped, looked around and found an entryway to a modern luxury building where she could stand and observe the door to Susan's building without being spotted. She settled in and waited. And waited. And waited.

The doorman where she stood was giving her the evil eye and her feet were killing her. She shifted her weight for the hundredth time in the last hour. Geez, maybe this was a dumb idea. Maybe Susan never left her apartment.

She'd give it one more hour.

She reached to pull her cell phone out of her pocket so she could at least play a few video games to kill the time when on the other side of the street she saw a flash of color and saw Susan, wearing a bright red dress, walk through the brass front doors, her doorman trotting behind. He pulled a whistle from his pocket and blew it shrilly several times. When that got no response, he ran the half block over to Columbus Avenue and blew it again. A cab swerved across two lanes of traffic and screeched to a halt in front of the doorman, who waved him toward where Susan stood at the curb, arms crossed, foot tapping impatiently, her mouth pulled into a tight line.

The cab made the turn, drove the half block, and stopped in front of Susan. She stepped off the curb and into the cab.

Candace grinned. Bye-bye, Susan. Dropping her phone back into her pocket, she ran across the street while the poor doorman stood on the corner catching his breath, and pushed her way through the double doors into the marble-clad lobby. Racing across the lobby and rounding a corner, she found the elevators. When she hit the button, an elevator door opened up immediately. She stepped inside, hit 14, and up she went.

Yes!

The elevator door slid open, and Candace ran down the hall until she found 14-F. She slid the key in the lock and opened the door. From the foyer, she could see the living room.

Wow. She knew the woman had expensive taste and the money to indulge her tastes, but geez. Everywhere she looked the place showed the signs of money spent. The antique armoire standing on the far wall surely cost a hundred thousand dollars. Flanking each side of a gray velvet sofa were several marquisette inlaid tables from the Louis XIV period. Odds were, they were real antiques. Over the massive scrolled fireplace hung a painting that looked like a genuine Erte. There were a couple of other smaller etchings she thought might be Degas. The ceiling... oh, my God, the ceiling was silver-leafed.

On her right was a closed door. She opened it to see a powder room. Next to that, the opening to a hallway, probably leading to the bedrooms. To the left a dining room. More expensive inlaid furniture. Traveling past the dining room she entered a humongous kitchen with Viking appliances, quartz counters, cherry cabinets, and a sunny dining nook. She'd heard from Fred that his first wife didn't cook, so what a waste, but still, only the best for Susan. Back to the dining room and through a wide archway on the left was a lounge with comfortable couches and a sixty-five inch television.

This must be a seven million dollar apartment, and this was one of three homes she owned. Susan spent most of her time in her eight bedroom house on the water in Miami Beach but she also owned a small four bedroom, four million dollar home in Laguna Hills, California. According to Wendy, Susan only came to New York City in the fall, when the weather was gorgeous, and December, ostensibly to see Gabe, but mostly to shop on Fifth Avenue.

Not bad for a girl who grew up on a farm in Iowa feeding pigs and gathering eggs.

Fortunately for Candace, the place was neat and not overly cluttered. That should make it much easier to search. She retraced her steps to the lounge and checked out all the shelves there as well as the drawers in the side tables. Nothing. She thought about checking in the kitchen, but it seemed like a remote possibility, so she returned to the living room.

She started with the bookcases on either side of the fireplace. After going through all the wicker baskets on the bottom shelf, she moved to the small collection of leather-bound books tucked between the knickknacks, pulling each book out and shaking it to see if anything fell out. Nothing. She checked her watch. Between the lounge and the living room it took forty-five minutes.

She quickly moved on to the spindly antique desk under the window. The drawers were shallow and held a few papers, pens, and some paperclips.

Hmm. Nibbling on a hangnail, she swept her gaze around the living room, looking for anyplace else she might search. There were a few books on the coffee table, so she looked through those. As expected, there was nothing. Next, she lifted all the pictures away from the walls, just in case something was attached to the back. Nothing. Well, shoot. Okay, that left the bedrooms.

She walked into the hallway. Four closed doors. She opened the one in front of her. Bathroom. Very luxurious. Marble walls and a million shower heads in the enormous shower, a soaking tub set into a platform. Closing the door, she opened the one on her right. It had the unlived-in look of a guest bedroom so she closed that door too. She opened the next one. It was filled to the rafters with clothing. Obviously, this is where she kept the spoils of her Fifth Avenue shopping. Which left the last door which was probably the master bedroom. She opened the door.

Ryowwlll! The Siamese cat leaped straight up in the air from where it lay on the bed. Candace screamed. The cat screamed. It landed on the carpet then ran straight up the wall for a few feet before flipping around and landing back on the carpet, back arched.

How the hell did it do that!

The cat sped around the room, screaming and yowling like a banshee having a tooth extracted without Novocain. After a few whirlwind circles it leaped back onto the bed where it crouched, tail puffed up like a bulrush, and glared at Candace, or at least one eye did. The other one looked fiercely off to the left somewhere, focused on something else entirely.

Candace quickly closed the door. If Susan came home and found the cat in the living room, she would know she was burgled. She approached the bed, hand out. "Here, kitty, kitty, kitty."

The cat spat at her. Okay, so they wouldn't be friends. As long as it didn't leap on her back and claw her to death when she searched the room, Candace didn't care.

Giving the room a quick scan, she determined Susan's real life took place in this room. To the right was a door that, when she opened it, disclosed a small closet. There were several large bookshelves along one wall. The bottom half of the bookshelves was all drawers, the shelves held hundreds of tattered paperbacks, as well as a large flat screened TV. On the other side of the enormous four-poster bed was a huge desk covered with piles of crap.

She walked over to the desk. The cat's eyes followed her, a low growl humming in its throat.

"Hush."

Surprisingly, it did. It blinked its slanty blue eyes then sat down on its haunches and began licking itself. Keeping a wary eye on it, Candace pulled out the first drawer. Oh crap, it was crammed full of stuff. With a sigh, she pulled the files out and began sorting through them.

By the time she looked through every drawer her back was in knots. She straightened, stretched. When she looked down the cat was at her feet, winding its lithe little body around and around her ankles. "Shoo."

"ROWW!"

Candace covered her ears. No wonder her mother hated this cat. Its meow had a decibel level equivalent to a 747 jet.

"Shoo!"

The cat looked up at her, sort of, and began purring. Oh for Christ's sake. The winding continued until her jeans were covered in black and tan Siamese hair.

"Go away!"

The cat jumped up on her lap. Candace jerked to her feet and the cat fell with a thump and another screech. One eye looked at her reproachfully. The other one stared off to the left and appeared to be glaring.

With a sigh, Candace crouched down. "I'm sorry." She gave it a tentative scratch between the ears. The sound of the cat's motor filled the room. Great, now the damned cat was in love with her. She glanced over her shoulder, wondering if she possessed the energy to sort through the piles of paper littering the desk top. No, she didn't, not and return everything to the correct place. She left the desk in favor of one of the bedside tables and opened a drawer.

She gasped. Shit! A gun. Susan had a gun! Maybe even the gun that killed Fred. Was it possible? Surely not, but the only way she would know was if the police tested it. She narrowed her eyes and stared at the gun. Did she dare? Would Susan notice if it was gone. Of course, she would. She was evil, not stupid.

Suddenly she heard a noise, the sound of the front door opening, then closing.

Holy crap! She looked wildly around the room, looking for a place to hide before realizing the only place was under the tall four-poster bed. She dove under it and pulled the dust ruffle back in place just as the bedroom door opened.

"Hi, Contessa," she heard Susan say.

Contessa? Like Fred and the chocolates? How weird was that?

The cat's motor sped up.

"What did you do while Mommy was gone, hmmm, sweetie? Did you have a good nap?"

Susan's feet thudded softly on the carpet then clothing rustled as she undressed. Candace's heart beat so hard it felt like it would break her sternum. What had she gotten herself into? She laid her cheek on the plush white carpet, her thoughts going round and round. What if Susan stayed home for the rest of the day? How would she escape?

Oh, God, she suddenly thought. What if Susan was one of those people who only went out once a week? Entirely possible since Candace doubted the woman had any friends, which meant she only went out to troll around the Fifth Avenue shops, and to get her hair done. Candace would starve to death under the bed, only to be discovered years later, a shriveled-up, desiccated *thing* they would have to do DNA testing on to figure out who she was. Heck, forget *who* she was, they would probably need DNA to figure out *what* she was.

She heard bare feet pad across the room and into the hall. The bathroom door opened. The shower turned on.

This was her chance! She started to slide out from under the bed and came face to face with the cat. The cat batted her across the face, claws and all.

"OW!"

The cat sat down on its haunches and stared at her. It was a cold stare, a lethal stare. Candace suddenly remembered in ancient Siam, Siamese cats guarded the palace, and no wonder; if they were as scary as this cat, no one in his right mind would try to invade the palace. Candace pulled her head back under the bed and thought for a minute then scooted around to the other side of the bed.

She poked her head out.

RYOWWWW! A clawed paw smacked her in the face. *Holy crap!* Tears rushed to her eyes. Doing a quick U-turn, she tried slithering out at the end of the bed. The cat leaped on her head, tangling its claws in her hair, and yowled.

The bathroom door opened. "Contessa? Is everything all right?" The cat raced out of the bedroom. "No, sweetie, you can't come in here while I'm showering. You get hair all over me. Sorry, sweetie." The door shut, and before Candace could get more than her head out from under the bed the cat was back at its post. It growled. Then, in a sudden turn-around, it lifted a front paw, licked it and began to purr. It was clearly telling Candace, "I like you right where you are."

Candace rolled up into a ball under the bed. She was so screwed. Why hadn't she listened to Gabe when he warned her? Hard as it was to admit, Gabe was right.

A light bulb went off. Lifting a hip, she reached into her pocket.

7 Birds do it, Bees do it

Gabe flopped onto his brown leather typical-bachelor sofa. Grabbing the remote, he turned on his flat-screen TV, put his bare feet on the glass and chrome coffee table and flipped the channel to ESPN. It was Saturday, he was exhausted, and he intended to spend the entire day parked in front of his television watching baseball, preferably the Yankees. If he ran out of baseball he'd happily switch to NASCAR racing or world-wide soccer. Hell, he would even watch golf if it was all that was available.

What he wouldn't do was think about Candace. Thinking about Candace inevitably led to him feeling agitated, irate, and turned on, not what he wanted to feel on his day off.

He popped the top on his can of beer and settled in. Then his cell phone rang.

He gritted his teeth and stared balefully at the phone sitting on his coffee table, determined not to let it interrupt his day. It continued to ring. Well, he would just outlast it. It rang several more times and finally went to voice mail. With a sigh of relief, he scrunched further down into the couch and took a big slug of beer. He held it in his mouth for a minute, enjoying the tang then let it slide down his throat. God, so good.

He lifted the can again. And his cell phone rang. *God damn it.* With a sigh, he picked it up. "Yeah."

"Hey, we're all going over to the high school to shoot some hoops. Come with us?"

His friend, Bill. Short, geeky, and an unbelievable basketball player.

"Not today. I've gone ten straight days without a break. I need some down time."

"Aw, come on. I'll take you out for a brewski afterwards." Blatant bribery, which usually worked, but his ass was dragging.

"I already have a beer. And I have the Yankees too, so no thanks."

"Yeah, but you don't have us."

Gabe sighed. "Look, my dad just died a few days ago and I'm not in the mood. Next time, okay?"

"Aw, shit, man. I'm sorry. I didn't know." He paused. "Hey, is there anything us guys can do? I mean, like, bring you food or anything?"

"Why the hell would you think I'd want you to bring me food?"

"Fuck, I don't know. It's what my mom always does, so, you know...."

"Thanks, but I just need some time.

"Okay. Right. Take care, man. I mean it. Catch you next time, though, right?"

"It's a promise." Gabe hung up, smiling, the conversation having cheered him up for some strange reason, then sobered. He still needed to do something about Contessa. He hated the idea he would be burdened with his father's legacy for the rest of his life.

He wasn't a kid anymore. He had grown up, developed his own ideas, and had his own ways of doing things but from the very start, Fred hadn't trusted those new ideas and new ways of doing things. Gabe had always felt that meant Fred didn't trust Gabe.

On the other hand, wasn't inheriting Contessa a sign his father did trust him?

Or, God forbid, maybe it was just Fred being manipulative. *You're going to run Contessa whether you like it or not. So there.*

Damn it, now that Gabe thought about it, maybe it wasn't about trust, maybe it was about fucking control. For the first time, Gabe began to put all the pieces together in his mind. For Fred, it was always either his way or the highway and even though he was dead now, he was still trying to control his son. He saddled Gabe with that damned albatross called

Contessa. Shit, he was so confused, but only about his father's motives. He wasn't at all confused about what he wanted.

Cheers blared from the television, pulling him out of the blackness he was in. Yes! The Yankees just hit one out of the park. He settled in for a good game.

The phone rang again.

Fuck! He gritted his teeth but picked it up. "Yeah."

"Hi, Gabey." The seductive voice scraped his nerves like a nail file on raw skin.

Son of a B. "Hey, Serena."

"You haven't called me in forever."

Gee, and why was that? Maybe because he didn't want to speak to her? "Sorry. I've been tied up. It's our busy season, you know. Summer and all."

"You had plenty of time for me last summer," she said, her voice just edging on a whine

"Business has picked up. I haven't had time to do much of anything but work." Really, he should just tell her the truth, that after the newness wore off and she'd shown her true self, it turned out her true self was possessive, vain, and hot tempered. It was the hot-tempered part that made him reluctant to say anything.

"But Gabey. I miss you."

Sorry I can't say the same. "Sorry. Maybe once summer is over, I'll have more time." *Coward.*

A hiss came over the phone. "Is it another woman?"

No. At least he didn't think so. Okay, maybe it was, since he couldn't stop thinking about Candace, although he couldn't swear he was thinking of her in a good way. "No. I just don't have time to see you right now."

"Are you dumping me!"

He sighed. He forgot, along with her other negative traits, she was also not very bright. "If you want to know the truth, Serena, I already did. You're just so self-involved you haven't figured it out yet."

She screeched, making his head ring then she called him a few foul names and hung up. He winced. At least she was gone. Hopefully.

With a sigh of relief, he relaxed back into his comfy leather couch. Suddenly the phone pinged, signaling a text message. He ignored it. After a few seconds, it pinged again. Irritated, he glanced at the message highlighted at the top of the screen.

Help! He frowned. Probably one of his buddies playing a joke.

Without bothering to look further at the message, he deleted it and went back to his game.

The Yankees just scored another run when the phone rang again! Damn it. This time he ignored it. It rang and rang then went to voice mail, but not before making his nerves jangle just as loudly as the phone. Really, he should just throw the damned thing into a fucking drawer until he was ready to talk to people. Leaning over, he picked it up, meaning to do just that. And it rang again!

He stabbed the receive button on the screen. "What!" he yelled.

"Gabe?"

The voice was so quiet he could barely hear. "Who is this?" He heard a mumble but couldn't distinguish the words. "Answer me or I'm going to hang up."

"NO!"

"Candace?" He held the phone out so he could see the screen. "Is that you? Speak up. I can't hear you."

He heard a sob.

"Candace? What's going on?"

"Help," said a tiny little voice, then the rest of the story came pouring out.

* * * *

Gabe roared up onto the ramp exiting off FDR Drive and took the overpass over the highway then over to Third Avenue and rode uptown. He slowed when he hit 68th Street, traveled across the park then up to 81st Street where he found a spot to park his bike. Dismounting, he stored his helmet and walked to his mother's apartment building.

"Hey, Mike," he said as he breezed by the portly doorman.

"Hi, Mister Jones. How are you today?" He tapped a finger to the brim of his cap.

"I'm good. You too, I hope." Not waiting for a response, Gabe jumped on the elevator and rode it up to the fourteenth floor.

He knocked on his mother's door. The door opened.

"Gabe? What are you doing here?" As usual, his mother looked perfect. Perfect hair. Perfect nails. Perfect clothes. It would be nice if, just once in a while, the woman exhibited a flaw.

"Well?" She lifted a perfect brow.

Oh. Right. What was he doing here? "I...uh, came to take you out for dinner."

Stepping aside, she let him in, shutting the door behind him then checked her watch. "It's only two-thirty."

"Right." He wracked his brain. "Uh, I thought we could go to the Met first. They've got a new exhibit of Impressionist artists and I thought you might like to see it." He groaned inside. Total bullshit.

Susan crossed her arms over her breasts and gave him a narrow look. "All right. What's going on? You never want to take me out to dinner and you hate the French Impressionists."

More brain wracking. Which resulted in a solution but not a solution he liked. "I, uh..." He squirmed. "...um... have a problem."

She furrowed her brow, puzzled. "What kind of problem?"

He could feel the red creep up his face. If it was possible to will oneself to die, he would die right on the spot. "I, uh... See, there's this girl..."

Her face lit up. "Really. Well, why didn't you just say so? Let me get some shoes," she said, and off she went to the bedroom.

He waited impatiently until she returned. He opened the front door then stopped, snapping his fingers. "Oh, shoot. I want to use your restroom before we go. Is that okay?"

"Certainly."

"Why don't you go on downstairs," he said. "I'll meet you in the lobby."

"What's wrong with me waiting right here?"

Shit. "Um, I just... you know. Um." Boy, that was articulate.

Her arms crossed again. "Oh, for heaven's sake. I've heard you go before."

His face flamed, but what could he say? He shrugged instead.

"Fine," she said impatiently. "Whatever. I'll meet you downstairs. Just push the button on the side of the door so it locks." She left and closed the door behind her.

He waited a minute to make sure she was gone then dashed into the bedroom. Kneeling down, he whispered, "She's gone, and I'm leaving in a minute. Give it five minutes and then get your ass out from under there and out of this apartment."

He heard a tiny squeak, like a scared little mouse.

"Once you're out of here, go home and don't you dare leave. I'll see you there at seven." With that, he left to go have what was sure to be the most humiliating experience of his life.

* * * *

Candace paced the length of the enormous (okay, it was only moderate sized...this was New York City, after all) living room. She hit the end of the room and turned, headed back in the other direction. She checked her watch. Seven-thirty, a full thirty minutes after Gabe said he would be here. He was late, as usual.

Not that she minded him being late. She wasn't in any hurry to die. She stuck her thumb in her mouth and chewed on the hangnail that was bothering her. She wished her mother was here to keep her company—and alive. Highly unlikely Gabe would commit murder in front of Wendy, but her mother was at her hairdressers so it was doubtful she would return in time to rescue Candace.

She hit the end of the room again and turned.

The doorbell rang. *Brrrrt, brrrrrt, brrrrrt, brrrrrt.* Without waiting for a response, the bozo at the buzzer banged repeatedly on the door. She dashed over to the heavy walnut door and flung it open.

He charged in, uninvited. He wore blue jeans and a gray long-sleeved shirt and had helmet head, which meant he rode his bike over, but it was his face that caught her attention.

Oh boy, he looked angry.

She shut the door behind him. "Please. Come on in."

"Don't give me that sarcastic shit," he yelled.

"Excuse me?"

"No, I won't excuse you," he answered, still yelling, but now the yelling was accompanied by a lot of arm waving as he strode toward her. "What the hell were you thinking?"

Candace retreated to the other side of the living room.

He followed. "I told you to leave my mother out of this." Two more steps brought him looming over her, his nose nearly touching hers.

Boy, he was really big.

"I told you no more breaking and entering. And what did you do?" he demanded.

Candace opened her mouth to answer but he didn't wait.

"You went to her apartment and nearly got caught!" One hand went to his head, fingers threading through his hair in frustration, making the dark curls wave wildly around his head.

And, boy oh boy, he was so damned sexy.

Without thinking, she threw herself at him, wrapping her arms around his neck, her legs around his waist. She locked her lips on his and gave him tongue.

He growled then groaned. His arms went around her, nearly crushing her, and his mouth opened, devouring hers.

"Damn it," he hissed at the same time that one hand went to her blouse and tore the front open. Buttons flew. She never believed that bullshit in romance novels about buttons flying off—she always figured the shirt would tear first—but apparently it could happen. *Hot damn!*

Reaching between them, she yanked his shirt out of the waistband of his jeans then popped open the buttons, baring his chest. He had such a great chest, just the right amount of muscles, sleek skin, and soft curly hair. She delved through the soft curls until she reached the nub of a nipple then made a circle around it. He shuddered, his skin jumping as if it was independent of his body.

One of his hands went to the waistband of her shorts. "Off," he mumbled against her neck, his teeth nipping all the sensitive spots.

Candace could feel herself getting wet. And hot, very hot. She wanted him to touch her there, where she burned.

"Touch me," she told him, pushing his shirt off his shoulders. He shrugged out of his shirt, one arm at a time then his hands returned immediately to her shorts. She heard the *ZZZZ* of her zipper going down.

"Off," he said again, and began to shift her in his arms, removing her legs from around his waist so he could remove her shorts. After that, her panties were no problem, he just ripped them in two then flung them over his shoulder. She felt him take a few steps until the cool wood of the long, low credenza hit the back of her legs. He lowered her butt to the surface as one hand swept off all the bric-a-brac and laid her back. She heard a couple of muted pops as he undid the buttons of his pants.

"If you don't want this," he grumbled, "tell me now. Otherwise, I'm going to fuck you until neither of us can stand."

He had to ask? "Geez, Jones, stop wasting time," she said and held her arms out.

With a deep growl, he slid himself inside.

She arched her back and panted with excitement. *Ohmigod*, it felt so good. He was thick and hard and hot as he pumped into her, slick and hot, his skin so smoo...

Eeeeek. "Stop!"

He jumped. Blinked. His head rose, his gaze met hers briefly, then his eyelids drooped, he gritted his teeth and groaned. His hips flexed.

"Stop, stop, stop!" She smacked him on the shoulder.

He jerked his head up again and stared at her, looking thoroughly peeved and unbelievably turned on. "Jesus Christ! What! You can't just tell a guy 'stop' once he's going."

"No condom," she said breathlessly.

His lips parted. She could see him trying to shift his thoughts from GO GO GO to STOP STOP STOP. His arms trembled, the skin on his back twitched. When he finally wrapped his mind around it, he looked pained. "Crap. Okay. No condom. Got it." He pulled out, swearing under his breath then twisted around and reached into his back pocket, pulled out his wallet and extracted a foil wrapper. He held it up. "Okay?"

She nodded. "Hurry," she told him. If the itch didn't get scratched soon, she was going to spontaneously combust.

He tore open the wrapper, quickly slid the condom in place and slid back home.

Home! Ack, shit.

"Stop," she yelled.

He was so startled he jerked out of her. "Jesus Christ, Candace! What now?"

"My mother's due home in a few minutes."

His head dropped. He muttered, "Jeez, Jones, is this really worth it?" then his jaw tightened, and he continued with, "Fuck yes, it is."

Straightening, he yanked his pants back up to his hips but didn't bother fastening them—with his huge hard-on jutting out she didn't see how he could—than scooped her up off the credenza. Following her instructions, he carried her through the connecting door to the adjacent apartment and her bedroom. He dropped her onto her bed.

"Don't you dare move a muscle," he ordered, pointing a finger at her. She wasn't so turned on she couldn't see that his finger shook.

She nodded. Assured she wasn't going anywhere, he hurried to the bedroom door. She heard the lock *snick* into place.

He returned to the bed, his face hard with passion as he stared at her spread out on the mattress like an all-you-can-eat buffet. The lust in his eyes said he was going to get his money's worth.

"Like what you see?" she purred.

His nostrils flared in response.

Reaching down, Candace touched herself. She was wet and touching herself felt so good. She ran her finger along her folds.

He groaned. "God, Candace, don't do that, you're killing me," he said, so she stopped. Looked at him. Then smiling, she withdrew her hand.

He swore under his breath. "Crap, Candace, don't listen to me. I'm just the drooling idiot whose brain is... You know." He pointed a finger at his jutting penis. "Don't stop now. Please."

She laughed and got her hand back to work.

His hands went to his jeans, and he pushed them down. Bending, he tried to pull them off his legs. She could hear him swearing as they got stuck on his shoes, then he was naked and all two hundred and some odd pounds were on top of her, and his magnificent hard-on slid inside her and it was good, so good as he plunged into her, moving her across the mattress with the strength of his movement.

She wrapped her legs around him, increasing the friction. She could feel him deep inside her, touching her womb. The soft hair on his chest stroked across her sensitive nipples as he moved in her. His mouth landed everywhere on her, on the tender skin of her neck, her breasts, then on her mouth, his tongue thrusting, matching the ebb and flow of his cock. The heat built, the need to come grew. She ran her hands over his back, feeling the muscles bunch as he worked her. He was hot and sweaty and all man. He groaned, murmured unintelligible words, his breath hot against her face.

Inside, need twisted, a burning itch, then suddenly it erupted, the release long and pulsing and so powerful she screamed.

He gave one last hard push, jamming her up against the headboard then, with a muffled shout, shuddered in release. He stayed on top of her for a long time, just breathing. Finally, with a soft apology, he slid out and rolled over to lie at her side. "Holy shit."

Candace let out a deep sigh. Wow, that was better than she remembered. Apparently, there was something to be said for getting older. She rolled onto her side, facing him, and ran a hand over his stomach, feeling the tight abs and, nestled in the slight convexity below his ribcage, his belly button. Even that was sexy.

He took her hand and put it back on her hip. "Don't think you're going to soften me up."

What! Candace jerked to a sitting position. "What do you mean, soften you up? I'm not trying to soften you up."

"Sure you are. Otherwise why jump my bones?"

Picking up a pillow, she smashed him over the head. He put his hands out to protect himself. "Maybe I jumped your bones because I like your bones, you big moron," she yelled furiously at him. "Maybe you make me hot. Maybe I think you're sexy."

He opened his mouth to respond but she lifted the pillow and jammed it over his face. He gurgled.

"You big dope. Maybe I just needed to get my rocks off."

He pushed the pillow aside and smiled up at her. "No, you didn't. It's because you like me. You really like me."

Unfortunately, he might be right. Frustrated, Candace tossed the pillow on the floor. "What, are you Sally Field now?"

Sure, all six-foot four of him. Tugging on her arm, he pulled her down so she nestled up against his side again then draped her arm across his waist. "No, I'm not Sally Field, but it makes me crazy when you do exactly what I tell you not to do."

"You're not the boss of me," she said truculently. Horrible man. She took her arm back and crossed both of them over her stomach, holding herself as far away from him as possible.

"I'm not trying to be the boss of you, I'm trying to keep you from getting yourself killed."

She had no intention of getting killed. "Susan wouldn't kill me." On the other hand, there was that gun.

He snorted and crossed his arms under his head, making the muscles in his chest flex enticingly. It was too much to resist. She spread herself along his side and ruffled the hair on his chest. "The worst thing that would have happened is the cat would have scratched me." She gave him her best smile.

* * * *

Oh God. That smile. A shiver ran up Gabe's spine. Okay, so he had an unbelievable letch for the woman, but why did she have to be so stubborn? "Candy—" he began.

She growled at him, his little lioness.

"Okay. Candace," he said more deliberately, knowing it wasn't worth the fight. "You've got to stop this. Really. I'm afraid you'll get hurt—or worse. Just let the police handle it, okay?"

He felt something hot and wet land on his chest. Oh, crap, she was crying. Candace never cried, not even the time she dropped a bowling ball on her foot and broke three toes.

"I can't," she sniffled.

Panic made his stomach quiver. "Sure you can." He gave her a gingerly pat on her shoulder.

"No, I can't. I have to do this." Her voice shook with desperation.

Oh, geez. He went silent, not sure what to say. Experience told him if he didn't say just the right thing she would do just the opposite of what he wanted. He gave her shoulder a squeeze. If only he understood better how her mind worked. Admittedly, he probably never would but at least he could try. "Okay, tell me why you have to do this."

The tenuous hold she had on her emotions seemed to slip. A sob hiccupped out. "The police just care about finding Fred's murderer. I care about that too, I truly do, because I loved your father even if he was an idiot sometimes, but I have to find *The Recipe*. Everyone's depending on me. Fred would never forgive me if I let Contessa fail."

Geez, another guilt-ridden victim of his dad's insane need to control. Gabe admitted he resented her for the last ten years or so but at this point he almost felt sorry for her. He knew what the man was like.

"Who's depending on you?" he asked softly.

"All those people. Everyone who works on the line and in the shipping center and in corporate. They're all looking to me to find *The Recipe*. Without that, we have no business, and with no business they have no jobs, and with manufacturing disappearing in New York City they won't be able to find work, except maybe at a McDonald's for nine dollars an hour and who wants to work for McDonald's anyway. Sarah, who works in accounting, is pregnant and her husband just lost his job so without Contessa they have no health insurance. Jamal, one of the guys on the line, his mother has Alzheimer's and he's her only support, and Jose in shipping has six kids to support, and his daughters Marina and Kristina are in college." She hiccupped again. "Fred would know what to do and I miss him so much. Why did he have to die, Gabe? Why did someone murder him?"

Gabe felt his heart twist painfully in his chest. Here he thought she was just being stubborn—okay, she *was* being stubborn—but it was more than that. She cared about her employees. He could understand, since he had twenty-five people who worked for him and he knew and cared about all of them, but until now, he hadn't understood the depths of her grief for Fred. He shared her grief, only his was worse because of his stupidity and stubbornness.

Gabe's childhood had been one of constant failure; bad grades, bad behavior, bad attitude. His father reacted predictably. The worse Gabe got, the harder Fred tried to control his behavior.

Why are you wasting so much time on video games? Why were you playing in the park when you should be studying? Your grades are a disgrace. How do you think you're getting into an Ivy League college? And last, *You're going to inherit a multi-million dollar confectionary company. Why are you wasting time with some rinky-dink saltwater taffy outfit?*

That had hurt. His father inherited a small but successful company and made it a huge successful company. Yet he hadn't understood Gabe's need to prove, if only to himself after his less-than-stellar beginnings, that he could succeed on his own.

They spent his entire adolescence and early adulthood fighting, and now his father was gone and he would never have another chance. Why? Why had they let something, that in retrospect was so unimportant, get in the way of loving each other?

He cleared his throat, trying to master the tremor in his own voice. "First of all, this is not your fault. Stop feeling guilty." Right, because he had enough guilt for the two of them. "Second of all, we'll find *The Recipe*, and when we find *The Recipe*, we'll find the guy who killed my father." His throat tightened and he needed to stop for a minute to collect himself again. "I promise we'll find the guy and *The Recipe*. We just need a plan. No more of this running around like a crazy person, breaking into people's homes and businesses."

He heard her sigh. "Okay, Sherlock. What's your big plan, then, if we can't break into people's houses and things? We already proved we're no good at grilling people for information."

He thought for a minute. Damn her, she was right. "Okay. Maybe we'll have to do a little breaking and entering."

She pumped her fist. "Yes!"

That was when Gabe knew he'd made big mistake number three.

8 Love and Loss

Gabe reached over to the other side of the bed, expecting a warm, naked female body. What he got was a fistful of stuffed bunny. He stared at the mangy pink fur, and the dog-chewed ears he recognized from his first time in Candace's bed, and tried to figure out how he ended up here again when he'd sworn he wouldn't.

There was this saying, *Live and Learn?* Apparently not in his wheelhouse.

But since he was here, the least she could have done after enticing him into bed was stick around afterwards, but she hadn't, and now he felt cheap and used and...

He snickered. Hah! Being used was the best thing that ever happened to him.

He waited for a few minutes, hoping she would come back and use him again, but when it became obvious that wouldn't happen he sat up and slid out of bed. Reaching for his pants, he slipped into them, commando-style. Not the most comfortable style when riding a motorcycle but it would have to do till he got home. He stuffed his briefs into his back pocket then reached for his shirt.

He was halfway into his shirt when, from somewhere in the pile of sheets and wadded-up comforter, he heard the sound of his cell phone. Using his free hand, he threw back the sheets, searching. When he didn't find it, he tore the comforter off the bed and threw it on the floor. At the foot of the bed he finally found his phone. He grabbed it up. "Jones," he said, trying to get his other arm into the shirt sleeve.

"This is Detective Dolan. You said you wanted me to call you when we were done with the autopsy."

Gabe gave up trying to get his shirt on; it was half wrong side out and one sleeve had twisted inside itself. He took it off and sat on the edge of the bed. "So you're done? Can I pick up..." He stopped, swallowing. "My dad's body?"

Dolan hesitated before answering. "Yes, we can release him this afternoon."

"What about the autopsy? Anything?"

This time the silence lasted longer. "We're still working on the test results. Shall I tell the coroner someone will make arrangements today?"

Okay, that was evasive. "Yeah, I'll make sure he's picked up today. Thanks." He got the address then hung up, feeling lower than he had since he first heard the news. Those feelings of guilt resurfaced, burning a hole in his stomach that matched the burning in his eyes.

He took a deep breath then blinked a couple of times to keep the tears from falling. He would never forgive himself for how things ended with his father, but he could make up for some of it by making sure his killer was brought to justice. Sitting here feeling guilty wasn't going to do it.

His resolve hardening, he stood and slipped into this shirt, buttoned it, and went looking for Candace.

* * * *

Candace jumped a foot when Gabe stalked into the breakfast room. He stopped right inside the doorway and stared at her, eyes narrowed as his gaze zeroed in on the remnants of eggs, bacon and an orange on her plate. He still wore his clothes from yesterday but no way did the wrinkled shirt and crumpled jeans detract from the sexy aura he radiated. Her throat suddenly bone-dry, she struggled to swallow the English muffin in her mouth but the damned thing stuck halfway down. Grabbing her glass of orange juice, she washed it down.

"Hi," she said brightly.

He growled. His stomach echoed the sentiments. "You couldn't wake me up?"

She shrugged but didn't answer. She was still dealing with his overwhelming hotness.

His jaw tightened. "Fine. I'll fix my own."

Turning away, he surveyed the kitchen, honing in on the stove still covered with the pans Candace had used to fix breakfast. He grabbed two small pans, took them to the sink, washed them, then walked to the refrigerator and took out eggs and bacon. Propping her chin in her hand, Candace watched him drop the bacon into one pan. He broke the eggs into the second pan then grabbed a spatula and, jaw clenched, beat the eggs half to death.

From where she sat, Candace had a great view of his ass, which was up there in the top three best asses ever, maybe even the top two. Okay, she had seen it naked and it was the best male fanny in the world. Except for maybe the guys at Chippendales, but they didn't count; everyone knew Chippendales weren't real people. She was tempted to throw him on top of the kitchen island and have her way with him. Instead, she took another bite of English muffin as he shook salt and pepper on the eggs, causing his yummy biceps to bulge.

Slapping the eggs and bacon on a plate, he sat down next to Candace and shoved a bite of egg in his mouth, glowering.

She picked up the pad of paper lying next to her plate. "Okay, so I'm thinking we should try Vanessa next."

He gasped, coughed, and finally grabbed her orange juice and took a big swallow.

At that moment Wendy breezed in, dressed in denim Bermuda shorts, a pink cotton blouse and espadrilles. She walked to the refrigerator, saying, "Morning," as she opened the door and stuck her head inside. She turned, carton of milk in hand, then pulled a glass from a cupboard and poured a glass.

"Gabe, it's so nice to see you again," she said. "I hope you and Candy had a good time last night."

Gabe spewed orange juice all over Candace's clean T-shirt.

Wendy grabbed a clean dishtowel and wet it in the sink. "Good heavens. What's the matter with you?" Stepping around the corner of the counter she scrubbed the front of Candace's tee.

Gabe looked constipated. "Um. Um. Um."

"Mom!" Candace sank down in her chair, effectively ending Wendy's scrubbing, wishing she could completely disappear under the table but since the table was glass, it wouldn't matter even if she did.

Still.

Wendy gave them both a look of disgust. "Oh, for heavens sakes. It's not like I don't know what happened here. You left evidence all over the living room." She rolled her eyes at Candace. "I found your panties hanging on that bronze horse statue."

Ohmigod! "Mom!" Candace protested again. She buried her face in her hands, too embarrassed to look at her mother.

"And it's not as if you're children." She paused. "Not like last time, anyway."

Gabe's head hit the tabletop with a loud *thud*. Wendy patted him on the head. "It's okay, dear. I always liked you, and I knew you'd take good care of Candy."

Candace couldn't even get her vocal cords working well enough to protest the nickname.

Picking up her glass of milk, Wendy took a long drink, blandly studying the two of them over the rim. When the glass was empty she set it down. "So who are we investigating next?"

Gabe hit his head on the tabletop again, deliberately, and groaned. His eyes were squeezed shut and his mouth drawn down, like a man with a severe case of indigestion. Candace had a better solution, she simply got up and went to her bedroom, but first she made a detour through the living room to collect her panties.

* * * *

When Gabe entered Candace's bedroom she was in bed, buried under a pile of sheets and the comforter. He approached the bed.

"You can come out now. I managed to divert her."

"I'm never coming out again," came the muffled reply.

He frowned at the lump that was Candace. "What's the big deal?"

"The big deal is I thought my mother thought I was still a virgin. Now I know she knows I'm not."

Long pause. "How old are you?"

"Almost thirty?" was her timid response.

He snorted. "If your mother thinks you are still a virgin at nearly thirty, she would have to be the dumbest person in the world."

Candace's head popped out from under the covers. She lifted a skeptical brow.

"Okay, so she's not a rocket scientist." Another pause while he studied her. "Apparently she's not as dumb as you think." Grabbing the coverlet, he pulled it down. "Come on, as much as I'd like to spend the rest of the day in bed with you..." He leered. "We've got work to do."

With a roll of her eyes, she slid out of bed. "Okay, fine. Then let's get to work."

His conversation with Dolan came rushing back. He squeezed his eyes shut. "But I have something else I need to do first."

"What's that?"

"I have to arrange for Fred's funeral." The quick burst of pain made him rub his chest. He heard the tremor in his voice and wondered if he would ever get used to the idea his dad was dead.

Candace looked at him, her eyes sad, then her arms went around his waist. She rested her head on his chest and held him. Her arms were warm and comforting, and some of the pain eased. He pulled her closer so her soft breasts were pressed against his chest and her head rested against his shoulder.

"I'm sorry, Gabe. I loved him like he was my own father but he wasn't, he was yours. I'm so sorry you're having to go through this."

Gabe felt tears prick his eyes. God, he wasn't sure if her sympathy helped or hurt. Bowing his head, he rested his cheek on top of her head. He decided it helped. "Yeah."

"You miss him, don't you?"

He cleared his throat. "Yeah."

"Me too. A lot."

He could hear the sadness in her voice.

"And you feel guilty, don't you?"

"Yeah."

"Don't. There's no need to. You didn't do anything to feel guilty about. He understood you needed to establish yourself as your own person."

"Sure he did."

"He did, but he was so stubborn…"

"Like father, like son," Gabe said in a low tone. "Stupid."

"Yeah." Her arms tightened around him. "Come on, I'll help you get this done."

With a nod and a sigh, he let his arms fall to his side and released Candace. He didn't want to because holding her this way was better than anything he could remember in recent history. Their hug wasn't sexual. They weren't male and female touching body parts. They were simply two people grieving who were comforting each other.

He wondered if he could hold her forever, but as much as he wanted to stay right here with Candace, there were things to do. "Okay. Let's get started."

After a few calls the arrangements were made. His father would be picked up and taken to the funeral home in a luxurious black hearse. Gabe decided not to have a big service. Everyone who was anyone in his life had attended the will reading and were mostly left out of the will so it was a forgone conclusion they would take their revenge by not attending the service. Anyway, he wanted those few moments alone with his dad. And maybe Candace. He hadn't decided.

He pinched the bridge of his nose, his head pounding.

"You okay?"

"Yeah, I'm okay. Just tired. Sad."

Candace nodded.

He stared at her. Just looking at her made him feel a little better. What they did last night made him feel a lot better. Typical male behavior, he knew, but he'd needed the distraction, he'd needed to feel something other than angry about his father's death and his own failure as a son. But now he felt too much, like maybe he wanted to fall into Candace's arms and cry. He didn't know if he could handle all this emotion. It was embarrassing. And wrong. Men didn't cry, at least not in public. What they did in the privacy of their shower was their own business.

He stood and walked to the window, staring outside at the traffic below then turned to face Candace. He smiled at her to mask his overwhelming sense of helplessness. "I think I'm going to go home now."

"But—" She stopped. A long silence followed before she finally said, "Okay, I get it."

She didn't, she couldn't, not really, but he let it go. "I'll call you, okay?"

There was no answer for a minute. Then, "Sure. Whatever."

He stood for a minute, feeling awkward, like his feet were too big for his body and his tongue too big for his mouth, but when she said nothing further, he shrugged. "Okay. See ya'," he finally said and left.

9 Shiny Pearls and Sparkly Showgirls

Candace ran to the window and stared out at the street below until she saw Gabe leave the building. He walked down the sidewalk, head bent, until he reached the corner. He made a right then disappeared.

She stood at the window for a few more minutes, as if she expected him to come back around the corner, walk into the building, come up the elevator to the apartment, and sweep her into his arms again.

Nope, not going to happen.

Not that she wanted it to. No way did she want a repeat of last night, because last night was...

Okay, what had it been? Well, it was fun, and heart-poundingly exciting. Yet so comfortable, like slipping into shoes worn until they molded to the exact shape of her feet. But how could you compare something that made her heart sing and her blood heat to a pair of comfortable old shoes? Maybe it was more like having a pair of shoes, complete with rhinestones studded heels and cute little ankle straps, custom-made to fit her feet. Even after all this time, she and Gabe just fit perfectly.

Still, no matter how wonderful, it had been a mistake. A big, fat mistake. Huge. One of those been-there-done-that-you-should-know-better-by-now mistakes. Because if she knew anything about Gabe—and she did—he'd had his fun and now he was running away, not to be seen again for ages, just like last time. Fine, if that was the way he wanted it that was okay with her. She hadn't needed him the last ten or so years and she wouldn't need him for the next millennium either.

He was too much of a distraction and she didn't need it. There was too much at stake. She needed to focus on finding *The Recipe*, and scratching an itch she had for a decade wouldn't do it. She needed to stop obsessing about something she shouldn't want and focus on what needed to get done. Okay. Good. Great. Decision made. It was full steam ahead and no more Gabe. So what if she hadn't told him about the gun his mother stashed in her bedside drawer. What he didn't know couldn't hurt him. Plus, now she had time to investigate her suspects further. On her own. Without Gabe. Really, he was just a hindrance, right? It was downright embarrassing how quickly she had succumbed again to the hotness that was Gabe.

Having talked herself out of thinking or talking about Gabe ever again, she left her bedroom and made her way through the connecting door into Fred's side of the apartment. She turned the corner and ran into Floyd. He stopped and stared at her, his face all hound-dog, like that dead actor, Walter Something-or-other. She dodged to her right, so she could get around him but he shuffled to his left, blocking her. He gave her a look that said it was all her fault. She sighed. That was the way it always was with Floyd. Obstructive and obtuse.

And now that Fred was dead, also rich. So why was he still here, living rent free in her mother's newly-inherited apartment. Eating her mother's food. Using her mother's soaker tub. Reading Candace's Wall Street Journal.

"Gee, Floyd. You look tired. Are we working you too hard?" A little sarcasm.

He looked at her. Floyd wasn't big on speaking. He didn't seem to be big on sarcasm either.

"Aw, I think we are. I mean, you have to drag yourself out of bed by ten then go to all the effort of going downstairs to get the mail. I know it's a lot of work which is why I know you need that nap at twelve. I think maybe all this work is getting to be too much for you at your age. How old are you now?"

"Sixty-two," he answered.

"Wow. Sixty-two. Retirement age. You could get Social Security now and everything."

He gave her a flat look then turned and went back to his room. Probably for a nap.

Floyd had to go, but she didn't have the time to worry about it right now. She continued down the hall to her mother's office.

"Mom."

There was a loud *thud*. Her mother yelped. "Candy!" she said as she backed her way out, butt first, from underneath her desk.

"Mom, please don't call me Candy."

Her mother stood, rubbing her head, looking a little perturbed. "I don't understand what you have against the name Candy. It's cute."

Candace narrowed her eyes at her mother. "It's not cute. It's a stripper's name. And a prostitute's name. Maybe, just maybe, it's a poodle's name, but it's never a responsible adult woman's name. It's right up there with Bambi for dumb blond bimbo names."

Her mother's mouth trembled. "It's not a prostitute's name."

"Geez, Mom, don't you watch TV? The smart girl is always named something like Kate or Jenny. The prostitute is always named Candy." Someone should shoot those writers for their lack of imagination, and for slandering her name.

"I like it," her mother said, pouting.

And she would continue to use it. There was no arguing with her mother. "What were you doing under your desk?"

"Oh, I was working on the bills."

"Under the desk?"

"It's the bills for the apartment, you know, so Fred always took care of those things, and I've never done them before so I was a little nervous about it and I was twisting my pearl necklace and it broke and all the pearls rolled under the desk." She took a deep breath. "I was looking for them. Most of them went down the heating duct."

Oh boy. "I'll have the super call the heating service company. If the pearls rolled down the ductwork, maybe they ended up in the furnace." Or maybe not.

Wendy's eyes suddenly filled with tears. "Oh, that would be good. I'd hate to lose my pearls. Fred gave them to me, you know." She sighed.

Yeah, you and all his other wives. Still, they were important to her mother which was the reason she would call the super. Although maybe she wouldn't call him. Maybe she would go speak to Anthony personally and check out his alibi for the time when Fred was killed. The super had keys to all the apartments, after all. She could check up on Tiffany, and Julian, who was his cousin, while she was at it.

"I'll do it right now."

Her mother peered up from under the desk where she had returned to search for pearls. "Do what, dear?"

Candace rolled her eyes and left. She exited the apartment, got on the elevator, and took it down to the basement.

"Anthony," she called as she threaded her way through the narrow cinderblock hallways. Her voice echoed back at her. She hated the basement, it was full of strange sounds, strange shadows and critters who had way more legs than they should, and it gave her the creeps.

"Anthony!"

Something touched her shoulder. Candace screamed and spun around. Anthony stood there, looking smug, having seemingly appeared out of nowhere.

"What 'chou want?" he said, and cracked his knuckles.

Candace put a hand to her chest, hoping to keep her heart from exploding, causing instantaneous death. "My mother broke a string of pearls, and they fell down the duct. I'm hoping they ended up in the furnace."

He cracked the knuckles on his other hand, considering her. Finally he shook his head. "Nah, I don't think so."

Candace narrowed her eyes. "Can we look?"

He grimaced, clearly put out that he was required to work. After all, wasn't that what the porters were for—work? Supers supervised. When Candace continued to stare at him, he finally heaved a huge sigh, turned and trudged down the hall. Candace followed, hoping he would take her to the furnace room and not some deep, dark crypt where he would chain her to the wall, have his way with her and then leave her until she died, at which time he would skin her and make her into a dress ala Silence of the Lambs.

He opened a door. Thank God. The furnace, a monstrosity with a million arms, was in the middle of the floor, currently cold and silent since it was summer.

"Be my guest," he said, and stood aside for her to pass by. Just not aside enough. He left a foot space so when she sidled through, her breast brushed his arm. He smirked. Letch.

She strode to the furnace door, and after a few minutes of struggle, managed to yank it open and look inside. There was nothing but cold steel and a light dusting of ashes.

"So," she said, pretending to look for the pearls. "Guess who I ran into the other day."

"Santy Claus," he responded sardonically.

Candace bit her tongue. "Guess again." Just as sardonically.

"Gee, I dunno, Ms. McCready. I can't guess no more."

Candace pulled her head out of the furnace. "Your cousin. You know, Julian." She racked her brain, trying to think of a way to bring the conversation around to discussing the murder.

He sneered. "Oh, yeah, him." He lifted a brow. "He still dating that dame, you know, the one what was married to Mister Jones?"

Wow, thank you, Anthony. "She was with him when Mister Jones's will was read."

His eyes lit up. "No shit. Guess he landed in clover after all."

"Clover?"

"Yeah, Julie always said she was his golden ticket."

His golden ticket, huh? Which could mean something or nothing at all. "I don't see how. Fred didn't leave her a dime and other than the small divorce settlement she got she doesn't have any money of her own."

A sly smile crossed his face. "That don't make no never mind. Julie's a smart guy. He has plans," he said, and tapped his nose with his finger. "Big plans."

Brother, who did this guy think he was? "Really. Like what?"

He tapped his nose again. "That's for me to know and you to find out."

Which is just what she would do. She shut the furnace door and dusted off her hands. "I don't see anything in there but thanks for letting me look." Exiting the furnace room, she walked back toward the elevator, Anthony trailing in her wake. She hit the elevator button and waited for it to descend. "Is your cousin going to share the proceeds of his 'big plans'?"

The elevator doors opened.

"Maybe. Maybe not." He threw her another smarmy smile.

Stepping inside, she turned to face him. "I'd say not, since I happened to overhear him say they planned to move to South America."

The door slid shut on his astonished face.

Candace grinned. That should cause a little dissension in the ranks. She took the elevator up to their apartment then walked into her mother's office. Her mother was back at her desk, staring at the bills with a look of complete befuddlement on her face. She swiveled around to face Candace when she heard her enter.

"Did you find anything?"

Candace picked up the phone. "No pearls, at least not your pearls but maybe a few pearls of wisdom." She punched in the number she wanted. "Anthony says Julian has some grand plan to make money."

Her mother blinked and opened her mouth to speak but Candace held up a finger—wait—then the phone was answered.

"Hello." The voice sounded sulky.

"Tiffany?"

"Yeah?"

"This is Candace. Hey, I just wanted to call and tell you how bad I feel about the way Fred treated you in his will. You didn't deserve it."

She heard a gasp then a pause, then a watery sob.

"No, I didn't. That dirty rotten dog. He should have treated me better." Her Georgia accent was in full swing as she complained.

Maybe you should have treated him better, Candace thought, and acted like a wife and moved to New York instead of staying in Vegas and putting your career—and Julian—first. Although, now that Candace thought about it, that meant Tiffany would have moved into Fred's apartment while Wendy and Candace were living there, which would have been intolerable, so better the woman stayed in Vegas.

"I totally agree. I feel like I should do something to help. Maybe I could come over and we could talk. What do you say, Tiffany?"

More sloppy sobbing. Yuck. "Oh, could you?" she burbled.

"Sure. I'll be right there."

There was a long pause. "Oh," Tiffany said. "Um, can it wait awhile?"

"Wait?" Why the heck would she want to wait? What was the big deal?

"I'm sorry. I just look horrible," Tiffany finally said. "I was up all night crying for poor Fred. Y'all understand, right? I need a few hours to put myself back together."

Ah. Vanity. Coming from the Vegas showgirl, it made sense. "Okay, how about I come over at three?"

"Sure. See you then." Hanging up, Candace turned to look at her mother. She raised a brow.

Her mother had returned to sorting through her bills but now she set it down with a look of relief. "You going to see her?" Wendy asked.

"Yep," Candace responded.

Worry flitted across her face. "Do they have any animals?"

"Animals?"

"You know, like Dobermans." Her mother gave her a look that said she thought Candace was the dumb one.

Candace shook her head. As if Wendy had room to talk. Anyway, it wasn't as if everyone they knew had a vicious animal. Okay, they might but Candace wouldn't let that stop her. "Not that I know of."

"That's good," her mother said, and turned back to her bills.

* * * *

Tiffany and Julian were staying at a moderate priced hotel in Chelsea, not the type of place one would stay if one had lots of money but maybe the kind of place one would stay if one had plans to have more money sometime in the future. After asking for their room number, Candace took the elevator up to the eleventh floor and walked down the hall. She was early but so what? It was hard to control arrival times in Manhattan, what with the traffic and everything. As she walked, ticking off the room numbers as she went, she saw the door she wanted was cracked open and loud voices were coming out. She slowed as the shouting grew louder. Right before she reached the door, she stopped and listened.

"You promised me you would take care of it so I would get the money," Tiffany yelled. Her words were clear to Candace even through the partially closed door, as if Tiffany was standing right next to it. Thinking about the standard layout of most hotel rooms, the woman was probably in the bathroom.

"I tried, sweetie," Julian responded. "I dunno what happened, but I'll fix it. I promise."

"I don't see how. Nothing you've done so far made a difference. You said you had a fix in with the attorney so I would get the money but the old bastard didn't leave me a penny, just a lousy lifetime membership to Gold's Gym. What the fuck am I going to do with that?"

Wow, this was a Tiffany she had never heard before. Even the Southern accent had disappeared. Candace pressed herself against the hallway wall, pretty certain she didn't want to go another step.

"Hey, baby," Julian said. "It just means you'll look fabulous for the rest of your life, right?" The sound of a slap echoed. Julian howled. "Fuck, whadja go and do that for?"

"Because you're a moron," the other woman said. "If I had the money I could buy my own damned membership. Shit, I could buy the whole gym if I had the money."

The sound of a closet door sliding open came through the room door, then it slammed shut.

"Oh. Right."

"So do something about it, Julian. I want to go to Europe. I want my gym. I want to have a big house and jewelry and nice clothes, and you promised I'd have them." Candace heard the sound of a drawer slamming. "I refuse to spend the rest of my life taking off my clothes and dancing for a bunch of drooling old men. I want my money, and I want it now," Tiffany screeched.

"Okay, okay. Just calm down, okay? What do you want me to do? It's not like I can go back and change the will or anything now that the old guy's dead." He sounded desperate and Candace almost felt sorry for him. Almost.

"I told you what I wanted you to do. I already did my part and..." Candace strained to hear as Tiffany's voice faded away. She must have moved farther into the room. Moments later, she heard curtains being drawn.

"I'll never figure out how you managed to get it." Julian's voice was clear, as if now he was next to the door.

It? What it?

"Don't...stupid, Julian. How... think... it? ...fucked... little turd."

Just getting bits and pieces of the conversation wasn't helping at all.

"Oh. Okay," Julian answered but he didn't sound happy.

"Hey, it's not like I enjoyed it." Her voice grew louder then receded again, as if she was pacing up and down the length of the hotel room. So irritating. Why couldn't the woman stand in one spot so Candace could hear her better?

"Why are you so hung up on doing this, Tiff? We could spend the rest of our lives in jail if we get caught, you know. I already been there once and I don't wanna go again."

"Because I deserve it." Candace heard this loud and clear. "Fred screwed..." Tiffany's voice dropped again as she evidently moved away from the door. "... owes me..."

"I dunno. I think he treated you pretty good. I mean, he paid you eight thou a month."

Tiffany let out a scream. "But he's dead, and now I get nothing. I deserve more."

"Well... but I ... not gonna...."

Damn it, now the Greaseball was talking too quietly to hear.

"Jesus Christ, Julian. ...I already have...but code... We need..." Tiffany's voice was so faint Candace could barely hear her. "...have to... office... not there. She must have..."

"Yeah, that old fart thought she walked on water and—" Yikes, the sound of his voice was right next to the door. There was the sound of the closet door sliding open which drowned out the rest of his words.

"She was his right-hand man, so I betcha she does. But how we gonna make her give it to us?" The door slid shut.

Candace held her breath. She had a bad feeling she knew who "she" was, and she didn't like the implication. What could she possibly have that they needed?

"Oh my God," the woman said. "Julian! Get with it. And while you're at it, turn the air conditioning on. I'm fucking dying of the heat."

"Christ, okay, okay. I..." At this point his voice faded as he moved away so Candace couldn't hear the rest of what he said. Darn it! She inched a little closer to the opening of the door but his voice was so quiet all she heard was, "...plan... Just need... Sure to work."

What? What about a plan? What did they need? *Grrr.*

Tiffany giggled, her voice so loud she must be close to the door again. "Oh, Julian, you're so smart. Get over here so I can reward you." Seconds later, Candace heard the loud smacking sound of kissing. Ick.

"That's me, Mister Smart Guy," Julian said, sounding breathless as he obviously came up for air.

"I knew you wouldn't let me down."

More kissing. More loud moans. Even though no one was there to see her, Candace stuck her finger down her throat, simulating gagging.

"Now remember what I said, sweetie pie," Tiffany said in honey-sweet tones now that she got her way. The closet door banged shut again. "Candace is going to be here any minute, and when she gets here, I'm going to play all sad but resigned, and stupid. You just do your part." Tiffany was silent for a minute then, "It's sure taking her a long time to get here. I wonder where she is."

Oops. That was her clue to get the hell out of Dodge. Candace scuttled down the hallway toward the closest exit sign—no way could she afford to get caught waiting for the elevator—opened the door and ran down the stairs. She hit the lobby running and raced outside and hailed a cab.

Boy, oh boy, did she have a story to tell Gabe. After giving the cabbie directions, she dialed Gabe's cell. "Gabe, guess what!"

"I can't guess. Maybe if you give me a clue. Or two. Or even three. 'Cause I'm kinda slow, you know." He sounded irritated.

"Sorry. Obviously, you can't guess so I'll just tell you. I went to Tiffany's hotel and—"

"You went to Tiffany's hotel? What were you thinking?"

Where had she heard that question before? She heaved a sigh. "Yes, I went to her hotel. I thought we could talk and I might learn something."

She could practically hear him gnashing his teeth. "I'll bite. Did you learn anything?"

Okay, this was the tricky part. Because, now that she thought about it, she hadn't learned all that much other than something about some kind of code. Candace had no idea what kind of code Tiffany wanted, and who had the code.

"So there's some kind of code for something and maybe they have it or maybe they need to get it, I couldn't tell for sure, but I think it involves Fred. Or maybe me." She rolled her window down since it was stifling in the cab. No air-conditioning. Geez. How did the drivers stand it?

Silence. "That's what you're excited about? Tiffany has some kind of code for something or needs some kind of code for something. And it might involve Fred? Or you? Or maybe it has nothing to do with either of you since no one mentioned any names, right?"

Shit, this was not going the way she wanted at all. She picked at a loose thread on her blouse. "Yes," she said meekly. "I guess."

"Go home. I'll meet you there." He hung up. After a brief pout, Candace dialed her favorite Chinese restaurant and ordered a shit-load of stuff to be delivered. If Gabe was coming over, she figured she would need it.

10 Fried Rice and Funerals

"Okay, tell me what you heard. The whole thing," Gabe said. He crossed his arms over his chest and glared at Candace who once again wore her innocent face.

Instead of answering, she pushed a large carton in his direction with one of her chopsticks. "Want some?"

He tried to close his nostrils against the tantalizing smell. "No." He paused, struggling not to drool. "I'm too mad at you to eat," he told her, but he couldn't stop his eyes from flicking down to the carton in front of him. The smell was driving him crazy. "Okay, what is it?"

"Fried wontons."

Oh, man. "I love fried wontons."

"It's from Tam Woo's, over on Lex."

"Oh, man. I love Tam Woo's." He knew he sounded pathetic, but he couldn't help it.

"I know," Candace said. Rising from the kitchen table, she went to the cupboard, got out a plate and put it in front of him. She handed him a set of chopsticks then sat back down.

Grabbing the carton, he shoveled a bunch of wontons onto the plate. "What else did you get?" he asked, sticking a filled pastie in his mouth.

"Sesame chicken, shrimp lo mein, pork fried rice, and hot and spicy soup."

"Not fair." Opening the flap of one of the cartons, he checked it out. Shrimp lo mein. He moaned then scooped a bunch of shrimps onto his plate and added several heaping spoonsful of fried rice for good measure.

She smiled. *Agghh!* There was the smile. It almost stopped him from enjoying the fried rice he'd just put in his mouth. Almost. He swallowed anyway and reached for a wonton.

"What's not fair?" She took a dainty bite of rice. Her rosy lips moved slowly, looking almost as tantalizing as the shrimp lo mein.

He jabbed a chopstick in the general direction of the cartons. "This. You did this on purpose."

"What?" Blink. Blink. Blink.

"Got Chinese food. You know I love Chinese food. You think you can distract me so I won't yell at you." His stomach started to churn.

She smiled again.

Gabe put his hand to his forehead. He was getting another headache. Normally, he would think it was the MSG, but he knew it wasn't. "Okay, never mind. Tell me what happened when you went to see Tiffany."

"They were fighting."

"And you were there while they fought? Geez, Candace, Julian's a gangster. With a gun. What if things got violent?"

"Obviously I wasn't in their room. I'm not an idiot. I was in the hallway, right outside their door." She folded her arms over her chest, looking indignant.

Gabe gulped down a bite of Bok choy and stuffed a couple more shrimp into his mouth. He figured he better eat as much as he could before he completely lost it and had to leave rather than kill her. "And hiding outside their door is better?"

"Sure, because they didn't know I was there, and they said things they wouldn't have said if I was."

His rising irritation made his jaw clench. He picked up his plate and crammed food into his mouth as fast as he could in spite of his churning stomach, which he knew he would pay for later. "Like what?" he said around a mouthful of rice.

"Frankly, I was having a hard time hearing them because they kept moving away from the door. It was more what they did." She speared a wonton and nibbled on it.

He looked down at his plate. Empty. And she wasn't done with her story yet. Grabbing a spoon, he put some sesame chicken on his plate. "Okay, what did they do?"

"I couldn't see them, so it wasn't so much what they did..."

"Candace!" Gabe roared.

She banged her chopsticks down on her plate. "Fine, just give me a sec to get my thoughts together." She squinted at the ceiling then said, "They didn't say much except the way Tiffany was acting was completely weird. Tiffany wasn't Tiffany, you know?"

Gabe shook his head.

"You know."

"No, I don't know. I never met the woman, remember? She was only married to my dad for four months, and she spent almost all that time in Vegas, not here in New York."

"Oh, that's right. So you wouldn't know she always acts dumb and clueless. And Southern. Well, guess what, she's not dumb and she's not clueless and she's definitely not Southern. She's the brains behind whatever they're up to. She said something about a code. I don't know what it's for but evidently she used nefarious means to get it."

"Nefarious? What kind of word is that?"

She threw him a look that clearly said, *Men!* "It's a word that means she traded sex for the code."

Gabe choked on a piece of chicken. "But you don't know what the code is for," he said when he could breathe again.

"No, but I think it has something to do with Fred's office because what else could it be?"

"Any idea how? Did Fred use security codes and things in his office?"

"Maybe. With Fred, I never really knew." She shrugged. She looked cute when she shrugged. Her blue eyes widened, and her pink lips puckered, very kissable.

He yanked his mind away from the thought and tried to focus. "Okay, so we have no idea if Fred used codes, or if he did what the codes were for. His computer? A safe? A locked room? Some kind of bank account? And if so, we have no idea if it's even Fred's codes they want or it's something totally unrelated. And we don't even know if they're up to something sneaky or if it's something totally legitimate."

"That's about the size of it," Candace said. Her look of indignation was traded for a more thoughtful one. "Except Tiffany said they needed something from me."

Gabe didn't have an answer. "Maybe they weren't talking about you. Did they mention you by name?"

Candace stared at the ceiling for a moment, thinking. "Well, no, they just said '*she* was his right-hand man.' That has to be me, right? If nothing else, we should spend some time thinking about what the code could be for, don't you think?"

No, what Gabe thought was he would be much better off if he hadn't answered his cell phone when Candace called. Now he was stuck.

He sighed. "Okay, I guess we need to check it out."

"Oh, good." Her blue eyes sparkled happily.

"But first I need to get my dad buried. Will you come?"

* * * *

Gabe winced, listening to the dismal funeral dirge the organist played. Wanting to avoid looking at the shiny wooden coffin at the front of the room, he twisted around and looked over his shoulder at the seats behind him. The small room where the service was to be held had folding chairs for around twenty people but, except for Wendy and the little Korean pizza delivery guy, the seats were all empty. Someone from one of the nearby churches was supposed to come and deliver a service but the guy hadn't shown up yet so they had simply sat here, staring at each other, for the last thirty minutes.

"No one came," Candace said. She took his hand and threaded her fingers through his. "I can't believe no one came." Her voice was high and thin with distress.

He took a deep breath. God, her hand felt good. It was like a lifeline in a sea of dismal. "Yeah, but to be fair, there was no public notice and no time to let anyone know."

Candace's lower lip trembled. "Sure, but they could have asked, you know?"

"If they don't care enough to ask, I don't want them here anyway." He felt tears prick his eyes but blinked them back. He seemed to do that a lot lately.

Candace glanced at him. Her eyes softened with sympathy. She leaned into him, pressing the warmth of her shoulder against his arm as she squeezed his hand. It helped, but his father was still dead, and he was still filled with regret and guilt over the past. His stomach hurt. His heart ached.

The organist finished the current gloomy song with a flourish and started on another one, equally as gloomy.

"This is bullshit!" Wendy burst out.

Candace turned and stared at her mother. "Mom!" She turned to Gabe, eyes wide. "She never swears like that. Honest."

"I'm sorry," Wendy said, slapping her thighs. "But Fred would hate this. All this depressing music and the candles and the Easter lilies. Fred hated Easter lilies, and he hated funerals. He liked parties and fun and laughing. This is just wrong." Standing, she marched down the aisle to the organ, her pink (she refused to wear black) chiffon skirt swaying around her knees. She jerked a thumb at the organist: Get out. The organist gaped at her.

"Move it, sister," Wendy said.

The organist moved it. Spreading her skirt, Wendy sat on the bench, limbered up her fingers and then pounded out ABBA's "Dancing Queen."

Great dance music. Gabe shot a look at Candace. She met his eyes. Her mouth began to quiver with a smile. Her foot began to tap.

Gabe looked down and found his foot tapping too. Wendy wrapped up "Dancing Queen" and swung right into "You Should Be Dancing." *Ohmigod.* "Saturday Night Fever," his favorite late-night movie. He tapped the beat out on his thigh. Candace sang the words to the song under her breath. Pretty soon she wasn't singing under her breath anymore. She looked at him and grinned. He grinned back. He remembered when he was just a kid watching his father do the worst boogie in the world at one of Murray's many weddings (multiple marriages seemed to run in the family). Fred's chubby hips swung, his arms waved in the air, and he whooped at the top of his lungs. He had fun.

Gabe jumped up out of his seat. Grabbing Candace's hand, he hauled her to the open space in front of Fred's coffin, swung her into his arms and danced her across the floor.

She laughed, head thrown back, eyes glittering with laughter.

"That's the way," Wendy yelled, and transitioned seamlessly into "That's the Way I Like It."

"Uh huh uh huh," Gabe sang.

"Oh, my goodness," someone said from the doorway.

Gabe spun around. A young couple gaped at him, eyes startled. Dressed in black, they looked both intensely funereal and astonished at the same time.

"What's going on?" the man asked.

"We're holding a funeral service," Candace shouted back. "Come join us."

They stared at her then the woman, petite and dark-haired, began to smile. "Come on, Jim. Let's," she said to her tall, slightly balding companion.

Jim returned the lady's look. Her foot had started to tap, and she already shimmied to the music. With a grin, the man stripped off his dark suit coat and threw it on a chair. The next thing Gabe knew, the couple joined them.

"Who'd you have die?" Candace yelled to the couple over the organ music.

"My great uncle Gordon. How about you?" the woman answered and completed a spin under her partner's arm.

"My dad," Gabe answered, and whipped Candace in a circle then dipped her.

"Gee, I'm sorry to hear that," Jim shouted.

"Me too," Gabe shouted back. "He loved a good celebration."

Wendy immediately switched to Kool and the Gang's "Celebration," and the other couple laughed. They danced around each other, lifting their arms in the air in celebration while stomping the floor as hard as they could. Together their voices rose in a shout of "Come on!" while Wendy pulled out all the stops.

"Stop!" someone shouted.

Wendy stopped playing. They all turned to look. A crowd had gathered in the doorway. Older couples dressed in conservative somber attire, younger couples, a little more fashionable but still in black. Regardless of age or attire, they all looked aghast.

"Lisa. Jim. Oh my God, what are you doing!" an older blond woman said.

"Celebrating life!" Lisa yelled back. "Come on, Mom. Join us," she added.

"Oh dear," the woman said. She blinked, frowned, then said slowly, "This isn't right."

"Sure, it is," Jim said. He grabbed Lisa around the waist again and danced her across the floor even though there was no music. "Life is for the living. And Uncle Gordon would be dancing if he were still here."

"Still, I don't know if we should."

"Why not," the man next to her said, then grabbing her by the hand, pulled her up front to join the party. Wendy turned back to the organ and struck up another song. Soon a dozen couples slipped off their shoes and jackets and joined the dancing.

Gabe twirled Candace then jerked her up against his chest. He grinned at her. She smiled back. He dipped her. "Now this is a funeral," she said as she came back up. "Fred would have loved it." She panted from exertion, but her cheeks were rosy, and her lips smiled in the widest smile he ever saw. He wanted to kiss her so bad it hurt but instead he dipped her again and then pulled her tight to his chest, so her breasts brushed him in the most provocative way.

Wendy decided to leave the '70s and visit the Caribbean. The next thing Gabe knew she was playing an old resort favorite, and everyone was swinging their hips and going through all the moves, arms crossing over their chests then back to hips.

The funeral director rushed into the room. "What are you doing?" he yelled. He pressed a hand to his forehead, looking horrified.

"The Macarena!" everyone shouted back.

The man stared. "Oh, my goodness," he said. "This is a funeral service. It's supposed to be dignified and quiet and respectful."

"Depends on where you're from," someone yelled. "The Irish throw a party, so today we're all Irish!"

The funeral director blinked then began to smile. "Well, as it happens, my name is O'Herlihy." He turned and left the room then came back toting a large cardboard box. He carried it to the front of the room and began to set bottles of whiskey on top of the coffin. Next, he pulled out some plastic cups. "Come and get it," he called.

Wendy stopped playing. There was a stampede in the direction of Fred's coffin and soon bottles were tipped, pouring out the golden elixir of life. "We need to have more services like this," O'Herlihy said. He tilted his glass to his lips and took a sip.

"Hear, hear!"

Glasses were raised, and raised again, until there was just one bottle left out of the case. The last bottle went around, everyone pouring an inch into their glass.

"To Fred," Gabe said, slurring his words a little as he saluted his father.

"To Uncle Gordon." The voices were quiet, respectful, just what the funeral director ordered.

Candace slipped her arm around Gabe's waist and leaned into his side. Gabe turned toward her and pulled her into his arms, feeling himself tremble. Tears burned the back of his eyes. He pressed himself against her, needing her warmth, needing her aliveness. Something wet—please, God, not a tear—trickled down his cheek and plopped on her neck.

She flinched, then turned to look up at him. "He loved you, you know," she whispered. "And believe it or not, he respected you."

"I never noticed. He was always yelling at me and calling me a dumbass." He tried not to think about Contessa and the fact that he owned it now and that maybe his father's will had set his feet on a path he didn't want to follow. He just wanted to mourn the father he loved but could never agree with.

Candace gave him a squeeze. "That was just Fred's way of saying he loved you. He was so proud when your business took off. He bragged about you all the time. Granted it was along the lines of 'That goddammed ungrateful kid' and 'Stupid dumb-ass idiot' or 'He's making a fortune. Can't figure out how he's doing it. Who the hell likes saltwater taffy?' But he said it all with affection."

A sob shuddered through him. Candace softly stroked her hand up and down his back, comforting him like a child.

"This was a great funeral," she said. "Fred would be proud."

He turned his head away, hiding his face until he could wipe the tears off. His throat grew tight, making it almost impossible to speak. Finally, he managed, "Yep. A hell of a funeral service." Pulling back, he studied Candace's face, looking for something, but not sure what that something was.

Her eyes were soft, compassionate. The tears he had nearly conquered welled up again. She swiped a thumb across his cheek, wiping away the wetness. Her eyes held his, and he found his resentment and anger falling away, which scared him because those emotions had been part of his life for so long. But he needed her comfort. He needed her. His jaw started to wobble, making him clench his teeth.

"Come on, let's go home," she said.

He took a deep breath, unlocked his traitorous jaw, cleared his throat. "Yeah, let's go home."

He spent the night in Candace's bed where they made slow, sad, and oh so sweet love. It felt like home.

11 The Usual Suspects

Candace let Gabe sleep in. He'd had a rough day and he deserved it. So, when she woke up early, she slipped out of bed and trundled down the hall to the main kitchen where she found her mother at the big five-burner stove making breakfast.

"Hi, Mom." She hiked herself up onto one of the counter stools.

Her mother looked over her shoulder, smiling. "Hi, sweetie. Fun day yesterday, wasn't it?" She turned back to the stove and resumed stirring.

Strangely enough, it was fun. Fred was gone so there were heartache and tears, but the tears were put aside for a few brief hours in favor of the laughter and the singing and the dancing.

"Yeah, we gave him a great send off."

Her mother turned and, reaching across the island, set a plate down in front of her that held a lovely omelet and hash browns. "Fred would have loved it," she said. "When I go, I want you to do the same thing for me. No tears, lots of singing and dancing."

"Mom! Don't talk about that. That's years away."

"Then you'll have lots of time to learn to play the organ, won't you?" She turned back to the stove and cracked a couple more eggs into her frying pan.

Shaking her head, Candace took a bite of her omelet. Delicious. Whatever else she could say about her mother, she was a terrific cook, and a heck of an organ player. Something Candace would never be.

"Have you heard anything from the police about the investigation?" she asked her mother as she speared another bite of egg. It was over a week since Fred's murder, and it seemed as if no one was doing anything to solve the crime other than herself.

Her mother walked to the window and opened the blinds. Sunshine streamed in, reflecting off the shiny granite counters and the stainless-steel appliances. Her mother lifted her face to the sun and took a deep breath. "No, so I called them and told them about the service in case they wanted to send someone. You know, just in case the killer decided to attend too. You know what I mean. The killer feels compelled to see the results of his crime so he attends the funeral but the police are there, lurking in the background, watching for something suspicious."

Candace shook her head. Her mother watched too many movies. "Did anyone from the police department come?"

Her mother turned and gave her a puzzled look. "I don't know. I didn't see anyone, did you?"

Gabe wandered into the kitchen, bleary-eyed, dressed in colorful plaid boxer shorts that left his long, hairy legs bare, and a tight t-shirt that left little to the imagination. Even hung over and slightly green, he was still yummy.

He held a hand up, squinting, as he came face-to-face with the morning sun streaming in through the kitchen window. "No sun," he whispered hoarsely.

Oh, for Pete's sake. Candace slid off her stool with an exaggerated sigh, went to the window and closed the blinds her mother just opened. She returned to her seat.

Gabe gingerly slid onto one of the stools, propped his head in one hand and gave her a pathetic look, like a puppy whose chew toy had been taken away. Okay, more like a puppy who'd eaten his chew toy and now regretted it.

"Coffee?" he whispered.

Candace rose from her seat again and went to the coffee maker. Pouring him a cup, she set it in front of him with a clunk then once again went back to her seat. She picked up her fork, intent on eating her omelet before it got cold.

"Aspirin?"

This time Candace threw him an evil look but got up again and got him a couple aspirin. Dropping them in front of him, she quickly sat down and picked up her fork. She stabbed a hunk of bacon.

"Water?"

Candace froze. "Okay, Mister Monosyllabic. Is there anything else you want before I get up again?"

He visibly shivered. "Clothes."

Oh, for God's sake. Fuming, she got up, got a glass of water, which she gently put in front of him, resisting the urge to slam it down because it might crack the granite counter tops, then went back to her bedroom and retrieved his pants and socks. She carried them back and dropped them on the counter.

"Anything else," she gritted.

He groaned, hanging his head. "Death?"

Candace craned her head so she could see his face. His eyes were closed, his face now an interesting shade of gray. Using her thumb, she lifted an eyelid, forcing him to look at her.

"Noooo," he moaned, one hand flailing feebly.

"Listen, bub," she snarled. "You want death? One more demand, and I'll personally see you get it." She let go of his eyelid and it fell shut. "Okay, now we have that out of the way, we need to talk about Tiffany." She still hadn't told him about his mother's gun, but she didn't think now was the time.

Gabe's head hit the counter, narrowly missing her plate of eggs. "Come back in a year or so and we'll talk." His eyes closed. Within seconds he slid into sleep.

Wendy left her spot in front of the stove and sat down next to Candace. She lifted her cup of coffee. "We didn't need him anyway, did we, dear?" she asked, taking a sip. "But I'm ready, willing, and able to help."

Ready and willing? Maybe. But able? "Mom."

"What you need is a fresh perspective, fresh eyes on the situation, someone who knows where all the bones are buried, so to speak."

Oh boy, it seemed if her mother couldn't be a suspect, she'd settle for being a detective. God help them all.

"We should make a list of our suspects," her mother continued, looking contemplative. "Think about their motivation then list everything we know about them to date including where they were the day of the murder. Once we have that, hopefully we'll start to see some patterns."

Candace blinked at her mother. Who was this smart, intuitive woman? Then she remembered this was the same woman who managed Fred's office for a number of years before they married. She wasn't completely without intellectual resources, it just seemed like it sometimes.

"Right," she said, still mystified. "Good thinking."

Wendy glanced at Gabe. His eyes were tightly closed, mouth slightly opened as he slept the sleep of the wicked. She patted him on the head. "We should let the poor boy sleep in peace. Come on."

They left the kitchen and retreated to her mother's special domain. Fred had wanted the apartment decorated in contemporary neutrals, the better to project the image of a serious businessman, but her mother's office was frilly and colorful and very feminine. Candace selected a squishy shabby-chic chair in peach and pale green. Her mother grabbed pen and paper from her desk and handed it to Candace. "Here, you take notes. I need my hands free to think."

Candace gave her a look.

Hands went to denim-clad hips. "Hey, I can't write and think at the same time."

Ah, the mother she knew and loved. "I bet you can't pat your head and rub your stomach at the same time either."

Her mother glared. "Smart aleck. Write down our suspects," she ordered. Plopping down on the frilly loveseat across from Candace, she curled her legs up underneath herself.

Candace wrote. "Gabe and I already started a list that has the obvious ones—the exes, Susan, Tiffany and Vanessa, plus Murray but can you think of anyone else?"

"Murray's son, Junior."

"Junior. Really?"

"You and I both know Murray can't walk more than ten feet without having to sit down and rest. No way could he have carried out something like a murder and a theft without some help."

"Right, I forgot about that." She wrote the name down.

"Let's not forget the Luckless twins."

How could she forget them? She hated them. For a lot of reasons, all of them valid. She mostly hated their tattoos and the nose rings but more than anything she hated Lance's stupid tongue stud.

She also hated the fact that, even after Fred and Vanessa got divorced, the twins would walk into the apartment without permission. Every chance they got, they sneaked in, snooped in her bedroom and went through her drawers. Years ago they found a box of condoms (Gabe leftovers) and she had to bribe them to be quiet with a year's supply of porn magazines (Lance) and all the naked pictures she took of Gabe (Lucy). Now that Fred was dead, maybe she'd be allowed to change the locks.

She wrote their names down and underlined them three times. "Okay, is that it?"

Her mother squinted at the ceiling as she thought then offered one last name. "Add Hillary Hickok."

"Mom, Hillary wasn't even here. She was in Tennessee."

"Maybe that's what she wants all of us to think." She tapped her temple with one finger. She looked wise, or at least as wise as she could look given the wide blue eyes, the soft blond curls and the kewpie doll mouth.

Candace rolled her eyes but wrote her name down since it wasn't worth arguing with her mother. Illogic always trumped logic. "What about Floyd? Shouldn't we add him?"

"Floyd," Wendy said. "Really? Why Floyd?"

"Don't you know? The butler *always* did it."

"According to you, Floyd's not actually a butler."

"Whatever," Candace said.

"I suppose it could be Floyd. Frankly, it could be anyone. Even me."

"Again, I'm not putting your name on the list."

Her mother looked put out. "Whatever."

Shaking her head, Candace added Floyd's name to the list. "Are we done now? If not, maybe we should add Juan the doorman or Park Lee, the

KATY BARRITT | 107

pizza delivery guy." She tapped her pen on the tablet as she waited for her mother's response.

Her mother sniffed. "No need to be sarcastic."

There was every need to be sarcastic. "If you think that's everyone, let's look at their motives. What about Susan?"

"Revenge." Her mother narrowed her eyes, apparently doing her best to look like she knew what she talked about.

"Revenge?"

"She never got over losing Fred to me."

Oh, for Pete's sake. "And it took her over ten years to think of a way to pay you back?"

Wendy's face flushed. "Okay, fine, then simple greed. She has an expensive lifestyle but somehow, she thinks she's entitled to more. I know Fred told her he was leaving her something in his will and she counted on it. Like I said, she has an expensive lifestyle."

"That I can buy." She wrote it down. "What about Vanessa?"

"Greed."

Rubbing the achy spot between her eyebrows, Candace asked, "Isn't that Susan's motive?"

"And Vanessa's."

Still rubbing the achy spot, Candace studied the list in front of her, trying to sort everything out. It wasn't easy, especially when working with her mother. "I think we can agree greed is probably all of their motives. So, let's move on."

"Fine, then tell me everything you've learned in the last few days," her mother said.

Candace told her mother about the results of each of her forays. Wendy thought for a moment. "That's not a lot to go on."

"What about Susan's gun?"

"Lots of people have guns for protection. And remember, Susan grew up on a farm. She probably was raised around guns. Did you check to see if she was in the building the day Fred was killed?"

Candace heaved a sigh. She needed an aspirin. "Come on, give me a break. I'm just getting started."

Her mother patted her hand. "I know, sweetheart, and you're doing a great job, but given what you heard when you went to see Tiffany, I think your top priority is to talk to her and what's his name."

"Julian," Candace murmured.

"Right. Julian. I think you should go see them again, only this time actually talk to them. See if you can get them to say something incriminating. While you're there, you'll need to bug their room."

Her heart nearly leaped out of her chest. The rest of her followed suit, bringing her to her feet. "What! Bug their room? Like wire taps and secret agents? How would we do that? Where would we get a bug? Are you crazy?"

Her mother smiled. "Don't you worry about it. I know people. All you have to do is get inside their rooms and place the bug without them seeing you."

Her mother knew people? What kind of people? Candace didn't want to think about the implications. She chewed on a fingernail, pacing nervously. "Mom, that's illegal. We could get in serious trouble."

"After breaking into Murray's business and Susan's apartment, you're worried about illegal bugs?" She snorted. Actually snorted. Candace had never heard her mother snort.

"Do you want to find *The Recipe* or not?" Wendy demanded.

"Of course I do."

"Well, then."

How did you argue with that? "Okay, fine." She threw her hands in the air in surrender. "I'll call them and say I'm coming over."

"No, why warn them you're coming. I think you should just drop by, catch them unprepared, but you can't go yet. I need a little time to get all those things." She thought for a minute. "You haven't spoken to Vanessa and the twins yet. Go see them. I should have the stuff by the time you get back."

Good God. "Fine. What else?"

"I think we need to find out about those deposits you saw in Murray's desk. I'll have to think about how we can find out more."

"Mom, call my friend Phoebe. She works for Greenbrook Savings where Murray has that account. She could probably find out."

Her mother tilted her head, considering Candace. "Isn't that illegal?"

Candace gave her a look. "Mom. After all the things I've done in the last few days? After suggesting we bug Tiffany, now you're worried?"

It was like water off a duck's back. "Won't your friend get fired?" Wendy asked, completely disregarding the issue.

"She's getting married and quitting her job. I don't think she'll care if she gets fired."

"But won't she—"

"Mom! Do you want to help or not?"

"Fine!" her mother answered, her mouth set in a mulish line. "Write down what you need and give me the deposit slip. I'll figure it out."

Satisfied she made progress, Candace jotted down everything she could remember about the other deposits and handed her list and retrieved the deposit slip for her mother.

Her mother took them then gave Candace a look, eyebrow raised. She nodded toward the door. Hint. Hint.

Yeah, yeah. "I guess I'll go talk to Vanessa then."

"Good idea," Wendy said, her attention already focused on her computer.

Huh, apparently they were done. Candace hauled herself out of her comfy chair.

"Oh, by the way," her mother said as Candace headed for the door. "That policeman was here again while you went to see Tiffany." Pause. "You know, the one who was here the day Fred died."

"Dolan?" *Crap! Dolan?* "What did he want?"

She shrugged. "I don't know. He just looked around."

Well, hell. That couldn't be good. "Around where?"

She shrugged again. "I don't know. Just around. He looked in the cabinets in both kitchens and all the bathroom cabinets then he looked in all our drawers and closets."

What the heck? "What was he looking for?"

"I don't know."

"Did he have a warrant?"

Her mother got a look on her face that told Candace she never considered that. "A warrant? Was he supposed to have a warrant?"

Oh, geez. "Bye, Mom."

Exiting the building, she caught a cab over to the West Side. When the cab pulled up to the curb, she got out and stared up at the building, which was a pre-war building, ornate and well maintained.

Vanessa lived in a walk-up! How the mighty had fallen. After ringing the downstairs buzzer to Vanessa's apartment and getting no answer, she rang a few other apartments and some idiot who should have known better buzzed her in. She stared up the narrow staircase, trying to decide whether dropping in on Vanessa was a good idea or not, however, since she had nothing better to do with her day, at least for the next few hours, she decided, what the heck, and started climbing.

For a second, she felt sorry for Vanessa then remembered how she'd rushed Fred into a quickie Reno wedding. Eight months later, the Reno divorce was even quicker.

By the time she reached the fifth floor, she was out of breath and having second thoughts about her visit with Vanessa.

She had this funny, lurking feeling this interview wasn't going to go much better than the one she and Gabe conducted with Murray. After all, what did she know about investigating? Nothing. Zero, zip, zilch. And it wasn't as if she would find a lot of clues just lying around Vanessa's apartment, waiting for Candace to find them. Any clues that existed would surely be hidden away, right? Now that she thought about it, this whole venture seemed doomed to failure from the get-go.

She reached Vanessa's apartment. Taking a deep breath—okay, she admitted it, she had to take more than one—geez, who knew she was so out of shape—she knocked on the door and waited. When no one answered the knock, she rang the bell. Still no one. She stood back, arms crossed, and stared at the door, thinking. After a minute, she reached out and turned the handle, just in case. After all, you never knew, right?

In this case, it turned out she knew. Locked. Trying to think what to do next, her eyes drifted upwards, following the stairs up to the ceiling. Hmmm. Abandoning her knocking, she climbed the last flight until she reached a door that presumably opened onto the roof. It opened under her push. The sun beat down on the black tarpaper roof, making her squint against the glare. The wide expanse was broken by several tall pipes and oddly enough a clothesline. Stacked against one of the chimneys were a dozen or so large plastic bags filled with beer cans. The smell of beer permeated the air. Party City. She wandered over to the short wall at the back of the building and looked down at the garden below, then something else caught her eye. Well, well, well, would you look at that.

Before she could change her mind, she hiked a leg over the wall and climbed onto the narrow metal structure.

* * * *

Gabe woke with a snort. He jerked upright, which made his head throb. Damn, he'd fallen asleep at the kitchen counter. His forehead ached where it rested on the cold granite and one foot was asleep from sitting on the hard stool for so long.

"Morning, sunshine," someone said.

He slitted one eye open to find Wendy entering the kitchen, a cup of coffee in her hand. Groaning, he closed his eyes against the bright light as it came in through the window, rubbed his face then held out a hand, silently pleading for the coffee.

The cup was placed in his hand, and he took a big gulp.

"Feel better?"

He cracked open an eye, testing the waters. His head didn't explode so he cracked open the other eye. "Marginally," he answered in a hoarse whisper.

Wendy took his cup and refilled it with fresh coffee. Gabe drained it and began to feel almost human. He waited a minute before saying anything, in case speaking caused him to backslide into the black pit he just escaped. Finally, "Good morning. I think."

Wendy smiled. "You too." She went to the cupboard and pulled out a package of Oreos.

Gabe carefully turned his head, watching Wendy, thrilled to find his head stayed on his shoulders where it belonged, and his eyeballs didn't bleed in protest. His brain still didn't work very well, though, grinding slowly from one thought to the next, but give him another hour or two and he might be able to have two consecutive thoughts without stopping in between to recover.

After a few minutes of blinking around the kitchen, something abruptly clicked into place. "Where's Candace?"

"Oh, she went to see Vanessa."

"What!" Gabe jumped up off his seat. His head immediately exploded, forcing him to hold onto it so it didn't topple off his shoulders onto the floor. "You let her go to Vanessa's?"

"I *told* her to go see Vanessa. She hasn't talked to her yet."

"I told Candace not to talk to anyone until we have a chance to strategize."

Wendy looked offended. "You're not the only person in the world with a clue, you know. Candy and I strategize just fine." She took a bite of the Oreo.

Gabe thought he would faint. The idea of Wendy and Candace strategizing was a scary proposition. No telling what the girl was up to, but he needed to find out before she did something she would regret, or worse, something he would regret. Carrying his pants, he made a beeline for Candace's bedroom where he grabbed the rest of his clothes, threw them on and left the apartment, but immediately stopped and rushed back into the kitchen. "Where does Vanessa live?"

Wendy gave him the address, and Gabe left again. He caught a cab, figuring it would the fastest way to get there, and had it drop him off right in front of her building.

Huh. She lived in a walk-up. Finding her name on one of the buzzers downstairs, he rang her apartment.

"Who is it?" a disembodied voice asked from the speaker next to the buzzers.

"Gabe Jones."

A long time passed before the buzzer sounded as someone let him in the front door. He climbed five long flights, his head pounding, until he reached her floor. Vanessa stood in the doorway, arms crossed over her meager chest, the door held open.

"I just got home." She sounded irritated but stood aside so he could enter. After standing awkwardly for a minute, she finally led him to the living room. When she didn't ask him to sit, he perched himself on the loveseat facing the two windows.

Vanessa lowered herself onto a beige couch opposite Gabe. They stared at each other for a minute.

"Well?" she finally said.

He opened his mouth to answer when he saw something move outside the window that nearly made him jump out of his skin.

Holy shit! Candace waved at him and smiled.

12 Fire and Ice

Uh oh. Given that Death stared her in the face, in the gorgeous form of Gabe Jones, it wasn't easy to hang onto her smile. Even through the barrier of the window, he looked apoplectic, with his face all red and his eyes popping out of his head like one of those weird rubber squeezee dolls. She figured she had two options, brazen it out and see what happened, or she could slink back up the rickety ladder of the fire escape to the roof, flee back down the staircase to the street and catch a cab to Kennedy Airport where she could buy a ticket to Brazil and disappear into the Amazon Jungle for the next thirty years or so, or at least until Gabe was too old to catch and kill her.

She decided to brazen it out. She waved at him through the window and smiled. She knew something about her smile pissed him off, but hey, what the heck, if you're going to go for it, go big.

He turned even redder. She could see his mouth open, and she knew he was about to—unwisely—say something to her even though she stood on the other side of a closed window, but he abruptly changed his focus back to Vanessa who sat with her back to the glass. He said something to her instead. Vanessa apparently said something in return because Gabe nodded, then she stood and exited the room. The minute she left, Gabe leaped from his seat and jabbed his finger at her. She could see his lips form the words, "Go! Go, go, go."

She shrugged and smiled.

His hands grabbed his head then he abruptly threw himself back into his seat just as Vanessa came into view carrying a glass of clear liquid. Candace ducked down, giving the woman time to reseat herself before poking her head back up above the level of the windowsill.

Gabe glared at her from across the room for a moment then shifted his gaze to Vanessa. With Vanessa now facing away from the window, Candace pressed her ear against the glass, hoping she could hear their words. No luck, just a lot of undistinguishable mumbling. Disgusted, she pulled away so she could keep her eyes on Gabe because he was certainly keeping an eye on her. Suddenly he jumped up again, said something to Vanessa and rushed out of the room.

Hmmm.

The screeching sound of a window going up made her jump. She turned.

"What the hell are you doing!" Gabe hissed as he leaned out of the window a few feet from the fire escape.

Candace shrugged. "I don't know." She did, but she certainly wasn't going to tell him.

"Then why are you here?"

More shrugging. "I don't know."

"Why did you do exactly what I told you *not* to do?"

"I don't know." Geez, why didn't she just play a recording of her answer? It would save her all that work.

"Oh, my God, do you know anything?"

"I'm not sure." At least it was different.

His eyes blazed. If the window was closer to the fire escape Candace figured she'd be dead.

"Get off this fire escape!"

Candace stared at him for a minute, thinking. Okay, so she could refuse to do his bidding—crap, his bidding? How archaic. What was the big deal about leaving anyway? It wasn't as if she'd learned anything hanging around on a rickety old fire escape.

"Okay, fine, whatever." Putting a foot on a rung of the ladder, she climbed back up toward the roof, barely pausing when the window slammed shut behind her. She hauled herself over the low wall and crossed the hot tarpaper expanse before jogging down the stairs to the floor below.

She reached Vanessa's apartment. Stopped. Stared at the door. Shook her head. That deep depression that had filled her ever since Fred's death threatened to engulf her. It was quickly followed by the usual anger. Damn it, why did her stepfather change his will? And what could she do to fix it? Maybe not much, or maybe she could keep trying. It wasn't in her to quit.

She rang the bell. There was the sound of footsteps approaching then the door swung open.

"Hi, Vanessa," Candace said and squeezed past her into the apartment. "I was here earlier but evidently I missed you so I'm glad you're here now. I have questions." She threw herself onto the beige brocade loveseat next to Gabe. She purposely didn't look at him, but she could feel his eyes burning holes into her.

Vanessa glared. Her foot tapped with irritation. As usual, she was dressed perfectly, makeup flawless, every hair in place. How in the hell did she end up with the Goth Twins?

"Did I invite you in?" she asked.

"No, I don't think so, but I know you'd never be rude enough to refuse to admit me." She heard a growl from Gabe but ignored it. "So, sit down. You're making me uncomfortable hovering over me."

Candace could see Vanessa's instinct for good manners warring with her loathing of Candace. Finally, good manners won out (as Candace knew they would, Vanessa's society family was good for something, after all) and she took a seat on the couch across from Candace.

"What do you want?"

Oh, lord, there was that question again. She wished people would stop asking her since she never seemed to have a good answer for it. She hoped the suspects would let their guilt get the better of them and blurt out the truth so she wouldn't have to ask any questions. She sighed. Apparently, she would never make it as a detective. Good thing all she wanted to do was be a chocolatier.

"Um..." she hedged.

"I think Candace wants to ask you about *The Recipe*," Gabe volunteered.

Right! "Yes, who do you think would benefit from stealing *The Recipe*?"

"How would I know?" Vanessa said in a monotone voice. Her eyes narrowed, and her mouth flattened into a long thin line then her tongue slid out from between her lips and flicked at the corner of her mouth. That, in combination with her pointy nose and greenish-colored eyes, made her look like a giant boa constrictor.

Candace stared, mesmerized. Yikes. Gabe poked her in the side with his elbow and her brain unlocked.

"Right. Really, that's not what I wanted to ask. I overheard someone say something about a security code. Did you hear anything about that?"

Vanessa's mouth thinned even more, if that was possible. "How would I have heard anything about a security code? Fred and I divorced seven years ago, and we were only married for a short time. I'm sure things have changed since then." She gave Candace a look that said she would love to tell Candace how she felt about those changes.

"Maybe you know something about some scheme Tiffany and Julian have to make some money."

"I've probably talked to the woman twice, and once was at the reading of the will. So again, the answer is no, how would I know anything?"

Okay, this was going nowhere fast. She better come up with some better questions or Vanessa would kick them out. She wracked her brain for something to say as she watched the older woman toy with the diamond necklace around her neck. The diamonds sparkled in the light.

"Are those real?" she blurted.

"Of course, they're real." Vanessa answered, sounding offended. She let the necklace fall back into place around her neck.

Wow, there were at least a dozen diamonds on the necklace, each diamond separated by a silver flower with a tiny garnet in the center. It was so unique Candace knew darned well she'd remember it if she'd seen Vanessa wearing it while she was married to Fred. Still, she had seen the necklace somewhere.

"Did Fred give you those?" she asked next, just to be sure.

Vanessa jumped to her feet. "What business is it of yours?"

Which meant he hadn't. "Since Fred gave my mom pearls and he gave both Tiffany and Susan pearls, I'm surprised he didn't give you pearls too. How long have you had the necklace?"

"I think you'd better go." Vanessa walked to door, opened it then stood aside and waited for Candace and Gabe to leave.

Gabe got to his feet and held out a hand for Candace. Together they walked past Vanessa and out into the hall. The door slammed behind them.

"Bye, Vanessa," Candace said, and wiggled her fingers at the door.

Gabe narrowed his eyes at her, not amused. Okay, fine, whatever. Turning, she went down the five flights of stairs. Gabe followed. When they reached the street, he hailed a cab. They climbed in.

"Where to?" the driver asked as he pulled out into the sea of trucks and other cabs headed downtown.

"67th and Park," Gabe said, and turned the volume up on the in-cab TV. Candace could see a muscle bunch in his jaw. Obviously, he didn't want to talk.

Tough. "Driver, change of plans. Tiffany's on Fifth," she said, contradicting Gabe's instructions.

Gabe's eyes went wide. Jabbing the TV screen with a finger, he turned it off then turned to face her. "What the hell are you talking about! No way are we going to Tiffany's," he growled through tight lips then reiterated his instructions to the driver.

"Yes way." She leaned closer to the Plexiglas partition separating the back seat from the driver. "Take us to Tiffany's on Fifth."

"God damn it! 67th and Park," he barked at the driver while glaring at her, his eyes shooting sparks.

"No, Tiffany's," Candace replied, staring at him as he ran his hands through his hair, glaring at her. Geez, he was big, and, she supposed, intimidating, at least for people who allowed themselves to be intimidated. Not that she was one of those easily intimidated people, she was more one of those people who found his glare a big turn-on. She wiggled her eyebrows at him, smiling. He slapped himself on the forehead.

"We're going back to your apartment," he gritted.

"No. Driver, we're going to Tiffany's," Candace said calmly.

The driver darted a wide-eyed look at them in the rearview mirror. His cab crossed two lanes of traffic and slammed to a halt next to the curb. "So, you tell me where we are going when you know where we are going and then we go there. Okay?"

Bowing his head, Gabe rubbed his temples with his fingers. He acted like he had a headache although Candace couldn't figure out why he would have a headache since she was the one being yelled at. "Okay, what's going on?" he asked, finally giving up the argument.

"Did you see that necklace?"

He blinked. "Necklace? Sure, I saw it. How could I not when you were making such a big deal over it. Why?"

"That necklace is from Tiffany's."

He blinked again, his thick eyelashes fluttering. God, so cute. But so clueless. Candace sighed. She forgot, he was a guy, so what did she expect. "I know that necklace." Reaching into her purse, she pulled out her iPad and typed in a web address. Once the site came up, she scrolled through several pages then held it up for Gabe to see.

"There, see?" She pointed. "It's the same necklace. And it costs over a hundred thousand dollars."

He stopped blinking, instead his eyes widened, then he frowned. "Okay, so it's expensive, but maybe Fred bought it for her."

"No, he was a pearl man all the way. Anyway, you have to remember Wendy and I lived next door while he was married to Vanessa. I would have known if he bought her diamonds."

"How would you know?"

"She never lost an opportunity to lord it over my mother. Believe me, I would have known. Anyway, he couldn't have bought the necklace when they were married. It's part of this year's collection."

"Right," he said faintly. "So where did she get the money?"

His wide-eyed look was sexy, too. "Exactly."

Candace could see the wheels turning in his head. "Driver, Tiffany's, please."

The driver stared at her in the mirror then rolled his dark eyes.

"I saw that," Candace said. She put her iPad back in her purse. "Go."

Looking abashed, the driver hit the gas and merged into traffic, once again on the way downtown.

* * * *

"Wow, Richard, this is so gorgeous."

Gabe tried not to watch as Candace held the dainty amethyst necklace up against her throat and looked in the mirror. Her slim neck was just too enticing. Tilting her head—*holy shit, don't tilt your head like that, it makes me crazy*—she smiled but it wasn't her usual evil smile, and it made his heart clench in his chest, and his breath catch in his throat.

He scowled back at her. He didn't want any heart-clenching and throat-catching. Heart-clenching and throat-catching just asked for trouble. Although it was safer than what he actually wanted, so maybe he should just give in and go with it.

After a minute, she sighed and handed the necklace back to the salesclerk. "It's beautiful but not today."

"You're such a spoilsport." Richard pouted but put the necklace back on its stand inside the glass case. "Is there anything else I can do for you?" He cocked a hip, striking a pose as he smoothed his bleached-blond hair.

Candace twisted a lock of her hair around one finger as she directed a sly smile at Richard, her whole demeanor changing from innocent Pollyanna to seductress Lilith in a moment.

Dear God, she was back. That headache lurking at the back of Gabe's head moved forward front and center.

"Now that you mention it, there is something you can do for me." On her iPad, she showed him the picture of Vanessa's necklace. "So, what do you think? Can you tell me who bought it?"

Richard shook his head. "I'm sorry, sweet cheeks, no can do. I would if I could, but I can't. Company policy."

Candace amped up her smile. "Not even a hint? Pretty please?" More hair twirling.

Richard took a step back; obviously afraid he would get burned by the sheer wattage. "You wouldn't want me to lose my job, would you?" he whined. One hand nervously fiddled with his red power tie.

"No," Candace sighed, that thing she had in spades abruptly dialing back to normal. "Of course not. Thanks anyway, Richard. See you soon, I'm sure." With a wave of her hand, she walked away from the jewelry counter and headed toward the front door.

"Come back when you're ready to buy the amethyst necklace," Richard called as she reached the door.

Candace waved again without turning. Outside on the sidewalk Gabe slanted a careful look from the corner of his eye. She had that stubborn bulldog look on her face again, and once again, he knew he should be afraid, very afraid.

"We need to go to the police," she said. "They need to know about the necklace and what I found in Murray's office."

It was all Gabe could do not to whine just like Richard. "First of all, the fact Vanessa has an expensive necklace means nothing. Secondly, how are you going to explain to the police how you know all that information about Murray? Are you going to tell them we broke into his office late at night and went through his desk?

Her face fell. "No, of course not. I'm not stupid, you know."

Really? Sometimes Gabe wondered. "Give it up, Candace. We're hopeless as investigators. Skulking around on fire escapes and breaking into people's apartments isn't going to make a bit of difference. Let the police handle the situation."

"Are you wimping out? Bailing on me before we've hardly gotten started? I thought you wanted to catch the murderer."

God, she was like a wasp near a bottle of Coke. No matter how many times you swatted her away, she just kept coming back. The impulse to slap his forehead became almost irresistible. He settled for running his hands through his hair instead. "I do. You know I do but we're not making any headway."

She bared her teeth at him. The expression was almost as scary as when she smiled. Almost but not quite. The teeth-baring expression clearly said there was something sneaky and horrible lurking in her mind, but when she smiled, there was no way to tell for sure what she was thinking. That's why it was so scary.

A lot more teeth became visible. "Fine then. I don't need you anyway. I planned on doing it by myself in the first place, so I'll just go back to plan A.

Okay, he took it back, the teeth-baring was just as scary. "Don't you dare. You could get hurt."

"You can't stop me."

"If you're going to go off half-cocked and do something crazy, I will too stop you."

"You're not the boss of me."

Jeez, the last time he heard that phrase he had gently tried to point out to her it wasn't a good idea to break into his mother's apartment, because look how that ended, with Candace trapped by an insane Siamese under his mother's bed. Why couldn't she just be some normal girl, all flirty and flighty and just happy to obey.

She needed someone to take a firmer hand with her. "You know what? You're a damned menace, to yourself, and to society. Being around you is like being trapped in a cage with a wild bear. You're such a menace you need a keeper."

"I'm a menace? I'm a menace!" Fury radiated from Candace's eyes. "You selfish jerk. You don't care about me. All you care about is yourself."

The unjust accusation frosted him. "What the hell, Candace. Of course, I care about you. I'm trying to help you."

"Bullshit, you've done everything you can to weasel out of helping me."

He opened his mouth to respond but she rushed on with, "I've worked my ass off for ten years. Ten years, Gabe." Tears glittered in her eyes. "I worked for your father at the same time I went to college, I graduated from college in three years instead of four, I worked as a stock girl, I worked on the line, I worked in accounting, all so I'd be prepared to someday do the top job, all while you did whatever. I've done everything...nearly every job there is at Contessa because I love the company and I loved Fred and I wanted to be worthy. And in the end, it didn't matter. He didn't keep his promise." A sob escaped.

Something painful twisted in his chest. He reached out a hand for her, wanting to take her in his arms, while he struggled to find something to say, although he wasn't sure what that would be.

She knocked his hand aside. "He didn't keep his promise, and you know what? It's not fair. And you know what's the worst thing?" She poked him in the chest. "You threw it away. Threw. It. Away. Everything I ever wanted; you threw away. That's why you're selfish. You got it all and you don't care. You got it all."

She squeezed her eyes shut for a moment and took a deep, shaky breath before opening her eyes again. Her bright blue eyes were dark with sadness and reproach.

"But it wasn't what I wanted," he protested.

"I know that, and I hate you for it!" she said. Shoving him out of her way, she ran into the street and jumped into a cab. The last thing he saw was her head in the back window of a taxi as it receded in the distance.

13 The Saggy Middle

God damn son-of-a-bitch! That asshole. How dare he? She was so angry, her stomach burned. Saying she needed a keeper then giving up right in the middle of the investigation when they had just started to make progress.

In just over a week they'd learned Murray had lost hundreds of thousands betting on the horses, but money was still being deposited into his bank from an unknown source (read criminal). They learned Tiffany and the Greaseball had some kind of scheme going that might—or might not—involve Fred, or Fred's office, or maybe a secret code or some kind of password to something in Fred's office. They learned Vanessa had a necklace she shouldn't be able to afford. They learned...

Okay, so maybe they weren't making spectacular progress. Maybe they were only making fair-to-middling progress.

All right, fine, she admitted it, maybe not even fair-to-middling progress since they didn't know what any of it meant, but they made *some* progress.

Maybe the fact that Vanessa was able to afford a diamond necklace that was worth as much as her yearly alimony meant nothing, and maybe Murray had a good explanation for all the deposits in his bank but knowing Murray, probably not. And maybe Tiffany and the Greaseball were just blowing smoke out of their asses, and maybe there was a legitimate reason for Susan to have a gun in her bedroom. Lots of people had guns. It didn't make them murderers.

The fact they were making so-so progress wasn't the issue. It was the fact Gabe didn't seem to care. She didn't understand how he could have what she would kill for, and yet he walked away from it. It was clear he didn't care for Contessa, and obviously not for her.

Her heart hurt from the blow he dealt her.

She counted on Gabe to support her, and just when things got tough, he bailed. Clearly a trend. Not happy with his relationship with his father? Don't speak to him for the next decade. Don't want the responsibility of running a billion-dollar company? Walk away. Don't like the idea of a relationship with a girl who adores you? Dump her.

Obviously, Gabe was a man not to be trusted. She thought she'd learned that eleven years ago but today just drove the point home.

She would never trust him again. Unfortunately, she still needed him. Okay, she didn't actually need *him*. What she needed was Contessa and *The Recipe*, in no particular order. However, *The Recipe* was no good without Contessa, and in order to get Contessa, she needed Gabe. But, damn it, she didn't want to need him.

Still, she felt terrible about saying she hated him because it wasn't true. Sadly, she felt the opposite.

Aaaaghhhh! She was so confused.

The elevator reached her floor. She got off and opened the door to the apartment, then stopped.

They were here. In her apartment...okay, in her mother's apartment but, really, who cared. The point was they were here, with their green hair, and their lip studs and tongue studs and nose rings, and the boogers they wiped on the furniture, and she hated them.

Goth Girl looked up at Candace's entrance. Her expression was flat as she blew an enormous bubble. The bubble popped. Still staring at Candace, Lucy slowly peeled the excess off her nose. It took her longer than it should have since she also had to peel it off the silver ring in her nostril.

"What the hell are you doing here?" Candace was out of patience today.

At her question, Lance managed to tear his eyes away from the video game he was playing... on her mother's TV!!!!... and looked at Candace. "Oh, hey, hi... um... er..."

Even after all these years Lance still couldn't remember her name. Another reason to hate him.

"What are you doing here?" Candace demanded again.

"Um... like, our mom..."

"...kicked us out," Lucy finished.

What a surprise. "So you came here? Why?"

Lance's eyes widened. "I mean, where else, uh..."

"...would we go?"

Her blood pressure went up. Most doctors would say she was too young for high blood pressure but then those doctors didn't know the Luckless twins. "Somewhere not here."

"Wendy said it was okay for us to stay here," Lucy said in a complete sentence. She was the only one of the two who could actually say a complete sentence.

Not bothering to respond, Candace marched down the hall to her mother's office. "What are they doing here?"

Wendy looked up from the book she held and stared blankly at her. Candace could see the wheels in her head grinding as her mother struggled to catch up. The light finally came on. "Oh. The twins. Vanessa kicked them out."

"I know that. However, it doesn't explain why they are here, in our apartment."

The usual state of confusion descended again. "Where else would they go?"

"I don't know. I don't care. I don't want them here, living in our house, eating our food, using our bathrooms, sitting on our couches like a couple of mooches. We don't need any more mooches, we already have our own resident mooch."

"We do? Who?"

"Floyd!"

"Floyd's not a mooch, he's our butler." Her baby blues were wide with befuddlement.

Candace caught herself just as she was about to slap herself on the forehead, a sure sign she already spent too much time with Gabe. Maybe it was a good thing he'd decided enough was enough and gone home before he completely infected her with his attitude.

She took a deep breath then let it out, giving herself a minute to control her temper. "Floyd is not a butler. When was the last time you saw him open our door to company?"

Wendy fiddled with the collar of her frilly blouse, stalling, before finally admitting defeat. "Not in recent memory."

"Right. And when was the last time you saw him organize a dinner party, or serve drinks, or do anything to manage our household, all tasks a butler would do?"

Wendy's mouth trembled.

"No, what Floyd mostly does is sleep half the day and the other half lie in your soaker tub with a bottle of champagne from Fred's expensive collection. He's a mooch but at least now he's a mooch who has his own money which means he can afford to leave."

"Are you telling me I have to fire Floyd?" Her voice squeaked in protest.

Candace heaved a sigh. Her mom didn't get it. Maybe this was an argument for another day, unlike the twins. They had to go today. "We'll talk about it later but right now you need to send the Goth Twins packing."

"I know you don't like them, and you know I don't like them either but..."

"Mom, Lance is out there playing video games on our TV but worse than that, Lucy is chewing gum and sticking it under the arm of the sofa."

"What!" Wendy's eyes blazed. "She is? That stinker. Okay, they've got to go." Jumping up from the chair, she marched into the living room, leaving a trail of lily-of-the-valley scent in her wake.

"Mom, wait!" Candace ran after her, but it was too late to stop the debacle.

"You," Wendy said, her voice promising doom as she pointed at Lance. "And you." The finger moved over toward Lucy. "Both of you. Out. Out of my house."

Lucy stared at Wendy, her mouth opening. A big glob of gum rolled out of her mouth and landed in her lap, proof of her culpability.

Wendy yanked the game console out of Lance's hand then rounded on Lucy. "Gum. You have gum in my house." She ran her fingers under the arm of the sofa. Her eyes widened. "You do! How could you?" She whacked the girl with the game console.

"But, Wendy—"

"That's Mrs. Jones to you." Her arm went up again.

Candace grabbed the game console from her mother. "Mom, stop. Calm down. Maybe we should work a deal."

Her mother didn't look like she was in the mood for any deals.

"Come on, Mom. Remember the list?"

The red slowly receded from Wendy's face. "Right. The list." She narrowed her eyes at the twins. "You," she barked at Lance. "Get your dirty clodhoppers off my good coffee table." Lance yanked his feet off and sat up straight.

Now that her mother didn't look like she was on the verge of murder, Candace turned back to the twins. "Okay," she said. "I'm going to ask you some questions. If you answer them to my satisfaction, you can stay until you find a place of your own."

"How are we gonna..." Lance whined.

"...find a place of our own? We don't have any money," Lucy said in a belligerent tone.

Okay, that could be a problem, Candace thought. It just wasn't her problem. "We'll discuss it later. First you need to answer some questions. Tell me about the diamond necklace your mom has. Where did she get it?"

"What diamond necklace?" Lucy responded.

"The expensive one."

The twins exchanged calculating looks. "How expensive? Like way expensive?" Lucy finally asked.

Okay. Switching gears. "Where were you when Fred was murdered?"

They looked at each other again, then shrugged. "What day was that?" Lucy finally asked.

"Last Tuesday."

"Tuesday?" Lance said, looking puzzled. Not that puzzled was unusual. "What happened last Tuesday?"

Candace needed to stick her hands into her armpits so she didn't strangle him. "That was the day Fred was murdered? Remember?"

"What was the question?"

Arrrrggggghhhh! "Where were you that day?"

"Like that..." Lance started.

"...was a week ago. How are we supposed to remember?" Lucy finished.

Sigh. Candace needed to remind herself of her goal, or she would kill them. "Okay. Fred always kept *The Recipe* locked in the safe in his office here in the apartment to keep it secret. Have you ever told anyone about the safe?"

Lance's eyes bulged. "Fred had a secret recipe?" he finally said, uttering the first full sentence she'd ever heard since she met him which didn't make him any less of a moron.

"All righty... Time to go." Candace stood, and grabbing Lucy's arm, propelled her kicking and protesting to the front door. Being a follower, Lance followed. Candace opened the door and pushed them out. They still stood there, mouths flapping, when she slammed it shut.

Her mother sent her a look.

Candace wasn't sure what kind of look it was, so she cut her mother off at the pass. "Don't say a word." She nibbled on her thumbnail in frustration.

"I wouldn't. They have a mother. They can go live with her."

Oh, good, it was that kind of look, the one that said she agreed. "And now that we are discussing it, since Fred is dead now, we should change the locks on the front door," Candace said with satisfaction, but her satisfaction didn't last long because, as it turned out, the Luckless twins were more than Luckless, they were Useless. She'd learned nothing.

God, Gabe was right. This was futile. She didn't know the right questions to ask, either that, or she didn't know the right people to ask them of. Sighing, she trailed her mother back to her office and flopped into her mother's shabby-chic loveseat. "What am I going to do?"

Her mother looked at her for a long moment, sympathy in her eyes. That was the thing about her mother, she might not be a rocket scientist when it came to solving problems, but she was always on Candace's side.

Making herself comfortable next to Candace, Wendy put her arm around Candace's shoulder. "Tell me what you found out at Vanessa's."

"Nothing," Candace grumbled. "The only thing unusual is she had this necklace from Tiffany's I know costs over a hundred thousand dollars. Given the fact she's living in a five-story walk-up I don't see how—"

"She's living in a walk-up?" Wendy interrupted. She clapped her hands together and started to laugh. "Oh my God, I need to hear about this. Is it a dump? Were there rats?"

"Mom, don't get sidetracked."

"But I want to know." She began to bounce up and down with glee.

"Okay, fine. It was actually in a nice neighborhood on the Upper West Side, in the Eighties, and it was a very nice apartment. Just no elevator. You know, with Fred and Vanessa only being married eight months, she didn't get much alimony, and with the prenup she signed, it kind of looks like that's all she can afford."

"What, ten thousand a month isn't chump change, you know."

"No, but it's not enough to keep Vanessa in the lifestyle she'd like to become accustomed to. Happy now?"

Wendy thrust her lower lip out, pouting. "Not as happy as I'd be if you told me she was living in the projects, but I'll let it go."

Her mother's reaction to Vanessa's problems might seem excessive to outsiders but they were justified. When Vanessa married Fred, she had naturally expected her predecessor, wife Number Two, namely Wendy, and her daughter Candace, to move out. Only they hadn't. Fred just moved Vanessa in, along with her twins, and they became one big happy family. Not. And Vanessa made sure Wendy paid the price.

"Okay, Mom, moving on. I went to Tiffany's—the store not the showgirl—to see if I could weasel Richard Read into telling me who bought the necklace, but it was a no-go."

Wendy thought for a long time. Candace could see from her face that thinking pained her. "Personally, I don't think Vanessa knows anything," her mother said reluctantly.

Candace gaped at her mother. "That's not what you said this morning."

"I've changed my mind."

"Mom!"

"Hey, I'm entitled to change my mind."

"So where does that leave us? Back with Murray?"

Her mother scratched her head. "I don't know. I called your friend what's-her-face about looking up those deposits for us. Know what? She's not your friend."

"What?"

"She said no." Her mother looked thoroughly put out. "Turns out she's not getting married and can't afford to lose her job."

Candace took a deep breath so her jaw would unlock. "Mom, you can't blame her for not wanting to get fired. There's still Floyd. And what about Tiffany and the Greaseball?"

Wendy jumped up from her chair. "Oh, that reminds me." She ran out of the office and returned carrying a small box and handed it to Candace.

Candace opened the flaps. Inside was a small plastic device resembling a tape recorder and several disks the size of dimes. She gave her mother a look.

"It's the bugs." Wendy preened, like a kid who'd just won first prize in a spelling bee.

Whoa. She had no idea her mother was serious. "Mom, this is so illegal." Illegal, yes, but it didn't stop her from removing the disks from the box and turning them over, examining them.

"What, are you chicken?"

Since not two hours ago Candace had thought the same thing about Gabe, she naturally took umbrage at the slur. "No, I'm not chicken."

This elicited a bunch of hand clapping and bouncing up and down. "Okay, let's do it."

Oh, crap. Tell me I didn't just hear what I heard? "What do you mean 'Let's do it'?"

"You and me. Us. Together. Like Mork and Mindy or Batman and Robin. You know, like a deadly duo." Her mother paced around the perimeter of the small office, rubbing her hands together in delight.

Mork and Mindy? Only if her mother was the alien. "Mom, there is no 'us.'"

"Naturally there's an 'us.' I got the stuff, so I get to go with you."

"No." The very idea horrified her.

Her mother's hands went to her hips. "And why not?"

If she was quicker Candace would be able to come up with a better answer but she wasn't so she couldn't. Instead, she said the first thought passing through her brain. "It could be dangerous. I don't want you getting hurt."

Her mother's mouth thinned. Her jaw jutted out in a Jay Leno imitation. "And why would it be any more dangerous for me than for you?"

Oh boy, the answer to that was liable to get her smacked into the middle of next week.

"Wellll..."

"It's because you think I'm too old, isn't it?"

"Wellll..."

"You think I'm old and out of shape and flabby." Wendy's chin trembled. "You think I'm too old to run if someone starts shooting at us. Admit it."

Oh, dear God. Shooting? "No—"

"I'll have you know I'm not old. I'm only middle-aged. I'm forty-nine—and a half—which means if I live to ninety-nine I'm smack in the middle. Got it? And I'm not too old to run either."

Candace eyed her mother's waistline which wasn't quite as svelte as it used to be, and her hips were a little wider than they were ten years ago. She was struggling for something to say when Wendy went across the hall to Floyd's room. She knocked. Floyd came to the door, wearing his usual plaid bathrobe and slippers.

Wendy pointed at Candace. "Tell my daughter I am not old."

Floyd stared at the two of them with that deadpan expression on his face. "She's not old," he said in a deadpan voice.

"Tell her I'm not too out of shape to run."

"She's not too out of shape to run." More deadpan.

"Tell her I'm not fat and flabby."

"She's not fat and flabby."

Her mother turned and glared at Candace. "Any other questions?"

Candace curled her lip. "You pay his salary. He lives here rent free. It makes sense he's going to agree with you."

"You shouldn't argue with your mother when she's right," Floyd interjected.

Boy, talk about being caught in the middle. "I never said you were fat and flabby. You look great..."

"You mean for someone who's *middle-aged.*"

"Mom," Candace whined plaintively.

"Okay, good, so it means we're going together. Let me get my purse."

* * * *

Lucy punched the button for the lobby as hard as she could. "That damned bitch. It's her fault."

Lance blinked while his hands roamed aimlessly through his all his pockets, in search of God-knew-what. "Who? Wendy?" he finally said. "You got any gum?" he whined as a follow-up.

Lucy glared. "No, dummy. Candace. And no, I don't have any more gum."

"Yeah. It's her fault. What's her fault?"

"Us getting kicked out of the apartment. And it should have been our apartment. I mean, Fred divorced Wendy to marry Mom. Why the hell were Candace and Wendy still living there, anyway?"

"Yeah, definitely their—"

"Fault. Yeah, but, you know, then Fred married—"

"I know, I know. He married Tiffany, but she doesn't count. He was married to her for only four months, and she's nothing but a tramp. She didn't want to live in New York anyway. We've been cheated, and it's their fault."

"Yeah, so they should pay. Just like..."

The sound of rap music filled the elevator. Lucy pulled out her phone. "What, Mom?" she said, holding it in front of her so Lance could also hear.

"Did you find it?" the disembodied voice asked.

Lance grimaced. "No, sorry, Mom, we kinda got—" Lucy's heavy brogue slammed into his shin. "OW!"

"What was that?"

"Nothing, Mom. Lance just tripped."

Lance glared at Lucy while he rubbed his shin. "I did not," he said.

"You need to get back in there and get it done," Vanessa continued, ignoring Lance's bellyaching.

The elevator doors opened, and the twins exited, Lucy still holding the phone so Lance could hear.

"Mom," Lance whined. "How are we..."

Lucy raised a hand for a cab. "Going to do that? That bitch threw us out and told us not come back."

There was a pause. "I don't care. You got in there plenty of times before, and you can do it again."

"But, Mom. Last time Fred—"

"Do it," Vanessa ordered and hung up.

Lance let out a squeal of distress.

"Oh, be quiet, you big baby." Lucy said, her mouth screwed into a sneer. "We need to get back in there."

Lance turned green, then leaning over, he threw up in the gutter.

14 Bugs and Bimbos

Candace stared at the door. She decided it wasn't a half bad idea to do what her mom wanted. First of all, maybe they would learn something, and B: someone would have to monitor the bug. That someone would be her mother which would keep her out of Candace's hair.

"So where are you going to put the bug?"

Her mother's head whipped around. "Me? I thought you'd know."

That produced teeth-gritting. "Mom, this was your idea."

Her mother blinked. That blank look indicated she was exercising her brain cells but that nothing was happening. "Under the bed?"

"How are you going to do that, crawl around on your hands and knees? Anyway, then we could only hear what they say if they're in their hotel room. What if they leave?"

"Right." Wendy took a deep breath. Her brow furrowed. More thinking, this time a little more fruitful. "Okay, so maybe we can put it in Tiffany's purse?"

"Okay, I'll distract them while you hide it in her purse."

Wendy's eyes widened. "Oh no. What if I drop it? Or they hear me?"

Candace had to bite her tongue. It wasn't easy when she acted as the parent more often than her mother. "Fine. Give me the darned thing. I'll get the job done."

With a nod, Wendy handed it over. Bug tucked into the palm of her hand, Candace knocked on the door. After a moment, it swung open.

Tiffany frowned. "What the heck, Candace. You were supposed to be here yesterday."

Oh. That's right, she was—supposed to be, and actually had been—but no point in telling their suspect. "Um, I got held up."

"Why is your mother here?" The showgirl's eyes narrowed suspiciously.

"Uh, because...uh..." Shit, because...? She hoped her face didn't wear that same blank look as her mother's. If so, Tiffany would catch on. "It was my mother's idea. She thought you might need some comforting."

Her mother threw her a panicked look then threw her arms around Tiffany's waist. "You poor thing," she said. "I feel so bad about how Fred treated you. You didn't deserve for him to refuse to give you the money you needed when he promised he would."

Candace thought she would gag, but Tiffany seemed to buy it. Candace heard her draw a shaky breath.

"Oh, thank you, Wendy. I was so disappointed. I don't know what I'm going to do."

Wendy patted her back. "Come on, let's sit down and talk."

Together they walked to the bed and sat. Candace stomped over to the lone occasional chair and slumped into it. A quick glance around told her the Greaseball had left. Hooray. He made her skin crawl, and his absence made it easier to distract Tiffany so she could sneak the bug into the other woman's purse which, fortunately, sat on top of the dresser just a few feet away.

She threw her mother a look. Her mother sent a look of desperation back. Lips tight, Candace jerked her chin at her mother... *Go on. This was your dumb idea. Do your thing!*

"So, what can we do to help?" Wendy said tentatively.

Tiffany burst into more noisy sobs. "He promised... and then he didn't... And now I'm... And no more alimony... And it's not fair..."

Wendy's eyes returned to Candace, this time with a frantic plea for help. Candace shrugged.

Her mother's lips tightened. If it wasn't for the fact Candace knew her mother was harmless, the glare would have incinerated her.

She glared back only to get a bunch of eyebrow wiggles, a sign of nervousness. *Oh, all right.* "Mom, can I talk to you in the bathroom?"

Her mother jumped up so fast Tiffany tipped over onto her back on the bed.

Together, they rushed into the bathroom. Candace shut the door. "Mom! You need to do your thing."

Her mother blinked. "What thing?"

"Oh my God! Distract her! Talk to her. I don't know. Comfort her. Do something so I can get at her purse and put the bug in."

"But she's crying. I feel so bad for her, and I don't know what to do with a crying woman. You never cried."

"Mom! It's all fake."

"It is?"

The temptation to bang her head on the wall was so great, Candace jammed her hands on top of her head to keep it still. "Yes, Mom, it is. Tiffany is about as sensitive as a brick, but play along with her so she thinks she's fooled us."

Her mother nodded, looking thoughtful. "Okay," she said but she still didn't sound certain.

"Try hugging her some more. If you can get her to put her head down, I can do what I need to do."

"Okay, let's get this done," Wendy said, this time sounding determined as she opened the door and led the way outside.

"I'm sorry," she said to Tiffany as the other woman eyed them suspiciously. "My, uh..." She waved a hand in the general direction of her chest. "Emergency. Sorry. Where were we?"

As if there were no interruption, Tiffany began sobbing loudly again. Wendy sat down next to Tiffany and put her arms around her. After a moment, she patted Tiffany's back, barely touching it, as if it were hot coals.

"There, there," Wendy said. "It's all right. Whatever it is, we'll fix it."

Tiffany sobbed. Her mother transferred her hand to Tiffany's head under the guise of caressing her hair but actually forcing Tiffany's face into her chest, giving Candace the opportunity to grab the woman's purse. After a hurried examination, she realized there was a leather tag hanging from the strap with the designer's logo fastened to it. Perfect. Prying up the little brass piece, she quickly shoved the tiny bug underneath and set the purse back on the dresser.

Her mother darted a look at her. Candace nodded. With a sigh of relief, Wendy shoved Tiffany away.

Tiffany squawked. "Hey!"

"Sorry. I was... you were..." She pulled her damp blouse away from her chest. "Why don't I get you a tissue, ok?"

"Sure," Tiffany said in a truculent tone. "Whatever." She glared at Candace as if it were her fault. Which it kind of was. "So, you said y'all could help me. What can you do?"

Oh boy. Candace hadn't thought that far ahead. "Uh." She wracked her brain for an answer. "Maybe we could talk to the attorney and see if we can't carve out something extra for you.

Tiffany gave her a look. "Geez, Candace, even I know y'all can't do that. Once the guy is dead, you can't change the will."

Candace gritted her teeth. "Maybe I can take something out of my share."

"What share?" Tiffany shouted. "You didn't get a share, all you got was that fucking recipe and you didn't even get that!"

Yikes! "Mom. Bathroom," Candace said, jumping to her feet.

"I don't nee—"

Candace grabbed her mother's arm and dragged her into the bathroom. "Sure, you do. Remember, you have that, uh, other thing... where you..." She shut the door since she had no idea what her mother's "thing" was, and if she tried to finish the sentence she'd sound like an idiot.

"We need to leave," she hissed.

"Well, duh," her mother said. "The last thing I want to do is spend any more time with Tiffany slobbering on my good silk blouse. Did you get the bug planted?"

"Yes, of course I did."

"Then let's go,"

"Isn't that what I just said?" Candace gritted her teeth. "Just give me a second to come up with an excuse for leaving."

"She doesn't want an excuse; she wants what she thinks she deserves."

Candace snorted. "No, she wants what's ours."

Wendy's eyes widened. "You're right! Well, fuck that."

"Mom!"

"Don't you 'Mom' me. I can say whatever I want." She grabbed Candace's arm. "Come on, we're out of here."

Wow. When the worm turned, it made a complete U-ee. "What are you going to tell Tiffany?"

"Who cares?" They exited the bathroom.

"Hey, Tiffany. We've got to go now."

Tiffany's lower lip went out. "You're leaving? But what about me? Y'all promised you'd help."

Candace and Wendy shared a look. Candace could see *"Fuck you"* hovering on her mother's lips. She shook her head. Wendy took a deep breath and then smiled the fakest smile Candace had ever seen.

"We're going to help you, but we need to talk first." Wendy picked up both their handbags and herded Candace in the direction of the door. "We'll let you know."

Shutting the door behind them, they ran down the hall and jumped onto the elevator as it opened on their floor, spitting out the Greaseball.

"Hi Julie," Candace wiggled a finger at him. "Bye, Julie." The door slid shut on his astonished face.

* * * *

"Sure, you'll help me," Tiffany sneered as she glowered at the hotel room door after it shut behind Candace and Wendy. If the door wasn't already shut, she would have slammed it.

A moment later, the door opened, and Julian walked into the room. "Was that Candace and Wendy?" he asked, looking confused.

Tiffany walked over to the still open door and did what she was aching to do. *Bam!* "Yeah. Stupid bitches."

Julian's eyes darted back to the now closed door as if he'd like to escape through it. After a moment, he ventured, "So, did you get the key?"

Tiffany rolled her eyes. "Of course, I got it. I told you, they're nothing but stupid bitches. They kept running into the bathroom and leaving their purses out here."

"You didn't forget to replace it with the one we made, did you, so Candace won't know we swiped it?"

She suppressed the eye roll. "Don't be ridiculous. Unlike them, I'm not stupid."

Julian nodded, and kept nodding. "Good, good, good." He still nodded as he said, "That's good."

"Fuck, Julian. I know it's good, but it only gets us into the factory, it doesn't get us into his office so we still need to figure that part out."

Julian's head jerked up and down: a bobble-headed gangster-doll. "We'll think of something."

"*I'll* think of something. You never think of anything but your dick and your stomach," she said, and went into the bathroom to run a bubble bath.

* * * *

They caught a cab back to the apartment, nervous energy making them giggle like a couple of two-year-olds the entire trip.

"I can't believe we did that." Candace buried her face in her hands, trying to hold back the hysterical laughter threatening to erupt, letting the cab driver know she was insane.

"I know! But it was so much fun."

"Yeah, but I feel kinda bad. Maybe she did need our help."

Her mother snorted. "Oh, fuck that, Candy."

OMG! Where did this potty-mouth come from? "Mother!"

"Hah. I just wish we could have stuck the thing up her ass, like she deserved," howled her mother, who didn't care what the world thought, much less the cab driver, who had tilted toward the Plexiglas partition in an effort to hear. "Then we'd be able to track her everywhere."

"Did you see her face when we said we were leaving? She looked like a constipated goose!"

More howls of laughter.

"Do you think..."

Candace shook her head. "No, I hid it really well."

"But what if..."

"Mom, stop worrying. What would she do to us even if she did?"

"Yes, but Julian is..." Wendy shivered.

"I know. He gives me the creeps too."

"I don't think I'd like it if someone put a contract out on me."

The giggle stuck in Candace's throat, but it was important to put up a brave front. "Julian wouldn't know how to put out a contract on anyone if his life depended on it. He's just a lowlife thug." The cab pulled up in front of their building. They paid the driver, who looked disgruntled because he would never hear the rest of their story, and they exited.

"Right," her mother said as they rode up the elevator to their penthouse apartment. She unlocked the door. Together, they walked back to her office. "Since we went to all that trouble, we may as well give a listen and see what's going on, right?" Sitting at her desk, she pulled out the little recorder they looked at earlier. She turned it on. Static.

Candace frowned. "Are we too far away?"

"No, it's supposed to have a range of ten miles." She shook the machine, like it was a vending machine and she needed to shake loose the M&Ms.

"Maybe if you tuned it to a different frequency?"

Her question earned her a look of irritation. "It's not a radio. It doesn't have frequencies."

"What does it have?"

Her mother turned it upside down and checked out the bottom, looking for a magic button apparently. "I don't know."

Candace suppressed a sigh. "So what's wrong with it?"

Her mother glared. "I *said*...I don't know. It should work. Unless you put it somewhere that would interfere with the signal, like on something metal."

Oh crap. "Um..."

"What?"

"I put it under that little horsehead medallion."

Her mother's mouth dropped open. "You mean to tell me I spent forty-five dollars in cab fare, was forced to listen to Tiffany drivel on with her 'poor me' speech, and got snot all over my good blouse, all so you could screw up the bug?"

Candace gave her one of her signature smiles. Because Gabe was afraid of her, her smiles always worked on Gabe. Her mother? Not so much.

She got up and left while she still could.

15 Cops and Cons

Candace hated him. She thought he was selfish. Gabe didn't know which accusation hurt more. In the last week, he'd spent entirely too much time on Candace's harebrained schemes to the detriment of his own business, yet she thought he was selfish.

Ahh, fuck.

He rubbed his sternum, unconsciously soothing the ache, trying to think it through, picking apart the allegations she flung at him, trying to find the truth in her claims. Just because he walked away from Contessa, did that make him selfish? Did that make him uncaring?

If he looked at it from Candace's perspective, it probably did. She desperately wanted exactly what he desperately didn't, and he wasn't sure he could explain to her why he didn't want it.

His only excuse was that last week had been horrendous.

Well, he needed to amend that. It hadn't been totally horrendous because he'd spent it with Candace. As much as she made him a little crazy, he loved being with her. She made life stimulating in more ways than one, although, if someone accused him of enjoying the time he spent with her, he would deny it. At a time when he felt lower than he could ever remember, she lightened his life. He didn't know how he would have stood the funeral service if not for her.

She thought he was selfish. Fuck!

It was just this damned week. His dad had been murdered and the police still hadn't said for sure what killed him (the current consensus said it was a bullet), never mind who. He was drowning in emotion. He didn't like it. It made his chest hurt and his stomach roil.

She thought he didn't care.

Damn it, he did care. He cared a lot. He cared about Candace. He cared about Contessa, just not the way she did. He cared about finding out how and why his father was murdered. He cared about making sure Candace got her due. Only then would he feel like he hadn't let his dad down, but so far, even with the two of them joining forces, they hadn't dug up a single real clue.

The truth was, when it came to investigating, two brains turned out *not* to be better than one. Their two brains together didn't even add up to one half-assed brain.

Damn, there was nothing productive about all this wallowing. Instead of wallowing, he should be doing something. After flagging down a cab—it wasn't rush hour so there were plenty—he sent the driver uptown.

* * * *

"Is Sergeant Dolan in?" he asked the uniformed cop at the desk after waiting five minutes for him to get his nose out of his computer.

The guy, short, fat, and bald, gave him the kind of look only a guy desperate for retirement could give. "I dunno." He went back to reading.

Gabe gritted his teeth. "Could you check?"

With a martyred sigh, the cop looked up. "Why?"

Geez, New York's finest. "I need to talk with him about my father's murder."

The cop curled a lip. "Yeah, okay. *Whom* shall I say is calling?" he asked in sugary tones as he reached for the phone.

"Gabe Jones."

The hand stopped. "Jones? Seriously?"

"Yes. Seriously." He looked at the guy's name tag. "Hey, not all of us can be lucky enough to have a name like Lipschitz."

The cop's pale blue eyes narrowed menacingly. He tapped a button on the phone.

"What!" blared through the speaker.

"Hey, Dolan, some smartass who says his name is *Jones* is here to see you."

"Send him up," the scratchy voice instructed followed by a click.

Lipschitz jerked his head toward the elevator, indicating Gabe should take it. "Third floor," he said then turned back to his computer.

Gabe rode the elevator and got off on the third floor. Dolan was waiting for him, and just like Baldy downstairs, he silently jerked his head, indicating Gabe should follow, and led him toward a desk toward the back of the room.

"Sit."

Gabe sat. So far, this was not going well, but at this moment, he could do nothing but obey, not if he wanted to get any information.

Dolan leaned back in his chair and steepled his hands together then tapped his lips with his joined fingers. He cocked a brow. "So?"

Gabe paused, debating whether he should try to weasel information out of Dolan or share what he knew in hopes it would help the investigation. He opted for weaseling since sharing might land him in jail. "I wanted to find out if you've learned anything more about my dad's murder."

A slight smile tilted the corner of Dolan's mouth. Anyone who thought that smile meant he was a friendly guy needed to have their head examined. The cop's eyes dropped, and he seemed to be thinking, before he finally said, "What exactly do you want to know?"

Gabe felt a spurt of irritation. "I want to know how my dad died and who did it."

"Who do you think did it?"

Holy shit. Did the guy think he was a psychiatrist? Answer a question with a question? He clenched his jaw, reaching for patience. "If I knew, I wouldn't ask."

"Sure, you would. Killers frequently insert themselves into murder investigations so they can keep track of how much we know." He smiled again. It struck Gabe there was something very familiar about that smile.

"I'm not trying to insert myself into the investigation..." For a minute, he'd thought maybe he should share what he and Candace had learned so far, but that was a big fat *no,* since the guy was being such an asshole. Or maybe he was just being a cop. Whatever, Gabe decided to keep the info to himself. "I just want to know what happened. Wouldn't you?"

"Sure. But you must have some thoughts about who it could be."

He began to get annoyed. "I have lots of thoughts. None of them useful."

"If I remember correctly, you were out of town when your father was killed."

What, that again? "You know I was. You confirmed it." He glared at Dolan. "Can we please talk about something relevant?"

Dolan's eyelids slid down, leaving a slit of silver. "You never know what might be relevant. For instance, we still haven't confirmed Miss McCready is innocent. She found the body, after all. Fifty percent of the time the killer is the one who 'discovers' the body."

Gabe snorted. "What a crock."

"And then there's her mother. Although, I've pretty well eliminated her mother."

Gabe lifted a brow.

The corners of Dolan's mouth tipped up slightly. "Turns out she was lying naked on a massage table so it would have been difficult to be two places at once." He snickered. "In addition to embarrassing."

And let's not forget the fact Wendy could just as easily shoot herself as Fred if anyone was nuts enough to actually give her a gun.

When Gabe didn't reply Dolan continued. "Then there's also your mother."

Just like when Candace added Susan to the list, Gabe bridled. "My mother didn't do it."

"We'll see."

Gabe leveled an unblinking stare at the guy. Was it okay to hate a cop? "There are plenty of other suspects. He had three other ex-wives, you know, as well as a brother who is bitter about the deal he struck with my dad twenty some years ago and maybe thought he'd get more if my dad was dead. Then there's Murray's son Junior, Tiffany's boyfriend, Julian, and the Luckless twins."

"I know. All on the list."

Oh, for Christ's sake. The guy was obviously not going to tell him who he suspected, but... "At least tell me this: how did my father die?"

"We're still working on it."

"I thought it was a gunshot."

"We're still working on it."

Shit. Candace was right. If they wanted to find *The Recipe*, which should lead to the name of the killer, they would have to investigate for themselves. All well and good except it meant he would to have to go back and grovel. He stood. "Gee, thanks," he said, then left, Dolan's "Don't leave town," trailing in his wake.

Yeah, thanks. For nothing.

He waved down a cab. Getting in, he reluctantly gave the driver Candace's address. On second thought, he changed the address to the offices of Mott and Mott. As much as he didn't want to, it was time he did something about his inheritance.

Damn it. If she hated him before, now Candace would hate him forever.

Of course, he could always take the coward's way out and not tell her. He sighed. Why bother, she'd find out soon enough on her own. He could feel his manhood shriveling just thinking about it. It didn't improve when he entered the attorney's offices and was ushered into their conference room.

Two nearly-identical bird-like visages stared at him from across the enormous conference table. Beaky noses, skinny mouths, and crow black hair.

"Hello," said Bird One.

"Hi," Gabe responded cautiously.

"Hello," said Bird Two.

Gabe bit back the *cheep* threatening to escape.

Simultaneously, they both folded their hands on the table. Two sets of beady eyes stared at him. Bird One pursed his lips. "So...?"

This was painful. Like pulling teeth where none existed. "The will?"

"Ah, yes. The will. Ahem, as you know..." Bird One said.

"Your father left you Contessa," Bird Two finished.

"Yes."

"But he left Candace *The Recipe*."

A headache bit at the back of his skull. This was more than painful, it was lethal. His heart thumped heavily in his chest as the finality of his father's death hit him. For the hundredth time, he castigated himself for letting his pride get in the way of speaking to his father during the last ten years.

If he could, he'd do the last ten years all over again, only differently, including how he treated Candace, because he knew once he signed the paperwork that made him officially the owner of Contessa, Candace would truly hate him. There would be no do-overs. Their relationship was complicated, but he wanted a do-over anyway. There were other girlfriends in the last ten years, admittedly lots of them, but they never seemed to last long because in the back of his mind there was always this image of Candace. The others weren't blond enough. They weren't leggy enough. They especially weren't feisty or argumentative enough, and he didn't even want to think about the sex. That went without saying.

Then again, they hadn't hated him.

But he had no choice.

"Look, I know all this. Candace filled me in. I just want to sign whatever I need to sign and get on with things."

The Birds exchanged a look. "But..."

"Just give me the papers so I can sign everything."

Finally, they pulled out a file and opened it to reveal a stack of papers.

"The estate, including the business, still needs to go through probate, but these papers will allow you to operate the business in the meantime. Please sign here." Bird One pointed to the bottom of the page. Gabe scribbled his name where indicated. "And here." More scribbling.

"And one more, right here."

Gabe signed, as well as the other half dozen places they pointed to.

"That's it then. You are now in charge of Contessa Chocolate and Confectionary."

Oh, yeah, real proud, Gabe thought. He sat back in his chair, feeling like crap. He never wanted this. Despite all the years of his father's pushing and prodding him to take his responsibility seriously, he never thought he'd be here, and yet here he was, taking on something he had no desire to take on, and killing Candace's dream in the process. Thinking about her grief made guilt pile up in his throat and choke him. A lump of lead settled in his chest. Sometimes life sucked lemons.

A thought hit him, because he suddenly remembered there was the saying: *when life hands you lemons, make lemonade.*

"Actually, there is something else I want done."

* * * *

Candace walked over toward the subway on Lexington Avenue. Now that she'd done what she could about Vanessa and Tiffany, her thoughts returned to the argument she'd had with Gabe outside Tiffany Jewelers. When she took the time to look back on her behavior, she realized it was inexcusable. She'd totally lost it. She was an absolute bitch and had said things she didn't mean. Okay, so yes, she resented that Gabe was the rightful heir to Contessa even though he hadn't done anything to earn that right. And yes, he kept putting the brakes on their investigation, but he wasn't uncaring. She knew she tended to go off half-cocked, witness her little adventure with the Siamese cat, so maybe she did need a...

No. No way would she admit she needed a keeper, which didn't negate that fact that she did need Gabe's help.

Okay. Okay. She admitted it; she actually *wanted* Gabe's help. The question was, would she get it? She felt awful about all the things she said to him. She saw the hurt in his eyes when she said she hated him.

She was wrong.

Maybe if she apologized, he would forgive her for the unforgivable words and things could go back to the way they were.

But probably not, because Gabe was right. It was hopeless. They were hopeless. She was totally inept when it came to investigating, and they were getting nowhere. Yet none of those problems eliminated that fact that she still had a business to run and that, as hopeless as it was, without *The Recipe* it wasn't possible.

She stopped. Shit. She didn't have a business to run. Gabe had a business to run. Tears sprang to her eyes. How could she have forgotten? In her obsession with finding *The Recipe*, she'd almost forgotten that the business wasn't hers.

This sucked.

Yet Gabe hadn't said a word about taking over. Had he forgotten, just like her, or was he just playing it cool? Maybe he would swoop in when she least expected it and take over. After what she said to him, she wouldn't blame him. Boy, that would suck.

Still, she owed it to her—okay, Gabe's—employees, to at least attempt to manage the place. Although she had filled the workers in on the details earlier this week, she hadn't told them anything since then, so they were probably worried about their jobs.

She sighed and finished her walk to the subway that would take her out to Brooklyn and the factory where she would try to allay everyone's fears. After that, would come the groveling.

It was getting late in the day, a day that had been crazy, what with visiting Vanessa, then the thing with the Tiffany's, both the store and the woman, so she needed to get to Contessa before they quit for the day. She rode the Number Four train to Union Square and changed to the L train out to Bushwick. Walking the few blocks to the factory, she slipped inside through one of the loading doors, hoping she could reach Fred's office on the third floor before anyone noticed her so she would have time to gather her thoughts.

Unfortunately, Manuel saw her as she headed for the freight elevator. He looked worried.

"Miss Candace, things they not so good."

"What's wrong?" As if she didn't know.

"Like I said before, two, three more days, no more chocolate. Lots of beans. Lots of cocoa nibs but after that…"

After that, they needed *The Recipe*. "But we can at least get as far as making the presscake, right? But then…"

"Si." He worried his baseball cap around in his hands. His dark brown eyes gazed at her with trust and hope.

Everyone counted on her. Her chest tightened. Without *The Recipe*, the press cake would be useless because the next step was where they added all the ingredients that made their chocolate uniquely theirs, and for that step, they needed *The Recipe*. She wondered how much longer they could continue if she didn't find it. "How many tanks of chocolate liquor do we have that are ready to send down the line?"

"Five."

Candace sighed because she knew when all the chocolate in the tanks was molded into bite-sized candies and wrapped, they were out of business. It didn't matter how many bags of cocoa beans they processed, without *The Recipe*, there was no chocolate. Not that it mattered anyway since, as the non-owner, she wouldn't have access to the company accounts any longer. That meant no money, no additional supplies, no way to pay the workers, all of which also meant no production.

She clenched her fists, trying to think. Focus. Remember the objective here. Find a way to convince Gabe to let her run Contessa. Find *The Recipe*. Apologize. Not necessarily in that order.

First thing first. "Do me a favor, shut the line down and gather everyone at the south end, okay?"

"But Miss Candace…"

"Just do it. Please."

He bit his lip, shadows clouding his eyes then turned and walked back into the production area, stopping to talk to people as he went. Soon the machinery went quiet, and a crowd gathered at the other end of the vast space.

Candace slowly made her way to join them. As a group, they all stared at her, their faces furrowed, their eyes filled with the same shadows as Manuel's, arms crossed over their bodies in a defensive position. Taking a deep breath, she marshalled her thoughts, searching for the right things to say. "Folks… It's not good news—"

"But we're going to get through this. I've inherited Contessa and I'm going to make sure things stay on track," a deep voice said from behind her. Candace spun around.

"You! What are you doing here!" she yelled. Oops. Not a good start.

Eyes wide, Gabe held his hands up, palms out, as if to ward her off. He looked alarmed. It was as if he expected her to attack him, like she was some kind of out-of-control lunatic.

She lunged at him.

"Stop," he yelped. He grabbed her arms, holding her at bay while she flailed, swinging wildly in an effort to inflict some damage. The fact she couldn't reach him pissed her off. She swung harder.

"Oh, my God, Candace, stop! You're going to hurt yourself."

"No. Only you." She kicked him in the kneecap.

"Shit!" He let her go and hopped around in a circle, swearing.

Candace crossed her arms over her chest, watching his gyrations, satisfaction a bright light inside, then reality hit her. Oh my God, she'd meant to apologize. Attacking him got her nowhere. She was a horrible person. What kind of rational person went around hitting, kicking people? Her only excuse was she was at the end of her rope, but that wasn't a good enough excuse for going off the rails like this. She really needed to calm down.

He finally stopped hopping. Straightening, he glared at her. "What the fu... heck was that for?"

"Why are you here?" Tears burned her eyes. It was all too much.

He didn't answer her. They both know why he was here but neither wanted to say it.

He took a step backwards, out of her reach, limping as he did.

"Why are you here?" she repeated. If he said he would take over now she would just die.

Sighing, he closed his eyes before saying, "I went to see the lawyers today."

"You son of a..." Betrayed! She'd been betrayed. And to think she had slept with him, comforted him, danced with him, laughed and cried with him. Was about to apologize to him. Once again, he proved he couldn't be trusted. She wanted to hate him, but she was just too exhausted.

"Congratulations," she said, bitterness a hard ball of acid in her stomach. "Enjoy your inheritance." She needed to leave before she killed him. Pulling out her cell phone, she requested an Uber then strode back toward the exit door, threading her way between the machinery. Behind her, she heard, "Candace. Wait," then came the sound of rapid—but limping—footsteps as he ran after her.

He caught up with her by the door. "Candace, wait, we need to talk."

"No we don't."

"Yes we do."

"No, we don't."

"Yes, we—"

She stomped her foot and glared, both totally useless in the grand scheme of things. All of her fight had petered away.

"God damn it, Candace, would you just listen to me?"

She crossed her arms over her chest again and waited, holding back the tears, while he rubbed his aching shin. He gave her a look of resentment. Like he was the victim here.

"Geez, Candace, I don't want the damned company."

"Well, you got it." She clenched her jaw. What an ass. How could he not want the company? Unquestionably, he wanted the company. He was just lying to her, trying to pull the wool over her eyes. It was so typical of him, tell her what she wanted to hear then betray her. Never again.

"Really. I don't want it. I already have my own company, that I built from scratch, and that I love."

Oh, for crying out loud. "You don't have a choice."

"Of course I do."

"No you don't," she said and jumped into the Uber car just pulling up. "Go," she told the driver.

The driver threw her a wild-eyed look over his shoulder because Gabe was climbing into the front seat even as the car pulled away from the curb. "Stop the car," he ordered, and damn him, the driver did.

"Gabe. Get out."

"No, I'm not going to do that. We need to talk."

"No, we don't."

"Yes, we do."

Candace gritted her teeth. Crap, this could go on forever. She turned her head to stare out the window.

"Listen to me," he said. "I want to talk about the business."

"Unless you can tell me that Contessa is mine, there is nothing to talk about."

Crickets.

"That's what I thought. Get out."

"Candace..."

She glared at him.

He winced. "Listen to me. We can work this out."

Right. Sure they could work it out... all in his favor. He'd already made that perfectly clear ten minutes ago inside the factory. She bared her teeth at him.

"Fine." He opened the door and got out of the car to stand on the curb but still held the door open so the driver couldn't leave. "Candace, you need to stop. What you're doing could be dangerous. Promise me you'll quit digging into things, at least until we can talk."

She took a deep breath. "I can't," she said.

With a sigh, he shut the car door, allowing the driver to leave.

She had nothing to do but think during the half hour ride into the city. Somewhere in the back of her mind she'd always known that her investigations could lead to trouble. A frisson of fear went through her because there was every possibility Gabe was right. Whoever had killed Fred probably wouldn't hesitate to kill her too if she got close enough to be a threat, but she'd never let fear stop her from achieving what she needed to achieve, and her need had never been greater than right now. Maybe Contessa was lost to her forever—maybe not—but she wouldn't see it destroyed, and all those jobs lost, all because she couldn't find *The Recipe*.

The driver pulled up in front of her building and she got out, rode the elevator up to the penthouse level and entered her mother's newly inherited apartment.

"Mom," she yelled as soon as she shut the door behind her. "I need to talk with you. We need to make plans.

Her mother meandered out from the kitchen, chewing on a chicken leg. "What? What's going on?"

Candace filled her in with all the latest details, finishing up with, "So it's just you and me. I might need your help going forward."

Her mother lit up like a sparkler. Uh oh. Candace had a plan in mind which probably needed a lookout. Too bad the only lookout available was Wendy. She wandered to the window, wondering if she had any other options. Across the street, a big, black SUV drove up and pulled into an empty spot next to the curb. Wow. How often did that happen in Manhattan, a parking spot right when you needed it.

Her mind returned to her current problem, that of how she could continue her searches without involving Gabe, and without using her mom. Yeah, she'd gone along with her mother's argument about the fat and flabby thing, but the truth was she couldn't see Wendy scrambling underneath a bed to escape a rabid cat, nor could she see her mom running for her life if someone was chasing her so, if at all possible, she wanted to keep her mother on the sidelines.

Because her next move could prove to be dangerous.

She frowned. Huh. What was going on with that big SUV? No one was getting out. No one approached it either, which would have been the case if he was picking up a rider. She looked closer. That SUV looked familiar. Actually, that SUV looked just like the one Gabe owned, right down to the Yankees decal in the rear window.

"Mom?"

Wendy joined her at the window, munching on a potato chip from a bag she held in the other hand. Yeah, so that fat and flabby thing? No wonder.

She pointed down at the street. "Does that SUV look familiar?"

Her mom peered at it. "No, should it?"

"I think it's Gabe's. I think he's spying on me." She gritted her teeth. "I think he thinks he's going to stop me from leaving here to do what I need to do."

"That rat," her mother said. "Maybe if we wait long enough, he'll get tired of waiting and leave."

They looked at each other, then they both looked at the SUV. Then they went back to the kitchen where Wendy fixed them something to eat.

* * * *

"Is he still out there?" Wendy asked.

Candace moved the curtain aside and peeked out at the car sitting under the streetlight, careful to stay hidden. "Yep, still there, and I need to leave soon, or it will be too late."

"You checked, right? She's not home?"

"I checked. Like four times."

"Darn it, is he ever going to move?" Wendy paced around the perimeter of the living room.

Mulling this over, Candace chewed on her fingernail, the one with the ragged edges needing filing. Why was he doing this? It made things so difficult. Didn't he have anything better to do with his time than to dog her. He'd been sitting on the street without a break since before dinner time.

He must be getting hungry and thirsty.

Lightbulb! "Mom. Let's do an Axel Foley."

"What's an Axel Foley?"

Candace grinned and picked up her cell phone. "You'll see."

16 Come on, Baby, Light My Fire

God, he was starving to death, and he needed to pee in the worst way. That was what drinking five cups of coffee would do to you, but without the coffee he would fall asleep and if he fell asleep, he knew damned well Candace would sneak out of her building and go haring off on one of her investigative jaunts without him to protect her.

Just today, he arrived at the conclusion they were going to have to find *The Recipe*, and hopefully, Fred's murderer, on their own. The problem was, like an idiot, he got mad after she kicked him in the shin then wouldn't talk to him, so he hadn't told her so, just like he hadn't told her about his plans for Contessa.

He was such an idiot.

So the fact he sat in his SUV outside her building starving to death, with his bladder about to burst, was totally his fault. He supposed he could call her and tell her about his plan but some niggling thing in the back of his mind said she wouldn't believe him. There was still resentment, and a certain level of distrust between the two of them. Okay, a lot of distrust. Which he deserved.

He needed to tell her about the steps he had taken for the company but unfortunately, it seemed lately all they did was either fight or make love. Neither time seemed like the right moment.

He drummed his fingers on the steering wheel. Nine o'clock and Park Avenue was pretty quiet, quiet enough the cop cruising by several times noticed him and gave him the fisheye. If something didn't happen soon, he would get arrested, then he would never find out what Candace was up to, or ever get to pee, at least not in a toilet that wasn't surrounded by low-lifes and creepy peepers.

Unable to turn on the overhead light in the SUV, Gabe did nothing but think and play video games on his cell phone, but that distracted him from his primary mission of watching Candace's building, so he gave up. To keep himself occupied, he tried to focus on the investigation, running over the obvious suspects in his mind but his relationship with Candace kept interfering. Okay, it was more the memory of the sex interfering. Candace turned him on like no one ever. Just thinking about what happened—or almost happened—on that credenza in her living room, made him hot. Thinking about what did happen in her bedroom made him even hotter. Shit. He turned the car on and cranked up the air-conditioning.

Okay. Think about the investigation.

They still didn't know why Murray deposited tens of thousands of dollars into his bank account. If Gabe could get Candace to tell him what bank Murray used, maybe he could find out who issued those checks, although Candace didn't seem to be much on sharing which meant he might have to force it out of her.

Torture her even.

Like strip her naked, tie her to the bedstead and do nasty things to her.

That sounded like fun.

He turned the air-conditioning up higher.

What about Tiffany and Julian? If he had to guess if anyone had a criminal personality, it would be Tiffany and her boyfriend. Obviously, Tiffany, with Julian's willing assistance, was after something, but Gabe hadn't figured out what yet. Possibly *The Recipe* but it could be lots of other things. Julian would do anything for Tiffany, maybe even commit murder for her since she had his balls in the palm of her hand.

Not that having one's balls in the palm of a woman's hand was a bad thing, at least not if they were in the correct woman's hand. It had definitely been the correct hand the other night.

Crap! Stop. He shifted in his seat, his lascivious thoughts causing a slight problem. The last thing he needed was for Candace to skulk out and catch him with his pants down. Metaphorically speaking, of course.

Still, Tiffany and Julian were possibilities needing further investigation as Candace's efforts in that direction had yielded no results.

Then there was Vanessa, although he had his doubts about her. She didn't seem the type to dirty her hands with criminal activities, but Candace was correct when she said she wouldn't put it past the twins. They didn't seem to have any compunction about walking into Wendy's apartment and helping themselves to anything they wanted. No one had bothered to investigate them yet, probably because, between the two of them, they only possessed one full brain, and that brain belonged to Lucy, so everyone underestimated them.

Bang, bang, bang. "Hey mister, mumble mumble mumble."

Gabe jumped a foot. He jerked his head around to see a man rapping on the window, holding up a brown paper bag. The tantalizing odor of Chinese food wafted through the narrow crack at the top of the window. He rolled the window down.

"What?"

"I got your order."

"I didn't order food."

The man pulled out a slip and paper and looked at it. "Your name Gabe Jones?"

"Yes." He frowned. What the heck? His nose twitched. Oh, man. Fried rice. His saliva glands kicked in. He licked his lips, afraid he was drooling.

"Then this is your order." He thrust the slip of paper through the narrow opening at the top of the window.

"I didn't order—" But he would have if he'd thought of it. Next time.

Across the street, a yellow cab pulled up in front of Candace's building. The front doors opened, and Candace and Wendy burst out of the building and jumped into the cab. It hooked a quick right at the next corner and disappeared.

God damn it all to hell.

He yanked his seatbelt around his waist and snapped it shut. He put his foot to the pedal and inched forward to pull out of the parking spot.

The delivery man banged on the back window. "Mister, your food." He waved the bag.

Oh, crap. Pork fried rice. And Cantonese Chicken. That was what it said right on the receipt. He backed up, rolled his window down and grabbed the bag then he hit the gas, making a U-turn at the next corner, and headed in the same direction he saw the cab go.

But by the time he made a right onto the same street as Candace's cab, they were long gone. With a sigh, he pulled over to the side of the street and turned the engine off, then he pulled out the bag of Chinese food and dug in.

* * * *

"Are you sure she's not there?"

"Mom, I said I was sure. I called again just fifteen minutes ago, and no one answered but still, we need to hurry. I want to get this done." She watched the sea of taxis whiz by, wishing they were at their destination, yet dreading their arrival.

"Maybe it's that she's just not answering the phone," her mother fretted. Her fingers nervously twisted and turned a button on the front of her blouse. "Maybe she's in bed and is one of those people who sleeps with ear plugs and can't hear the phone."

"I checked with Floyd—you know he's still tight with her—and he said she left to visit a friend in Westchester and wouldn't be back until tomorrow morning."

Her mother frowned, not looking convinced.

"Mom, relax. It'll be fine." The cab stopped at a red light. Candace peered out of the dirty cab window, looking up at the street sign. Only a few more blocks. *She couldn't wait.*

"Are you sure this is the only way? Maybe we should wait until she goes back to Florida, or maybe we could just ask her."

For someone who rarely had any deep thoughts, her mother certainly could be obsessive. She was like a pit bull when she got hold of something—latch on, lock jaws.

The light turned green. The cab jerked forward, and Candace's stomach threatened to rebel as they approached Susan's address. What she wouldn't do for an antacid. But desperate times called for desperate measures. "We can't afford to wait. We need to solve this now and there's no telling when Susan will go back to Florida, and she might take it with her."

Her mother huddled next to her. With nothing else to do, she gave the button another twist and it came off in her hand. Her eyes widened. "Oops."

Candace knew exactly how she felt. If it wasn't for the fact her mother would never let her forget it, Candace would call it off. "Listen, if you're nervous, I can have the cab take you home and I'll do it by myself."

The nervous look disappeared to be replaced with narrowed eyes and an outthrust jaw. Now she not only acted like a pit bull, she resembled one too. "Are you still harping on that?"

"What?"

"That I'm too old. Too out of shape to help with the investigation."

Oh, brother. That again. "Mom, I never said that but if you want to help you need to stop complaining."

"Fine, but why do we have to do Susan? Why can't we investigate Vanessa or go back to Tiffany's and replant the bug?"

On the list, Mom, on the list. Fortunately, she was spared having to explain—for the tenth time—as they pulled up across the street from Susan's building. Candace paid the fare and they got out.

"Now what?" Wendy asked, her eyes trained on the doorman standing guard at the entrance across the street.

"Go talk to the doorman."

Wendy swiveled her head to stare at Candace.

Her stomach calmed down a little, at least enough to remember her strategy. "Come on, you said you'd do what I told you to do if I let you help. Just get him to look in the direction of that streetlight." She pointed at the light on the corner. "Keep him talking for at least a few minutes. Remember the plan."

"Fine. Whatever. I know my job." She marched across the street, shaking her head, mouth compressed into a thin line, but the minute she reached the older, uniformed doorman, the other Wendy—the one who was charming and engaging—took over. Candace could hear her laugh. With a toss of her blond curls, and a coy moue, she wiggled a finger inside the placket of her blouse where she twisted the remaining button until it popped out of the hole, exposing a rather large slice of breast, which was still pretty good even at her age. The doorman looked mesmerized.

Candace raced across the street to a spot about twenty feet to the side of the building's doorway. She pulled a bundle of newspapers out of her tote bag and set them down. Striking a match, she lit them. The fire flickered then burst into bright flames. She breathed a quick puff to make sure the flame didn't go out then raced back to her spot across from the building entrance.

"Oh!" Wendy squealed. "Oh dear." She pointed at the fire. Her hands fluttered helplessly.

"Shit," the doorman yelled and raced down the sidewalk. He beat at the flames with his cap. Candace ran across the street, grabbed her mother's hand, and pushed through the doors of Susan's apartment building. She hit the elevator button, the door opened, and they jumped in. Her mother started to giggle. Candace felt a nervous tee-hee bubble out. Pretty soon they were both laughing. The elevator door opened, and they spilled out into the carpeted hallway.

"Shh," Candace whispered, holding a finger to her lips.

Her mother giggled some more.

"Shhh. Shhh," Candace repeated, but she giggled too. She had no idea why. She wasn't a giggler but the whole situation was so absurd. Her thoughts went back to her Axel Foley tactic, and she laughed harder.

"What?"

"Axel Foley."

Her mother clapped her hands over her mouth. "You don't suppose the delivery guy remembered to stuff the banana in the exhaust pipe, do you?"

"I doubt it, but it doesn't matter. We lost him."

Still giggling, they made their way down the hall. Reaching into her pocket, Candace pulled out the keys Floyd had given her last time and opened the door. They tip-toed inside and shut the door behind them.

"Where do we look?" Wendy asked, looking around then, "Oh. Wow. I'd forgotten how gorgeous this place is." She reached for a light switch.

"Don't!" Grabbing her mother's hand, she pulled her into the bedroom. She gave a fleeting thought to locating the damned cat, but the sight of the bedside table kicked the thought out of her mind. She made a beeline for it and drew open the drawer. The gun, silver and shiny and lethal looking, lay inside, still in the same position as last time she saw it. From her pocket, Candace pulled out a handkerchief and a small paper bag to deposit the gun in. She wasn't a cop, but she didn't consider herself a novice either since she watched plenty of shows on Investigative TV and knew it was important to save the evidence in a paper bag, not plastic.

Her mother edged closer and peered over her shoulder. "Goodness. That could be the murder weapon, couldn't it?"

Gingerly, Candace picked it up, using the handkerchief, and opened the paper bag, prepared to drop it inside. "Maybe. Hopefully. We'll know soon."

"What the hell do you think you're doing?"

Candace shrieked. Wendy was right behind her in the shriek department.

"Susan!" Candace said when she could catch her breath. "What are you doing here?"

Susan lifted a brow. "I think the question is: 'What are you doing here?'"

"Ummmm..." Awkward. "You're not supposed to be here."

Susan's eyes widened in disbelief. "No, *you're* not supposed to be here. So, come on, Candace, why are you here?"

Without meaning to, Candace glanced down at the gun in her hand. "I... uh, the gun..."

"Lunatic," Susan muttered under her breath then she said out loud, "Okay, fine, don't move. I'm calling the cops."

Susan reached inside her handbag, obviously rooting around for her phone.

Without thinking, Candace raised the gun and pointed it at Susan. "Stop!"

Candace had to give the woman credit; she showed a lot of grace under fire. It must be her magic because Susan just slowly shook her head as if she was impervious to bullets.

Candace wished she had a little of that magic because the hand holding the gun shook right along with her arms and her legs and her stomach. Her mother cowered behind her, little bird-like peeps coming out of her mouth every few seconds.

They stared at each other for a minute than Susan reached into her purse again and pulled out her phone.

"STOP!" Candace's hand shook, bobbing up and down and sideways. She hoped she didn't have to shoot the thing as she was just as likely to take out the bedside lamp or her big toe as Susan. She put her other hand on the gun, trying to steady it. "Give me your phone," she finally squeaked once she could get her vocal cords working again.

Susan rested a hand on her hip and leveled a flat stare at Candace. "Why don't you come and get it?"

Okay, this wasn't working. When Susan continued to stand there, one hand on her hip, the other holding the phone, a smirk gracing her face, Candace knew she needed to do something. Ah, shit, if Susan wouldn't turn it over, she would need to take it from her. She took a step forward.

"Rrrrrooooooowwwwww!"

"Aaaaack," Candace screamed as the cat leaped on her leg and used its claws to climb up her thigh. She dropped the gun and grabbed the cat's tail, yanking on it to unhook the tiny little blood-sucking barbs. In the background, her mother echoed her screams as she climbed up onto the bed and jumped up and down in a panic.

"Aaaack. Off, off, off." Apparently, Susan's magic only worked for her because the cat quickly scrambled the rest of the way up Candace's body and sat on her head, digging its claws into her cheeks and biting her ear.

"Rrrooowwww!"

"Get it off, get it off!" She spun around in circles, swatting at the cat perched on her head but the harder she swatted, the deeper the claws dug into her cheeks.

Susan calmly bent down and picked up the gun then she scooped the cat off Candace's head and set it down on the floor, making sure to keep the gun pointed at Candace and her mother. Unlike Candace, she held the gun like a pro. Her dark eyes turned steely.

"Poor baby," Susan murmured, and Candace began to believe the woman wasn't going to aerate her torso with bullet holes but then Susan continued with, "Did the big bad burglar scare you? Shall I hurt her for you?"

Wendy stopped jumping and screaming. "How dare you?" she said, arms akimbo as she glared at Susan.

Susan lifted a dark brow and turned on her phone. "Oh, you'd be surprised at what I dare."

"No, I wouldn't," Wendy muttered, her lips pursed.

The insult bounced off Susan like bullets off the Man of Steel. Although, maybe that wasn't such a good comparison, Candace thought, given the big silver thing in Susan's hand.

"You could just let us go, you know. We'll go away and never bother you again," Candace suggested—okay, begged—hoping she sounded meek and contrite. It wasn't as if she was meek and contrite, but she figured sounding aggressive and uncontrite would just get her shot full of holes.

Susan laughed. One manicured hand stroked a stray lock of hair behind her ear.

Damn, probably she didn't sound meek and contrite enough or Susan just didn't give a shit. Either way, the hard-hearted bitch tapped something on the screen of her phone and held it out so Candace could hear.

"Mom?" a voice said. "What's going on?"

Oh, rats. How did she get herself into these messes?

"Gabe, darling? Where are you," Susan asked.

"Uh. Why?"

"Candace and her loony mother are here."

"Where here?" Gabe asked, his voice filled with trepidation.

Susan smiled. The smile was pure evil. "My bedroom. How soon can you get here?"

There was a long pause. Candace could feel Gabe's fury even over the phone.

"Ten minutes," he finally said, and hung up.

Ten minutes? Candace wasn't sure whether she wanted him to hurry up and save her from his murderous mother or never show up at all and save Candace the embarrassment of explaining.

He got there in fifteen minutes. Late as usual. But when he walked in, Candace decided she would have been happy if he never arrived. His face was red, and his eyes shot flames.

"Jesus Christ," he said, giving her a look of disgust. He glanced at Wendy, still standing in the middle of the bed. "And you. I thought you at least had more sense."

Wendy climbed down off the bed. "I told her not to do it. I told her we would get caught. She just never listens to me. You'd think she would listen to her mother just once, wouldn't you?"

What! Candace whirled around to glare at her mother. "Mom! You traitor. You begged to come with me."

"Nuh uh," Wendy said. She continued to shake her head, her eyes wide so she resembled one of those Disney cartoon heroines with the unrealistically humongous eyes and no noses.

"Oh, stop!" Susan said. "All of you."

They stopped.

Gabe cleared his throat. "Okay, Mom." He scratched his neck, looking supremely uncomfortable as he groped for words. "I know this looks bad, and I know you're upset but I'm sure Candace is sorry about the whole thing." He crept around his mother, giving her a wide berth, the coward, and went to stand next to Candace and Wendy. Candace felt his hand land on her shoulder. "It's late so why don't we just leave, okay?" he said. "Tomorrow we'll all just laugh about this, right?"

"Oh, I don't think so," Susan said. She lifted the gun and arm outstretched, pointed it at them, eyes narrowed. As usual, not a hair was out of place.

Eeek! They were going to die.

Gabe thrust out a hand, his face white as a ghost. "Mom!" he said. "Don't."

There was a click as she cocked the gun.

Gabe threw himself in front of Candace. Candace threw her hands up to cover her face. As if it would stop a bullet.

"Bang," Susan said, her voice flat.

After a minute, Candace dropped her hands, cautiously opened her eyes, and peered around Gabe's torso.

A yellow flame flickered at the end of the muzzle. Looking bored, Susan picked up a cigarette sitting on her nightstand and held it up to the flame. She took a puff. "Okay. Let's talk."

Sure. Just as soon as her heart restarted.

17 Déjà Vu...

"We need to talk," Gabe said, pacing around the living room. His mind went around and round, trying to put his thoughts in order of what he wanted to say when. He needed to tell her about his plans for Contessa, although his plans weren't done yet. Still, he needed to tell her something so she'd stop this insanity. Unfortunately, there were a lot of legal issues and tax issues and blah blah blah, that needed to be dealt with, so maybe he should wait. Maybe not. Maybe he'd just call the attorneys and tell them to hurry it up.

Right now it was more important to stop her crazy investigative jaunts. They were dangerous.

He asked Wendy to leave them alone and she was more than willing to scuttle out of the room and retreat to her own space, leaving Candace to take the hit. Wendy might be a ditz, but she was smart enough to know when to flee.

Candace winced. "Couldn't we have life-affirming sex instead?"

A flame flared in his groin. Good God! He was tempted, really tempted but he shouldn't. He was furious with her and having sex would send a mixed message. On the other hand, he was so tempted.

"What's life-affirming sex?" he asked, stalling.

She gave him one of her much-practiced puppy dog looks. "You know, the kind you have when you just had a life-or-death experience and you survived."

His heart triple-timed every time he remembered the click of the gun...okay, so it was a lighter, but that small detail didn't lessen the terror he'd felt. So maybe life-affirming sex wouldn't be such a bad thing.

Still, there was that mixed message thing. "We weren't going to die."

"We didn't know that," she said, and then she smiled that smile of hers and his heart squeezed in his chest again. He had begun to wonder, given all the heart-squeezing, if maybe he should make an appointment with a cardiologist.

He shook his head. Back and forth, back and forth, struggling to get his heart beating normally again and to lower his blood pressure and to shake the idea she could have been killed. Mixed message. Mixed message. But it didn't help, and she wasn't helping either. She pouted and heaved a sigh. That luscious lower lip gleamed. Her blond hair shone in the lamplight, and her eyes held that come-hither look...

Oh, the hell with it. He reached her in one stride, grabbed her and slung her over his shoulder.

She squealed, then giggled. "This doesn't change anything," he said and strode down the hall to her bedroom. "We still need to talk."

"Make sure you use a condom, dear," Wendy called as they passed her closed door.

"Yes, Mother," Candace called back, still giggling.

Gabe growled. He reached Candace's bedroom, pushed the door open and tossed Candace on the bed.

"Take that off," he ordered, pointing at her blouse while he toed off his shoes and kicked them aside.

Propping herself on her elbows, she sent him a coy look. The fluffy pink featherbed billowed around her, heightening her femininity so he thought he'd die.

"And if I don't?" she whispered in a husky voice.

He jerked his shirt off. "Then I'll tear it off."

"Oooh." She thrust her chest out then she thrust out that pugnacious jaw. Honestly, he was much more interested in the chest. "Go ahead. I dare you," she taunted.

No one dared Gabe and lived. Okay, that was bullshit. No way would he kill her, not now when he had her right where he wanted her. Truthfully, his entire being had focused on that life-affirming thing in the form of sex. Ripping open the front placket of his pants, he released the enormous hard-on he had for Candace and leaped on her. She gasped then laughed. Her shirt went one direction and her jeans were jerked off over her feet and tossed aside. The sight of her nearly naked body, in combination with the adrenaline still surging through his body, made his heart thunder in his chest and his nether regions burn like a Boy Scout campfire. With trembling fingers, he retrieved the condom he put in the back pocket of his pants—be prepared, another boy scout move—and covered himself.

He couldn't even wait to take off her undies—utilitarian white cotton—but who the hell cared. He just shoved the crotch aside and pushed his way inside.

She moaned. *God, she's beautiful,* he mused, but it was probably his last coherent thought.

Her arms went around his neck. She was tight and hot and slick and divinely female. His whole body went up in flames, the feel of her inner muscles around his cock making hot blood pound in his head and his heart. Sweat dripped down his temples, moistened his chest and stomach, making a sucking sound as he pounded into Candace's body.

She was as eager as him, her body writhing under his, her hands everywhere, his name constantly on her lips.

He was hot, he was cold, he shivered from the intensity as her hands stroked his ass and his back, tugging at his hair and biting his lip as he desperately covered her mouth, wanting, somehow, to inhale her essence into himself.

There was this thing surging inside he couldn't identify. It squeezed his heart in a painful fist and made his head ache as he tried to name it but in the end it had no name and he pushed it away from his heart, down his body and reduced it to physical desire.

"Gabe," she groaned. His name, moaned low and guttural, went straight to his groin and the orgasm he desperately held at bay, erupted, hard, and painful in the best possible way.

She wailed, and he knew she'd come too.

For a minute, he couldn't move. After what he just experienced, who the hell had the strength, or would even want to move? She damned near killed him. If he had to go, this was definitely the way.

He lay on top of her, as boneless as a slab of bacon. She didn't seem to mind. Her mouth continued to move over his chest, and her tongue took an occasional taste, creating little aftershocks of desire.

Finally, he rolled off her and flopped to the side. Somewhere in the back of his lust-fried brain he thought, *we need to talk*, but his lips didn't want to do anything except plant kisses on her neck and her shoulder and her stomach.

He turned to face her. She smiled and his heart did a triple-time again. Damn, he was in so much trouble.

"Hey," she said, her voice slurred with after-sex throatiness.

Keep your mind on business, he told himself. "We need to talk," he forced out.

"Can't we have some more life-affirming sex instead?" she asked hopefully.

"I'm already as affirmed as I need to be," he informed her.

"Nobody's ever that affirmed."

He suppressed a sigh. Sadly, she was probably right. But if she thought she would get out of *the talk,* she would soon learn differently. "I am. Now sit up."

Heaving a sigh of martyrdom, she pulled herself up and leaned against the headboard. The sheet, that she made no effort to catch, slipped down to her waist, leaving her exposed.

Rats. His resolve waivered. Maybe it wouldn't hurt to have life-affirming sex again.

She smiled that smile and he knew she knew his thoughts, and he knew he couldn't let her think she could lead him around by his dick, either literally or metaphorically.

"Cover yourself." Crap, he sounded like an old Victorian schoolteacher, but it was all self-preservation. Those perky little boobs with their pink tips and the tiny mole on one reminded him of the first time he saw her.

Apparently, she agreed about the Victorian part, although probably not the rest, because she crossed her arms over her chest, hiding all her feminine glory, and made a face. He hoped like hell she couldn't read his mind.

"What a prude."

"Yeah, yeah. Whatever."

Giving him a look of disdain, she said, "Fine. Say your piece."

He took a deep breath. A few opening forays flitted through his mind only to be discarded. This was one of those tricky conversations with Candace that could go south in a hurry, leading to bodily injury, most likely his. They already had the argument where she hated him and thought he was selfish, and he didn't want to go back there. Regardless, however he said it, and whichever way the conversation went, he should probably take precautions. He grabbed one of the fluffy throw pillows sitting at the foot of the bed and covered his sensitive parts.

She smirked.

"Okay," he said. "This thing you're doing? It has to stop."

Anger flitted across her face to be replaced by a cunning look. "What thing is that?"

He sighed. It seemed like no matter how prepared he thought he was, somehow, she managed to turn it around on him. That was because he tended to think in straightforward ways whereas Candace's thinking was as crooked as Richard Nixon.

"Don't play games. I'm talking about how you—and apparently your mother—are investigating on your own. I thought you understood you weren't going to do that." He waited and watched as a variety of emotions crossed her face, anger, rebellion and finally despair.

Her lower lip trembled. "Did you see their faces?" she asked in a quiet voice.

"Whose?" he asked, although he knew.

"At the factory. Manuel and Rosa and Layla and everyone from the line. Kristin and Jack from accounting and Janie and Meghan in the front office. Almost five hundred people. I can't quit. I have to find *The Recipe*. You know that."

He knew. "Candace, I didn't say to give up. I just don't want you searching on your own. It's dangerous. Whoever stole *The Recipe* might be the one who killed Fred which makes him...or her...a dangerous person."

Hope sparked in her eyes. "What are you saying?"

He paused for a minute, convinced he was insane to propose what he was about to propose. It was like having a death wish or something. Unfortunately, he already admitted to himself he wouldn't mind meeting his demise this way even though it made him an idiot. No need to let Candace know, though.

With a sigh, he gave in. "I went to see Dolan yesterday to see if he made any progress."

She nodded eagerly. "And?"

"That son of a bitch wouldn't even tell me how my dad was killed. What's the big secret anyway?" Thinking about it made him mad all over again.

Her face fell, which angered him, but only for her sake.

If used constructively, anger could be a good thing. It made him more determined than ever to find out who killed his dad. Candace was focused on *The Recipe* but, truthfully, their goals were the same. "And since we're not going to get any help from the cops it's obvious we're going to have to find out who killed Fred and stole *The Recipe* on our own."

Her face lit up. She pumped a fist. "Yes!" Then she threw herself on him.

And they had more life-affirming sex.

* * * *

Candace stared at Gabe's profile. God, he was cute. Irritating as hell, but cute. That must be why her heart gave a little jump every time he walked into the room. That was why she just couldn't stay mad at him. Because irritating people always did that to her, right?

Speaking of irritating, what the hell was wrong with Gabe, sleeping when there were important things to discuss. Just like a man. She gave him a little poke. He gave a soft little snore.

Damn it.

She gave him another little poke. She got another snore for her efforts. God damn it. She poked a little harder.

He came awake with a sputter. "What! What the fuck!" He looked around wildly before spotting Candace with her finger still raised. "God damn, woman, what the hell's the matter with you?"

What was wrong with her? What a lot of nerve the man had. "It's five o'clock."

He blinked his eyes to clear the sleep out of them then looked at his watch. He groaned. "Christ, it's five o'clock. In the morning."

"Didn't I just say that?"

"Why are we awake at five o'clock?"

See. So irritating. It was a good thing one of them—namely her—in this relationship was patient. "We need to talk about our plan."

Now he looked peeved, although she couldn't imagine why. He was the one who'd said they needed to talk and then fell asleep.

"At five o'clock? In the morning?" he said plaintively. "We didn't get to sleep until three." He thought for a minute. "That's only two hours of sleep." He flopped back on his pillow, groaning. "Go away."

She poked him again. "Get up!"

"Alright, alright, I'm up." Grabbing a pillow and stuffing it behind his back, he propped himself against the headboard. He crossed his arms over his chest. "Okay, okay, if you insist on talking, we'll talk. We can talk about what we know so far." He reviewed all the information they uncovered ending with, "So we still need to verify where Murray got all that money, how Vanessa paid for that necklace, and what Tiffany and Julian are up to." He glanced at Candace. "I think we can agree my mom has been eliminated, right?"

As much as she would love to keep Susan on the list—magic or no magic, the woman was scary—she admitted Gabe was right. His mother had nothing to do with Fred's murder. As it turned out, she was in Europe when *The Recipe* disappeared.

"Fine. Now how are we going to do all this?"

Gabe dug the heels of his hands into his eyes. "God, I can't believe I'm going to say this but..."

"What?"

"I think we need to try to plant another bug on Tiffany."

Candace jumped out of bed and ran to the hall. "Mom!"

* * * *

"Just remember, don't put the bug under anything metal. You already did that, and it obviously doesn't work."

Candace threw her mother a glare. "Cut it out, Mom. It wasn't my fault since *you* never told me it would be a problem."

"I'm just saying," Wendy responded.

"Yeah, you're always just saying."

Gabe sighed. "Really? Are we two-years-old?"

Candace exchanged a look with her mother, then they both slapped him on the back of his head.

"Ow!"

It helped to have a common enemy.

The elevator opened. They got out, walked down the hall to Tiffany's room and knocked. They heard footsteps inside before the door swung open. There was a brief flash of surprise then another flash of something dark and unpleasant before Tiffany rearranged her face into its usual pleasantly vacuous façade.

Candace shivered because she knew, for that one brief moment, they had just seen the real Tiffany. It further convinced her Tiffany could be the one. It hardened her determination to prove it and make her pay.

"Hi, Tiff," she said, and breezed through the door. Wendy and Gabe followed.

"What are you doing here?" Tiffany asked with that wispy little girl voice Candace hated. Fake, all fake, like her boobs. And her eyelashes. And her fingernails. For that matter, Candace didn't think her nose was hers either.

"Remember, we told you we'd think about how we could help so we thought we'd stop by and let you know what we came up with."

For a moment greed and satisfaction flickered across her face to be replaced once again by her vapid look. One thing you could say about Tiffany, she was consistent.

"Oh, that's wonderful. After the way you left last time, I thought you'd decided not to help."

Candace emitted a light titter. Fake, like Tiffany's voice. "Gabe, why don't you show her what we came up with."

"Absolutely." Pulling out a sheaf of papers, he waved Tiffany over to the small desk in the corner. He spread the papers out and began to talk.

The minute her back turned, Candace jumped up and made a beeline for the lamp sitting on the bedside table. She reached under the shade and stuck on the bug then gave a quick glance around for another place to stick the second bug her mother had managed to get. Tiffany's purse was again sitting on the dresser. She tiptoed over. After quickly checking it out, she realized the shoulder strap was doubled so it could be shortened. She stuck the second bug between the two straps then returned to her chair and gave her mother a thumbs-up. Her mother beamed and returned the gesture.

"So what do you think, Tiffany?" Gabe asked. He threw a look over his shoulder as he did. Candace nodded.

Tiffany straightened. "Oh, I don't know. Fred was going to leave me a lot more than that."

No, he wasn't. "Well, why don't you think about it, Tiffany," Candace suggested. Yeah, you go ahead and think about it, she thought, because you're never getting a dime no matter what your answer is.

With one finger, Tiffany twirled a strand of her long golden hair, which upon further inspection turned out to be a hair extension. Was anything about Tiffany real?

"What do you think, Gabe?" She smiled up at Gabe, a lustful gleam in her eye, and leaned into him. One fake-fingernailed hand stroked his arm.

Okay, if nothing else, her avarice was real.

Pure panic crossed Gabe's face. "I think you can call me when you've made a decision." Slithering out from underneath her stroking hand, he thrust the papers at her. "Here, you can read them at your leisure." Two steps and he reached Candace. Grabbing her hand, he yanked her out of the chair and headed for the door. Wendy followed on their heels.

"Let us know, okay? Bye," he said, and slammed the door behind them.

They ran down the hall and jumped onto the elevator. Gabe shuddered. "Oh, my God. Those nails."

"I know," Candace said.

"You know," Wendy said as they left the elevator and walked out to the street to hail a cab. "If she agrees to the settlement, I think we should give her a check as bogus as her boobs."

They were still laughing when the cab dropped them off at Park Avenue.

18 ... All Over Again

They decided to meet in the living room to discuss their next move. For once Floyd wasn't hanging around watching television in his bathrobe. No, instead he scared the crap out of Candace when she went into the kitchen and found him at the stove, cooking in the altogether.

She jerked to a halt, quickly swiveling her eyes up to stare at the ceiling. "Geez, Floyd. What are you doing?"

He grunted. "Making breakfast."

"With our food?"

"Who else's am I going to use?"

As usual, his attitude pissed her off. Without thinking, her eyes dropped. Eeep! She rolled her eyes back up to the ceiling, hoping to avoid seeing any more of his naked body, but it was useless. She'd already seen too much. Despite that, or maybe because of that, she couldn't keep her eyes from drifting downward again.

Floyd didn't respond to her snarkiness, just dropped another strip of bacon—*their* bacon—into the pan with no regard to his dangly bits right in the line of splattering grease.

In her mind's eye, Candace held her fingers out in the shape of a cross, hoping to ward off the evil that was Floyd. Unfortunately, the sight of his naked body intruded. "When are you going to leave?" she asked, her eyes involuntarily returning to Floyd's naked ass.

"When I get my money." He dropped an egg in another pan and gave it a stir. His man boobs jiggled.

She quickly returned her eyes to the ceiling. "Really?" A girl could hope.

"No."

Useless. She turned and went back to the living room. "Mom, you have got to make that man leave."

"What man?"

"You know what man. Floyd."

Her mother looked confused. "Why would I make him leave?"

Darn. The real Wendy was back. "Because he's in *our* kitchen, cooking *our* food, using *our* stove, and eating at *our* table. On *our* kitchen chairs." Oh, ick.

Wendy blinked.

"Without his bathrobe, Mom." No reaction. "Naked!"

Wendy jumped up and ran down the hall toward the kitchen. Gabe glanced up from his cell phone to gaze at Candace. "Floyd is naked?"

Candace grunted.

Turning off his cell, he stuck it into his pocket. "How'd he look?"

"Geez, Gabe, I was trying *not* to look."

Dipping his head, he stared at her from under his eyebrows.

"Okay, fine. He looked old and wrinkly and like a guy who was very well-fed. On our food."

"Aha. You did peek," he crowed.

She wiggled her eyebrows at him. "Yeah, but I tried not to. Why would I want to look at Floyd when I've got you to feast my eyes on?"

Gabe smirked. "Any time, babe, any time."

Wendy marched back into the living room. "Darn, that was a bust."

"What are you talking about?"

"He put his bathrobe back on."

Oh, my God. Why would her mother want to see Floyd in the raw? Personally, Candace would give anything if she could erase the image searing into her brain, killing off all her good brain cells.

Putting aside the issue of Floyd for the time being, she turned to Gabe. "So what's our next move?"

"I think we need to go back and talk to Vanessa again because I think there's something going on with the twins, but this time, let's make sure we have some specific questions to ask because I don't think she'll give us another shot if we blow this one."

"What about Junior," Wendy interjected. "We haven't investigated him, and you know Murray wouldn't be able to do anything unless Junior helped."

"She's right," Candace admitted.

Gabe nodded. "Agreed. We completely forgot about him. If something's going on with Murray, Junior will be involved, and he'll be easier to crack than Murray but give me a second first." He pulled out his phone and made a call.

"Hey, Frank, it's Gabe Jones." He listened for a minute. "Yeah, I know but I'm actually more interested in Junior. Have you seen him this morning?" Pause. "So he's coming back when?" He listened some more, then hung up. "Junior went out for a while, but the doorman said he'd be back in an hour or so. If we time it right, we can wait for him outside his apartment building and catch him by surprise. That should give us an advantage."

He slipped his phone into his shirt pocket. "That leaves Vanessa for now. So let's figure out what we want to find out from her."

Grabbing paper and pen, they jotted down a number of questions they wanted answers to. They even went on the internet to look up what kind of questions the police might ask. Apparently, it was important to ask the suspect if they committed the crime. Who knew? Also, hypothetically, if the suspect committed the crime, how would they have done it? And who else did they suspect? And why someone would want to kill Fred? They hadn't asked any of those questions.

And Candace still wanted to know where that expensive necklace came from.

With nothing else to do, Candace grabbed her purse. "Okay, we're going to go now," she told her mother.

"How about me?" her mother responded.

Gabe shook his head. "No, you have to stay here."

Wendy crossed her arms over her chest, looking miffed. "That's not fair. What am I going to do?"

"You're going to monitor the bug," Gabe told her. "You should turn it on now since we don't want to miss anything. Oh, and take notes. You never know when something they've said will make sense later even if it doesn't right away."

"Right!" Wendy ran out of the room.

The minute Wendy disappeared, Candace grabbed Gabe's hand and dragged him out of apartment. "Are you on your motorcycle or do you have your car?

"Bike. It's around the corner."

Yikes! Again? But she bit her tongue and followed him to where the beast was parked and climbed on board. All for the greater good.

It took them a few minutes to ride crosstown, minutes they spent trying to discuss how they would get Vanessa to talk but the wind and the noise of the motorcycle engine was deafening, and they finally gave it up in favor of going with the flow.

Once again, they walked up five flights of stairs, this after ringing the buzzer then waiting five minutes while Vanessa hemmed and hawed over the intercom while she decided whether or not she wanted to let them in.

She met them at the door, her usual stick-up-her-ass attitude radiating off her, evident by the arms over her chest and the sour expression on her face. "Why are you here? Again."

Okay, this wouldn't be easy. "We just wanted to ask a few more questions." No response. "Please, Vanessa?" *Ouch. That hurt.*

Hearing the nicely phrased (but totally insincere request), Vanessa didn't look any more welcoming, but she stood aside and waved them in.

They sat on the same loveseat they sat on last time. Vanessa took the same couch as before and gave them the same look as their last visit. It was like reliving one of Candace's nightmares, the one where she was falling and woke up just before she hit bottom.

A long, excruciating silence ensued where no one said anything, then Candace finally ventured, "We had a few questions?"

She stared at them, mute.

All right, not working. "So, that necklace you wore last time..." Darn, she hadn't meant to start there.

Vanessa's eyes narrowed. "What about it?"

Shit. Now what? She could see Vanessa was already annoyed. Next step, they were out the door.

"Oh, nothing. It was just so pretty." Oh, boy, a totally thumb-twiddling answer. She cleared her throat. The questions she really wanted to ask were somehow stuck there. She cleared it again and gave Vanessa a wide-eyed look. She was trying for cocker spaniel cute but was pretty sure she came across more like strangled Boston Terrier, all bug-eyed and drooly.

Vanessa shook her head, looking irritated but resigned. "Can I get you something to drink?"

Really? You have to ask? After five flights of un-airconditioned stairs in ninety-five-degree weather and me sitting here choking to death?

She nodded. It was clear the woman wasn't being hospitable, she just wanted to escape. Candace could relate.

Rising, Vanessa retreated into the kitchen.

As soon as she disappeared, Candace hissed, "You need to ask her if she did it."

He grunted, his eyes roaming around the apartment, looking everywhere but at Candace. That did not sound like the kind of response a man after blood would make.

"What's the matter?"

Gabe didn't answer; instead he finally turned to stare at her, his eyes reflecting resignation. "Okay, I'll make sure to ask her. I just don't think it's going to do any good."

"I thought we were committed to doing this. Did you change your mind?"

"No, but I don't think we're going to get anything out of Vanessa. She's already PO'ed at us and all you've asked about is her necklace," he said in the flat tones of defeat. "We're just lousy at this." One corner of his mouth quirked wryly.

Candace suddenly realized the last week was nothing but setback after setback, with nothing accomplished except the oddness of his father's funeral, broken by a few stolen moments of making love.

She wanted to reach out and hold him and heal him and never let him go but what she did instead was say, "No, that's okay, I'll do it."

Vanessa walked back into the room, carrying two glasses of water. Sitting, Vanessa sat back on her couch, arms crossed over her chest, and returned to giving them the stink-eye.

Candace took a big gulp of water. "Thanks. We're sorry to bother you but we just had a few more questions since the other day," she said for the third time. If this were baseball, they would be out.

"Fine, ask your questions."

Candace waited a second, glancing at Gabe to find him staring back, those chocolate eyes filled with encouragement and something else she was afraid to define. There was a sharp pang of lust deep in the pit of her stomach, with Gabe Jones she always felt that sharp pang, but this was more. That flop of silky dark hair slid down to curl over his warm brown eyes.

A corner of his mouth then turned up, amused, and she suddenly couldn't breathe. There was a sweet melting inside and turning her world upside down as she suddenly realized she wanted him forever. She found herself wishing the investigation would never end because once *The Recipe* was found he would go back to making his taffy, and Candace would hopefully become the chocolatier of her dreams, and she had no idea if that was what she wanted anymore.

Oh, damn. When had she caved to Gabe's all-around wonderfulness? Too late now.

Every logical thought she ever had suddenly disappeared from her mind and she found herself asking the stupidest question ever.

"How are the twins?" Oh my God, she'd just asked about the twins? Proof positive her brain had turned to mush.

Gabe groaned and grabbed his glass of water, gulping down most of it, staring at Candace over the rim. She could see the question in his eyes, *Are you crazy?*

Candace shrugged. Fine, so they were lousy at investigating. More specifically, *she* was lousy at investigating. She picked up her own glass and gulped down some more water, stalling, wracking her brains for something worthwhile to ask.

Finally, something managed to crawl to the surface. "So, Vanessa, did you kill Fred?" Shit, she didn't mean to ask it quite like *that*. At least not yet.

Vanessa shot to her feet. She pointed at the front door. "Out!"

Candace stubbornly stayed seated. "Hey, I had to ask."

Gabe looked horrified and gulped down the rest of his water. Damn it, if he was so horrified, then why didn't he ask something?

"Come on," Candace said, smiling while inside her stomach churned, wanting to throw up the water she'd just gulped down. "I know there's no way you could have done it." She didn't know any such thing. "Theoretically, let's say you did."

Vanessa's jaw clenched. "Let's say I didn't."

"Yeah, yeah, I know you didn't but we're just dealing in theoreticals here, and since you're so smart I thought you could theorize with me. So, if you wanted to kill someone, how would you do it?" Not wanting Vanessa to realize how stupid she felt, she sipped the last of her water.

The other woman watched, smiling, that sly look so much a part of Vanessa on her face. "Let me see." Pause. Crafty look. "*Theoretically*, if I wanted to kill Fred, I would have used poison."

Oh, brother, every woman's weapon. No creativity at all. Candace sighed. "Okay, what kind?"

"Calcium gluconate," the woman said smugly. "It causes a heart attack. You can put it in water. It has no taste and leaves no residue."

Holy shit! Candace turned to look at Gabe. He stared back at her, his eyes big. Candace was sure hers looked the same. As one, they turned and stared at their now-empty glasses of water. They both jerked to their feet. "Gee, thanks for your time, Vanessa, but gotta run." They edged toward the door.

Looking like the cat that ate the canary, Vanessa led the way. She opened the door, only to find an older, distinguished looking gentleman standing on the doorstep, hand raised to ring the bell.

"Vanessa?"

Vanessa's mouth tightened. "Arthur." Not a warm and fuzzy greeting.

"Guests?" he asked, silver-gray eyebrow raised in inquiry.

"They were just leaving."

"Yeah, we were just leaving. Right now," Candace said and darted toward the stairs, Gabe hot on her heels. They raced down the five flights to the street where she yanked open her purse and dumped onto the sidewalk her wallet, her keys, her make-up case, her checkbook, her new packet of breath strips, and everything else in her quest.

"Dammit, where's my phone?" she demanded.

"Never mind, I'm on it." Gabe tapped something into his phone, sweat dripping down his temples, his face ashen. "Quick, what was the name she said?"

"Calcium gluco-something or other."

He tapped some more. "Got it. It's calcium gluconate." His eyes moved back and forth as he read the information, then he let out a sound of annoyance. "It's only lethal if it's injected, and then, only if given in high doses. Taken orally, it would just cause constipation."

Thank God. "What the hell! What a bitch. She let us think..."

Gabe ran a hand through his hair. Even though, not two seconds ago, Candace believed she would die, now she was immediately turned on. She couldn't help it. It was his hair, and his sexy masculine hands that knew just where to stroke and caress her. Also, there were those taut buns and the firm pecs and... Oh, hell, it had become obvious she could live to be a hundred and Gabe would always turn her on.

"Yeah, I know," he growled, his eyes meeting Candace's. "She was fucking with us."

"I don't know how, but somehow I'm going to get her," Candace said, but what she thought was, dear God, she could have died. Okay, she wasn't actually going to die but still, it was a great excuse to have more life-affirming sex again.

She nudged him and smiled.

He glanced at her, did a double take and paled. "No!"

Oh, crap. She sighed. "Come on, let's go find Junior and see what he has to say."

They turned to walk back to Gabe's bike when who should appear, but Lance, blithely sauntering down the street, Lucy-less and vulnerable. He had dyed his hair blue from the green he sported last time they saw him, but the studs and black makeup were still in full force.

He jerked to a stop when he saw them, his head swiveling in both directions as he searched for an escape route, before abruptly turning to run.

Candace leaped forward to grab him, but Gabe beat her to it and captured Lance's arm.

Lance squealed, looking remarkably like a New York subway rat faced with a train barreling down on him, all pointy nose and wide eyes.

"Hello, Lance," Candace crooned.

Lance gulped loudly then coughed. His face turned red as he tried to swallow, his Adam's apple bobbing up and down. "Ack. Ackackack..." Gripping his throat, he coughed again.

Good God, swallow the damned gum.

He swallowed and the red slowly receded.

She waited for the boy to gather his thoughts then decided, what the heck, why wait, as they might be here all day, or even all year if they waited for that. "So, Lance, let's talk..." she started. "We were just up to see your mother. We had something important to discuss."

A crafty look slid over Lance's face, making him look more rat-like than ever, or maybe more Vanessa-like. It was hard to tell since there was so much similarity.

Surprisingly, he spoke first. "Oh, wow, really, so did you bring her stuff with you?" he asked, the question coming out of the blue.

Wow. A whole entire sentence. With no help from anyone.

Gabe looked intrigued. The arm holding Lance's arm now draped over the younger man's shoulders, holding him in place. "What stuff would that be, Lance?" He gave Lance a squeeze.

Lance's eyes bugged as he looked wildly around. "You know, that stuff of my mother's. She really, really wants it."

Candace had no idea what he was talking about but admitting her cluelessness would make Lance clam up like...well, like a clam, whereas pretending she was in-the-know might garner some important information. "I'm not giving it back," she said even though she had no idea what *it* was.

His mouth dropped open, exposing that nasty stud he wore through his tongue. *Ick.*

"But, but, but..." He was back to Mister Speechless. "Why not?" he finally whined.

Gabe stepped in, continuing the game. "We might think about giving it to you if you were willing to give us something in return."

Those black-liner rimmed eyes narrowed. "Like, what do you want?"

Candace waited for Gabe to respond. It was his idea, frankly a great idea, so she let him play it through. In the meantime, she could stand here and imagine those manly hands on her, rather than Lance.

"We want to know—"

"Don't say a word, Lance," the strident voice ordered as Lucy clomped down the street, her face blazing with fury.

Well, shit.

Lance jerked away from Gabe and Gabe let him. "Luce, I wasn't—"

"—Going to say anything. Yeah, sure you weren't, Lance."

Lance hung his head but unlike her brother, Lucy wasn't at all intimidated. She walked right up and stuck her face in Gabe's. "We've got nothing to say," she told him. "Got it?"

All they could do was nod.

"I think you're done here," she told them.

Gabe apparently thought so too. He grabbed Candace's hand and they retreated, retreat being the better part of valor. Or something like that.

It was an ignominious retreat, yet the visit wasn't a total loss as Candace had learned three things,

1. Vanessa knew how to kill someone with poison.

2. Lance thought Candace had something Vanessa wanted.

3. And Candace was in big, big trouble. Because it had become clear she no longer resented Gabe. Damn it!

19 Froggie went a'courtin' he did go, uh-huh

They mounted his motorcycle and roared off. As before, the motorcycle was too loud to discuss their upcoming visit to Murray's place, or talk about their strategy either, but given their total lack of success at Vanessa's why continue strategizing?

Reaching Murray's street, Gabe slowed, looking for a spot to pull over and park but as they approached Murray's apartment building, Candace whispered, "Gabe, look! It's the Tadpole." She pointed as Junior walked out of the door.

Gabe hit the brakes and stopped. He turned and gave her a look that he hoped said, *Are you sure you're perfectly sane, and if not, am I safe with you?*

She looked right back, then she smiled.

He recoiled but managed to unlock enough of his frozen brain cells to ask, "The Tadpole?"

"You know. Ribbit Junior."

It took a minute, but he finally got it. Not that he was dumb or anything, but Candace's mind worked in wondrous ways, or weird ways, and his didn't. Okay, sometimes his mind didn't work at all when he was around her. Look at what just happened when she smiled at him. He turned into a drooling, incoherent idiot. He wondered if he would survive their time together. The good news was it seemed as if she'd forgotten their little tiff.

"Fine, why don't you jump off and go talk to him while I park."

Candace didn't answer. Instead she watched Junior as he stood on the sidewalk, hands in the pockets of his saggy pants, dirty T-shirt barely covering his hairy belly, shoulders hunched as his eyes darted furtively around.

Gabe watched Candace watching Junior because he loved looking at her face while she thought. He could see every thought as it flitted through her brain because her face changed. He particularly liked her face when she arrived at a solution. It lit up. Watching her, he knew damned well what he wanted to do with her, and it wasn't tracking Junior down on a hot summer day.

With difficulty, he reined in his lurid thoughts. "Candace," he reminded her.

"No. Something's up. We should follow him instead."

Gabe narrowed his eyes at her then turned back to watch as Junior skulked down the street. "You're right." Breaking every law on the books, he made a U-turn, going the wrong way on the one-way street, and slowly coasted behind Junior as the guy stomped toward the avenue going downtown.

When Junior grabbed a cab, Gabe sped up and followed. "Lucky we're on my bike, right?" he yelled to Candace, weaving in and out of traffic on the tail of the cab. She just whined, apparently still not a fan of the motorcycle. Gabe totally disagreed as he enjoyed the feeling of her pressed against him, her breasts smushed against his back, her long legs hugging his, although he wasn't a fan of the sharp fingernails she dug into his stomach. Any other day, he would turn the motorcycle around and take her back to bed and make love to her until her eyes crossed. Sadly, not today.

They reached the East Village and the cab slowed then made a turn onto a narrow street lined with old tenement buildings, each with a street-level store with apartments above. The stores included a clothing store, a porn shop, a tattoo parlor and a basement shop with a sign in the window stating, *"Madame Occult, Specialist in spells and omen. Your future for $25."* It was easy to tell they were in the East Village because uptown a psychic would charge at least forty bucks. The pedestrians walking by with blue hair, nose rings and tattoos were another clue.

Junior's cab stopped. Gabe slowed about thirty feet behind him and pulled over at the curb. They watched as Junior rolled out of his cab with a grunt and entered a store across the street.

"*Chain Gang*," Gabe said as he read the sign over the door. "What's that?"

Candace shrugged. "No idea."

They waited. Traffic crawled around them, on the way to parts unknown. Most of the pedestrians threw them sideways glances since they didn't fit into the environment, being a little too normal.

Gabe moved restlessly then cleared his throat. "Listen, about Contessa—"

Junior exited the store with a length of chain slung around his shoulder. In his hands, he held a pair of handcuffs that he opened and snapped closed several times before dropping them into a paper bag looped over his arm.

"What the hell?" Gabe muttered. Candace didn't answer since it was a question with no answer.

Junior walked down the street toward First Avenue, and they slowly followed. After crossing First, Junior went into another store.

Gabe pulled over on the opposite side of the avenue to watch. "*Another You*," he said aloud, again reading the sign. "Quick," he told Candace. "Go see what that is."

Why me? her look said, but she obediently got off the bike, trotted across the avenue, dodging traffic as she went, before stopping in front of the shop. Cupping her hands around her eyes, she pressed against the window and stared inside. The short skirt she'd insisted on wearing rode up, revealing her long, slim legs and her heart-shaped fanny just begging for some masculine attention.

The hot summer day suddenly got torrid. He dismounted the bike, the seat suddenly too uncomfortable to sit on. Discretely, he adjusted his jeans.

Candace suddenly raced across the street and threw herself into his arms.

He held her tight. "What did you see?" He could feel her slight tremble, but mostly he could feel her breasts through the thin fabric of his T-shirt.

The sensation gave him some very specific ideas and kind of made him want to go back to that last store and get some chains of his own.

"It was horrible. Just horrible," she said as she buried her nose in his chest, rubbing.

"What? What did you see?" She scared him and he found himself running his hand up and down her back, each time, his hand dipping a little lower until his fingers managed to curl up under the hem of her short, short skirt and touch her inner thigh. He figured she wouldn't notice.

She did. She leaned back in his arms and, eyes narrowed, gave him one of her Candace looks. He waited for *the smile* but at that moment Junior exited the store, carrying another big shopping bag, still with the chain slung over his shoulder. He looked up and down the street, then scuttled toward the next street corner as fast as his fat little legs would take him. Taking out his phone, he made a call.

Gabe's head swiveled to follow Junior's progress, but he couldn't keep his hand from still stroking her back, and her fanny. "Candace, tell me, what did you see?"

She snickered. "Nothing. It was too dark inside to see anything. I just like how you get all cute and cuddly when you're worried." That smile finally appeared. "Mostly, I didn't want Junior to see me as he left."

Damn it. She'd done it again. If he wasn't so in lust with her, he'd kill her. Gabe mounted the bike and revved the motor. "Get on!"

A car pulled up next to Junior. He jumped in and the car drove back uptown, Gabe and Candace right behind. After a long ride and a few weird turns to avoid traffic jams, the car pulled over to the curb and Junior got out.

After bringing the bike to a stop across the street, they sat there, idling, while Junior entered another store.

Gabe cocked his head. "Lane Bryant?"

Candace shrugged. "No idea."

After twenty minutes, Junior exited carrying several more big bags, hailed a passing cab and traveled back to the apartment where he and Murray lived. They watched while Junior got out of the cab, dragging the shopping bags with him, and walked through the door the doorman held open.

"What do you think?" Gabe asked. "Should we go in?"

"That's why we came, isn't it?"

"Yeah, I guess so. But..."

"But what?"

Gabe didn't answer. He just kicked the bike into gear and rolled down the street until he found a spot to park. Candace dismounted, took her helmet off, and shook out her hair. Gabe tried to focus on parking but clipped the bumper of a car backing into a spot because his eyes were on Candace and that glorious hair rather than his rearview mirrors.

Seeing where his eyes were focused, she grinned and began the walk back to Murray's building, waggling her tail as she went. Gabe trailed behind which was fine with him since it gave him an excellent view of her ass. When they got to the building the doorman just waved them through since he knew Gabe. Right on their heels walked a reject from the 1950's, a skinny guy with a wispy goatee, wearing a beret, lugging a humongous black bag that looked like it weighed more than the guy, and a mousy looking girl with an over-bite. They all trekked to the elevator, got on and rode up together, getting off on the same floor.

Gabe exchanged a look with Candace. She shrugged.

They walked down the hall. The odd couple followed. They arrived at Murray's door and stopped. So did the odd couple.

What the hell? He wanted to ask them what they wanted but he guessed it wasn't his business, it was just weird. While he attempted to decide what was going on, Beatnik Boy reached under Gabe's elbow.

"Hey, dude. Move," he said, and rang the bell.

Who did that guy think he was? Gabe glared at him and growled. Seeing his irritation, Candace leaned against the door, arms crossed over her chest and grinned impudently at him. The door flew open, and Candace fell inside with a loud *yeep*.

She lay on her back in the foyer, looking vaguely like sexy roadkill. Junior stared down at her. "What are you doing here?"

Candace didn't answer, silent for once in her life.

Instead, Beatnik Boy answered indignantly, "I have an appointment."

"Not you," Junior answered, and pointed at Candace lying on the floor. "Her. Them." He waved a hand vaguely in Gabe's direction, but Gabe ignored him as it finally occurred to him he should probably help Candace up off the floor, although he was loathe to do that since her skirt was wound around her hips, revealing her lacy pink panties.

Which no one should see but him. Bending, he reached out a hand.

"Junior? What's going on? Is that the photographer?" It sounded like Murray's voice coming from the bedroom, and yet it wasn't. It seemed more of a froggie falsetto than the usual deep croak. The falsetto was soon followed by the clicking sounds of high heels walking on hardwood floor.

Hearing the footsteps, Junior spun around, hands up as if he could stop the approaching disaster. "Dad, wait!"

Too late. Murray entered the living room. And what a Murray it was.

"Holy fuck," Gabe gasped, and dropped Candace back on the floor.

Junior buried his head in his hands and groaned.

"What are you staring at?" Murray falsettoed.

"Um," Gabe muttered, his hand still extended to help Candace to her feet, a useless endeavor since the sight of Murray, clad in a lacy peignoir as he swept a masculine hand through his enormous platinum blond wig, stunned both of them senseless.

Gabe gave his uncle's fat form a quick once over from top to toes. "You need to shave your legs if you're going to wear short skirts," he blurted out.

Murray leaned over to survey his legs, squishing his enormous fake boobs down with one hand as he did so they didn't get in the way of the view. "Hmmm. You're right. Can't have my picture taken with hairy legs." The falsetto was still in full force. "Shoot, I'm out of razors. Junior, go on over to the Duane Read and get me some razors."

Beatnik Boy dropped his humongous bag with a thump. "Hey, are we going to take these pictures or what?"

Murray turned to glare at him. "Listen, jerk-off, I'm paying you by the hour." His voice had lowered to his usual basso croak. "I'm not having my picture taken until I shave my legs. What would my fans think if they saw me like this?"

"Fer fuck's sake," the photographer muttered, but plopped his butt down on his big black case with a sigh. His assistant, losing interest in the whole thing, went into the living room where she sat on one of the gilt bedazzled couches and proceeded to file her nails.

Murray turned back to Junior. "Well, what are you waiting for. Hop to it." The voice was back in soprano territory.

Junior hopped, like the junior frog he was.

Candace snorted. Her whole body shook as she tried not to laugh. Her breasts jiggled. Very enticing. Gabe could feel heat rising, and was tempted to forget their mission, grab her hand, drag her out the door and home to find the closest bed.

She ruined it by gaining control of herself and getting to her feet. She brushed her hands over the back of her short skirt so the cloth pressed against her tight ass. So, okay, she hadn't ruined it, she just changed his focus, that's all.

Damn, he was in serious lust here.

"Hey, Murray. How's it going?" she asked, grinning at his uncle. Gabe was grateful to see it wasn't her usual smile, the one that said, *I want to have sex with you but first I want to drive you crazy.* Directed at Murray, that would be totally inappropriate, and make Gabe jealous as hell. No, this smile was just a normal smile, one filled with unmitigated glee at the situation which caused a bubble of hot emotion to fill his chest.

"Cute shoes, Murray," she said next, nodding at the pink mules—size thirteens—covering Murray's feet.

Gabe shuddered. Yeah, the shoes were very cute. Less cute were the long hairy toes hanging out of the open-toed slippers.

"You like?" Murray simpered, sticking out one foot for Candace to survey, twisting and turning it so she could get all the various angles.

"Absolutely."

Gabe could hear the laughter in her voice.

"You have great taste in shoes," she added.

Murray frowned. "Hmm. Not so much in dresses, though. I always have trouble finding the right silhouette, but, you know, maybe you could help in that department." He picked up the Lane Bryant bag Junior left sitting on the floor when he fled and pulled out a garment. Shaking it out, he held it up to his chest. Murray being Murray, the dress was the color of algae, perfect for the pond. "What d'ya think?" he asked, his face showing his anxiety. "Is the color right for photos?"

Candace gurgled. One finger went into her mouth, and she chewed on one of her nails as she tried to hide her smile. He wished she wouldn't do that because it made him want to replace her finger with his tongue. The way things were going, he thought more and more about Candace, and less and less about finding out who killed his father. He still cared, but he was getting distracted.

"Very pretty," she said. "Er...I like the fabric."

Murray nodded, then bending, he grabbed the other bag, the one labeled Chain Gang, and pulled out the chain Junior had looped over his shoulder. Murray draped it around his neck like a feather boa and turned to Gabe. "So? Will this give the right impression?"

Gabe struggled for words. He wasn't a fashion critic. He wasn't a hairy-legged, cross-dressing lunatic either. "Uh...what kind of impression are you trying to make?"

"A quick one, I hope," the photographer muttered unhappily.

They both ignored him since—you guessed it—he was getting paid by the hour, so if they wanted to waste Beatnik Boy's time, they would.

Murray twirled a hank of blond (fake) hair around one finger as he stared up at the ceiling, obviously turning the question around in his mind. "I ain't sure. Something that shows my fans who I am, I guess."

At his side, Candace snickered. Again. Another thing Gabe wished she would stop doing since it made it nearly impossible to quell the rising hysteria the sight of his uncle in a pink peignoir induced. "And, uh...who exactly are those fans?" *Please don't tell me it's a bunch of cross-dressing Hell's Angels.*

Murray threw him a look that clearly said, *Are you stupid, or what?* "My readers, naturally."

Readers? "Um. What readers would those be, Uncle Murray?"

Again, that look of irritation. "For my books."

Getting information from his uncle was a little like pulling teeth, slow and painful, but at this point, Gabe wasn't sure he wanted the answers. Because, unfortunately, he had begun to figure out what the answers were, and what he suspected might explain those big checks they found in Murray's office. If true, it would be the sole good news of the day. "So, uh, you write books." His gaze dropped to the chain Murray still had in his hand. He massaged his forehead, trying to make the headache go away. "Let me guess. Erotica?"

Murray drew himself up. "Damned straight. Erotica sells like hotcakes. I'm making a bundle."

Of course he was. "Uncle Murray..."

Murray gave him the fisheye, or maybe more accurately, the frog eye. "What's with you? What are you saying?"

"The dress, and the wig, and..." He glanced at Murray's hands and winced as he saw the inch-long lacquered nails.

Candace gave him a nudge. "Oh, leave him alone. I think it's cute." She giggled.

Cute. Just the idea made him nauseous. "But the getup. Why? Why the thing with the dress and all?"

"My fans are all women. Women read books written by women. They ain't reading no stuff written by men, especially romance. If they knew I was a guy, nobody would buy my books."

Sure, fine, he got it.

Okay, truthfully, he didn't. It was just too weird. The whole thing. "But... the dress. And..."

Murray's chin went up, a good thing since at least two of his multiple chins disappeared. The man should remember this trick when it came time to shoot his photos. Much more flattering.

Oh, crap. Did he just think that?

Murray's arms crossed over his amply padded chest as he glared at Gabe belligerently. "Hey, you little shit. If dressing as a dame was good enough for your father, it's good enough for me."

There was no answer for that since it was true. Shaking his head, Gabe gave up. "I just have one question, and I want a serious answer."

Still looking angry, Murray nodded.

"Did you kill Dad?"

All the air went out of Murray. Grabbing the lapels of his peignoir, he pulled it tight around himself again as he hemmed and hawed. Finally, "Nah. Your father was a selfish prick, but I loved him. I wouldn't never hurt him."

In spite of Murray's previous evasiveness and attitude, Gabe believed him.

Junior returned, out of breath, with razors in hand. He tossed them at his father. "Here. Go shave."

"Thank God," Beatnik Boy growled.

"Oh, good," his assistant shrilled, finally coming alive from her semi-comatose state on the couch. "Can we get this done now. I've got a date in two hours."

With nothing left to say, or ask, Gabe reached for Candace's hand. "Come on. We're out of here."

And they were.

20 The Plot Thickens

Wendy tapped her fingers on the arm of her peach-colored chintz chair. The voices the bugs were picking up droned on, Tiffany and Julian saying nothing that Wendy hadn't heard already in the last four hours.

'I want to buy this dress, what do you think?'

'You'll look adorable, baby.'

'Are you sure? It won't make me look fat?'

'No way, babe. You'll look fabulous.'

'Teehee. Teehee.' Ugh.

Then: *'Once we're done here in New York, I want to go to California.'* Sounds of kissing. *"You'll take me to California, won't you, my big handsome man?'*

More kissing. Ick.

'You bet.'

'And if I want to buy a yacht and go to Catalina, you'll take me, right?'

'A small one, babe, a small one.' Gotta make the money last.

Followed by more of the same.

Wendy rolled her eyes. I want, I want, I want, and blah, blah, blah, blah, blah. Not that any of this surprised her, but goodness, it was so repetitive you would think it was a recording and not the real Tiffany and Julian.

Oh! Oh, oh, oh. What a good idea.

The machine she'd purchased had recording capabilities.

With nothing interesting being said, Wendy switched it to record and went to the kitchen to make a late afternoon snack which she enjoyed sitting at her kitchen table basking in the sunlight streaming through the window. She sipped her tea and leafed through the latest edition of *Ladies Home Journal* and thought about her blessings. A wonderful daughter, and a previous job that led to marriage to Fred Jones, the love of her life even though he hadn't felt quite the same way and divorced her for that awful Vanessa Luckless.

Sad, but Wendy had no complaints. The person who should complain was Vanessa since she was thrown over for Tiffany when she expected to be set for life with Fred and hopefully have the apartment all to herself.

Speaking of Tiffany... She glanced at her watch. Oops. Almost seven. She'd sat daydreaming for over an hour, ignoring the bug when she should have been listening. Oh, what the heck, she could just play it back on the tape machine. That would work just as well, but first, she wanted to have some of that apple pie she bought at Zabar's. She would heat it up then get right on the thing with Tiffany.

The sun was getting low in the sky when she returned to her office. The tape recorder was silent, which meant either Tiffany and Julian were asleep or just not talking to each other, which was a distinct possibility given Tiffany's bitch factor.

Oh, that was a nasty thing to say even if it was true. Even so, she shouldn't use bad language. It wasn't nice, but then, neither was Tiffany.

Okay, never mind. She could listen to the previous hour's recording without worrying. Setting the recorder on the table next to her, she turned it on playback, then settled down in her chair to listen.

And...it was more of the same. Gee whiz, what dreary people they were. After another half hour, Wendy finally got so bored she was about to fall asleep, but she knew if she did, Candy—and what was wrong with the name Candy, anyway—would never forgive her so she needed to find something to keep her awake.

Standing, she stretched and then went to her desk drawer and pulled out her needlepoint. That always took a lot of concentration. Returning to her chair, she curled up and spent a few minutes sorting through the embroidery threads and picking out the right colors. In the background, she tuned one ear to the recorded sounds of Tiffany kvetching. She picked up her needle, threaded it and began the soothing task of moving it in and out of the mesh. Pretty soon, the voices receded, just another annoying noise in the background like the street noise down below and the sound of the dishwasher in the kitchen.

She stuck the needle through the next hole. "OW!"

Holding her hand up, she stared in disbelief at the blood running down her finger. Oh, darn, now she'd done it. Heaving a sigh, she rose and walked to her bathroom to get a Band-Aid. She ran water over the puncture, wanting to make sure it was clean, then carefully dried it off and applied some ointment. Last, the Band-Aid. Darn, it still hurt but there was nothing she could do about it. Hopefully it wouldn't affect her ability to finish her needlepoint, and hopefully, she hadn't gotten blood on it either since it was almost done, and she wouldn't want to ruin it after all her work.

With that thought in mind, she hurried back to her office and checked out her work. No, it looked fine.

In the background, *'blah, blah, blah...go to Contessa.'*

Wendy reseated herself and picked out a nice blue for the sky.

'Blah, blah, are you sure it's the right key?'

She held the canvas mesh out in front of her. It was looking very nice. Once it was done, she had the perfect spot for it in the kitchen.

'Mumble, mumble, mumble.'

Picking up a green thread, Wendy compared it to the darker shade she'd selected for the trees. She glanced at her watch. Seven forty-five. She hoped the recording ended soon as she wanted to watch her favorite program.

'How do we get her there?'

She took a sip of her tea. It was surprising what hard work needlepoint was. Listening to Tiffany and Julian bicker wasn't much more fun either.

'But what if Candace won't cooperate? I don't want to have to hurt her.'

'She'll cooperate or else.'

'Or else what?'

'Oh, my God, Julian. Or else Candace is dead, what did you think?'

Wait! What!

Wendy grabbed the recording machine and held it out in front of her. "What did you say?" She shook it.

'*...Don't think I can...*'

Wendy couldn't hear the rest. She turned up the volume and the next words blared.

'*No, we can't wait. It has to be done now, tonight, before Candace realizes her key is missing.*'

Wendy pressed her ear to the recorder, wanting to make sure she didn't miss a word.

'*But...*'

'*No but. It's tonight or never. So call her right now.*'

Her hands trembling, Wendy rewound the tape for a few seconds then re-listened to the conversation. When it got to the same place, Wendy didn't wait to hear the rest. She turned the volume down and picked up her phone.

* * * *

"Why my family?" Gabe complained as he stomped down the street toward his motorcycle.

Candace giggled. "Hey, every family has its eccentrics. I mean, look at my mom."

He threw her a look. "Your mom is a little odd, but she doesn't dress up like some overweight drag queen."

They reached the motorcycle. Gabe rubbed his forehead, massaging it as if he had a headache. Which he probably did.

"Hah, I thought it was cute."

"Cute? You thought Murray in a silk robe with his chest hair popping out and false eyelashes was cute?"

Candace took the helmet and put it on. "At least he... she... whatever, has good taste, something I'm not sure my mom with her plaid shorts and hippie muslin shirts, has." That didn't mean she didn't love her mom, just that she had truly bad taste in clothes. Candace much preferred what Murray chose. All except the algae green color of the dress. The color had made Murray's skin take on sort of a bilious hue. Hmmm. She probably should have told him before the pictures were taken. Next time she'd offer to do his styling. Wouldn't want to disappoint the fans, after all.

"At least we can stop investigating Murray, since we know now where all his money came from."

"Yeah." Gabe scrubbed harder at his forehead.

"Are you all right?"

"No. I have a mother of a headache." He glared at her. "I'm probably never going to recover from today."

Poor baby, today was hard on him but she knew just what he needed. "Let's go get a drink," she offered. "And talk about our next move."

He nodded. "Yeah. And while we're at it, I want to talk about Contes—"

Lips tight, she smacked his arm. "I'm not discussing that!"

"But..."

"No! We just need to find *The Recipe*, that's all." Turning, she stomped off in the direction of his bike.

He sighed and followed her. He didn't know what her problem was, but they needed to talk soon. Putting on his helmet, he started the engine as she mounted behind him and they coasted down the street, heading back uptown until they reached the Seventies where there were tons of cute little restaurants with sidewalk tables. They found a likely one and parked.

After settling at a table, they ordered burgers, fries and a large, very large, Scotch and water for Gabe. Candace eyed the humongous size of the meal, mentally calculating the calories but she figured the diet coke she ordered would atone for the trillion calories in the burger and fries. Okay, it didn't, but it made her feel more virtuous to drink diet.

While they ate, they went over their list of suspects, which had gotten progressively smaller.

"So, cross off Murray, right?"

"Right," Gabe said, wiping ketchup off his chin.

"I guess it means we can eliminate Junior too."

"Yeah, Junior doesn't sneeze unless Murray tells him to."

"I guess your mom is off the list?"

Gabe gave her a threatening look from under his brow.

Candace rolled her eyes. "Right. Naturally she's off the list. Now, what about Vanessa? I'm still unsure. What do you think?"

He sat back and patted his stomach, apparently finally full. What an appetite. He ate his mammoth burger, plus half of hers, both orders of fries and a huge helping of fried onions. She hoped he didn't run to fat when he hit *manopause*.

She stopped, her coke halfway to her mouth. Holy crap, did she just think that? About Gabe. And her. And getting old? Together?

She didn't know what was scarier, the idea of them being together in twenty years or the idea of being old. Upon reflection, it was the thought of being together, because she just didn't see how it would work. He would have his taffy factory and the chocolate factory, and she would have... nothing.

She watched him eat the last fry on her plate. A speck of catchup dotted his lip and his tongue darted out of his mouth and licked it off. Heat pooled between her legs.

Okay, so she could probably get over her resentment.

He looked up and caught her staring avidly at him. He grinned and his dimple showed. Under the table, his foot stroked up her calf and settled in between her thighs. Oh, damn. He'd taken his shoe off. His bare foot nestled warm against her inner thigh as he coaxed her legs apart. His toes worked their magic.

All right, she could definitely get over her resentment, especially if he continued to do what he was doing.

She closed her eyes and moaned.

He removed his foot, leaving her hanging.

She opened her eyes and glared at him. "You shit," she whispered. There were people listening, after all.

He cocked an eyebrow, looking too damned pleased with himself, but she could forgive him since he was so cute. His foot returned to its proper place between her thighs.

"So. Vanessa," Gabe said, continuing as if his toes weren't playing with her lady parts. "I'm still not sure of her either. There was that business with the poison." He shivered. "Jesus, that was just plain cruel."

Her nerve endings still hummed, and most of her brain power was still pooled between her legs but she made an effort to focus. "Yeah. To my way of thinking it puts her high on the list." She paused, thinking back on their interview with the Stiff, especially that older man they almost ran into in the hallway. Something about him bothered her.

"That guy. I feel like I've met him before."

"What guy?" Gabe pinched his nose, looking perplexed.

"You know. Arthur. The guy visiting Vanessa."

"I don't know him. Why do you care?"

"Because he looked familiar."

"Why does it matter?"

She opened up her tote and dug through it again until she found her phone. Not knowing where else to start, she typed in Vanessa's name. Lots of hits.

"Oh, my God. Look." She held the phone out for Gabe to view. "She's dating Arthur Middleton."

Holy shit. Arthur Middleton. The guy who helped build the new sports stadium out in Brooklyn. The guy who owned the largest chain of jewelry stores in the country. The guy who was born in the projects and was now as rich as Croesus. That Arthur Middleton?

"Darn," she said, slumping in her chair as her heart sank. "It probably explains the necklace. So I guess you can take her off the list too." How depressing. She'd wanted it to be Vanessa. Really, she'd wanted it to be the twins. Having them as the culprits would just seem like justice after all the shit they pulled over the years, including stealing her Boy George CD collection. So what if no one listened to Boy George anymore.

"How do you figure?" Gabe asked.

"Well, if she's got a rich guy on the hook, what does she need with *The Recipe*, and why jeopardize her relationship by killing Fred." She couldn't stand the woman, but fair was fair.

Gabe frowned. "Yeah, but what about the stuff Lance said she wanted back. That sounded like a big deal."

Right! "Okay, then keep her on the list, along with the twins." Thoughts of the twins invoked her usual response. She curled a lip. "So our list now only has Vanessa and the twins. Or just the twins. Or just Vanessa, depending on how you look at it. Plus Tiffany and Julian. My money is on the latter."

Gabe nodded. "Speaking of Tiffany, I wonder how your mom is doing monitoring the bug."

"Crap! My mom. I forgot all about her."

He gave her a look.

"I know, I know. I'll call her now." She pulled out her phone again but before she could make the call, it beeped an incoming call.

She checked the screen. She didn't recognize the number, however, that didn't mean anything. Any one of a dozen unknown people could be calling her about a dozen different things, but she didn't have any stalkers that she knew of, so she answered it. "Hello?"

"Is this Miss McCready?"

She glanced at Gabe. He stared at her, chin in hand as he picked through the remains of her dinner. Lord, how could he be hungry again? "Yes, this is Candace McCready."

"Of Contessa Chocolates?"

She sat bolt upright in her chair. "Yes. Why? What's going on?" She put the phone on speaker and held it out for Gabe to hear.

Gabe leaned forward, worry furrowing his brow.

"This is Lieutenant Jacobs from the New York City Fire Department. There's an active fire at your location in Brooklyn, and it looks pretty bad. Are there still employees on the premises?"

Her heart stopped. "No, we only have one shift working right now and they've already quit for the day, but—"

The caller hung up.

"Shit!" She hit redial but it just rang and rang, with no one picking up.

"Never mind," Gabe barked as he threw several twenties on the table to pay the tab. "We need to go."

They grabbed Gabe's motorcycle and headed out to Brooklyn. For once, Candace was thankful they rode the beast as they were able to roar past all the cars crowding FDR Drive, cross the Williamsburg Bridge into Brooklyn in record time and reach Bushwick just as the sun was lowering behind them. Candace hung onto Gabe's waist the entire ride, her heart racing in her chest in time with the throb of the motorcycle's engine, her stomach churning with apprehension. She had a nearly irresistible need to nibble on a fingernail or two, but she settled for digging them into Gabe's stomach instead. She'd bite them later when she knew everything was all right.

Right now, overwhelming anxiety ruled. After everything else, how could this have happened? The factory, although in an old building, was just rewired two years ago. They had new sprinkler systems and they did daily maintenance checks to make sure nothing combustible was left lying around.

Why? How? If she wasn't on the back of Gabe's bike, she would have thrown up.

They turned the corner. In front of them sat the factory, a forty-foot sign emblazoned with CONTESSA CHOCOLATE stretching across the front of the long, low building.

Gabe stopped the bike. Candace dismounted and took off her helmet. "What the hell?"

No lights showed through the grated windows and the factory was quiet. Most especially, there were no fire engines or firemen on the premises.

After parking and shutting off the bike, Gabe joined her on the sidewalk, his expression grim as he stared at the closed doors of the brick building. "Something weird is going on."

Candace nodded. Now that she knew her baby wasn't burning down, the panic subsided so she was able to think a little more clearly. "No shit, Sherlock," she responded wryly.

He wrapped his arm around her neck and squeezed gently. "Smart ass."

She pinched the skin under his arm, and he let go with a yelp. She trotted across the street with him on her tail as he ran to catch up. Reaching the front door, she pulled out her keys then sorted through them, searching for the key to the front door.

With a frown, she looked over her shoulder at Gabe. "Hey, my key to the main door is gone."

"What do you mean, gone?"

"Just what I said. My key is missing." She supposed it could have fallen off her key ring, but she had carried it that way for years and never had any problems. She took a moment to dig through her tote but found nothing.

After studying the door for a minute, she reached out and turned the knob. The door swung open.

"Damn. This should be locked."

"Yeah," Gabe said.

She thought about it for a minute. The door being unlocked in combination with the call she received, and her key being gone, made her uneasy but everything seemed quiet and there were no cars in the parking lot so maybe everything was okay.

"You know, Manuel has forgotten to lock the front door a few times in the past when he was in a hurry. Maybe he forgot again."

"Maybe, but we should be careful anyway," Gabe said, putting his hand on her shoulder, stopping her from entering. "We need to check things out."

"Okay. So let's do it."

"No, just me. You wait outside and I'll go in and check around." He ran a hand through his hair.

His beautiful hair. She never got tired of looking at his hair, or touching his hair, or smelling his hair. She turned to face him, leaning against the doorjamb, and wrapped an arm around his neck. "I know something you could check out right now." Winding one of her curls around a finger, she smiled up at him.

His eyes widened, surprise sparking, then his eyelids slid down to half-mast and the deep chocolate of his eyes smoldered. He edged closer to her until his hips touched hers. He widened his stance so her hips were pressed against the bulge in his jeans. "Oh, you do, do you?"

"Uh huh."

"What do you have in mind?"

Oh, she had lots of things in mind. For instance, she knew the big leather couch in Fred's office was big enough for two.

Before he could remember he told her to wait outside, she stepped through the door and backed into the cavernous interior, tugging Gabe with her. His hips were practically glued to hers as was his mouth, which seemed to particularly like the dip right above her collar bone. She backed, one step at a time, one kiss at a time, one heat-inducing thrust of Gabe's hips at a time. She couldn't see where she was going but she didn't need to, she knew the way by heart, and her heart was a one-track mind when it came to Gabe.

It was a short trip through the winding lengths of conveyer belts filling the building, the long stretches intersected by enormous black machinery. Candace maneuvered them between the enormous tanks usually filled with chocolate liquor waiting to have sugar and milk added but all now stood half empty. Now they were only a short distance away from the staircase leading to the administrative offices, then the way would be clear to the couch. She had even inched up her skirt—a girl had to be prepared, right, even if she was never a girl scout—when she ran into something hard.

"Ouch."

Gabe bit her shoulder. "What ouch?" he murmured, his lips sliding up to suck on her neck.

She enjoyed Gabe's lips on her skin but the thing in her back stopped her progress and right now progress was important. She tried to move away from the sharp object, but it followed her. What the hell. She turned to look over her shoulder.

Oh. Crap.

"Hello, Candace," Tiffany purred.

Gabe jumped away from her, his lips leaving a wet spot on her blouse, and spun Candace around to face Tiffany. And her gun.

Tiffany smiled, and even though it was an evil smile, it was probably the first real emotion she had ever displayed. "I wasn't expecting you to bring Gabe," she said. "But what a nice bonus."

21 The Chocolate Thickens

He couldn't believe his stupidity, to get caught flat-footed by Tiffany, of all people, all because he let his dick overtake his brain.

He stared grimly at his father's fourth wife, wishing the man had stopped at number three and saved them all this trouble. Out of the corner of his eye, he saw Julian standing behind her, supposedly ready to assist but looking like a scared rabbit who would dart away if someone said boo. It was obvious who was in charge, so Gabe directed his question to Tiffany.

"Okay, what do you want?" May as well ask as they had nothing to lose and maybe everything to gain.

She smiled. It wasn't her usual vapid smile, the one she used to prove she was stupid and harmless. Neither was it the kind of smile Candace used, the one that scared the crap out of him, but in a good way. No, this smile was an Attila the Hun smile, a Vlad the Impaler smile, a Hannibal Lecter smile. This smile said they were about to die in unpleasant ways. He suppressed the shiver shaking him to the core.

After smiling and pointing the gun at them for another minute, Tiffany finally deigned to answer. "Oh, I want what I deserve," she said. "And I'm going to get it."

Gabe could feel Candace tense. He could see her jaw tighten and her eyes narrow. He laid a hand on her shoulder and squeezed, hoping she got the hint. *Don't mess with Tiffany.*

She continued to quiver under his hand but kept her mouth shut, thank God.

"And what would that be?" he asked.

"I want the contracts, right, Julian?"

"Uh huh," Julian answered but his voice shook with fear.

Candace's head tilted. "What contracts?"

Tiffany laughed. "Are you that stupid?"

Gabe wrapped an arm around Candace's shoulders as he could feel her getting ready to launch herself at the other woman. He jumped in with, "She's not that stupid, but I don't know what you're talking about, so why don't you clue me in?" Like now, before Candace could say something and maybe get them both shot.

"Fred hedged his bets by investing in futures contracts against the price of cocoa beans," Tiffany told them.

It seemed, no matter the danger, Candace couldn't keep her mouth shut. "So?" she said in a snide tone. "Everyone in our business does that. So what?"

Tiffany sighed. "Oh dear, you truly are that stupid. When I talked to Fred last week, he couldn't stop gloating about how smart he was because the price of the raw beans just skyrocketed and he was going to make a killing with those contracts. Droughts in the rain forest, you know. He explained the whole thing."

"Did you kill Fred to get the contracts?" Candace asked.

Tiffany smirked. "Nope. Lucky me, someone was nice enough to do the job for me, but I'm certainly going to take advantage of it."

Candace didn't say anything, just continued to stare at Tiffany, her brow wrinkled as she thought. Gabe could see her trying to work everything out, which surprised him, because as devious as her mind was, apparently it wasn't devious in a criminal way.

Sadly, his mind apparently was, because he got it right away. "If Tiffany has the contracts, she can buy the beans at the agreed-upon low price and then resell them to Godiva at a huge profit. She'll do it all simultaneously, so she doesn't have to pay for the beans in advance," he pointed out.

Tiffany snapped her fingers, the equivalent of clapping since one hand was still busy holding a gun. "Hah, close but no cigar. Teuscher will pay more, and I don't need to buy the beans, they're already bought, they just can't be delivered to Teuscher without the contracts to prove ownership." She lifted the gun and pointed it at Candace. "Now. Where are they?"

Candace crossed her arms over her chest. "Where are what?" she asked, her words saying *I don't know what you're talking about,* but her body language saying, *No way in hell am I telling you.*

"Oh my God, Candace. Don't play stupid with me. The contracts. I want the contracts. They were in Fred's desk drawer last week but now they're gone."

Candace slanted Gabe a look before answering, "They weren't secure in Fred's desk, so I moved them to his safe."

God help them. Now they really would die.

"My, my, my, that wasn't very smart of you, was it?" Tiffany said, her eyes shooting darts of fury.

"Why do you say that?" Gabe asked. As if he didn't already know the answer.

"Because if the contracts had still been in Fred's desk, I wouldn't have needed you guys, would I?" She pointed the gun at Gabe. "Unfortunately for you both, the desk was empty so now I need your help opening the safe. So let's take a walk." She waved the gun at them, forcing them closer to the stairs.

Gabe took a reluctant step. This was bad, really bad. There was no way they could give Tiffany what she wanted and not end up dead in the end. He could feel the tension radiating off Candace, tension mirrored by his own. Dear God, he thought—and for once, he didn't mean it as an epitaph but as a prayer—if something didn't happen soon, they were going to die.

Like the answer to his prayer, Candace's phone rang.

Julian yelped, making Tiffany jump.

So Gabe jumped too. Grabbing Candace's hand, he ran, dragging her down the aisle behind the row of huge molding machines, his goal to reach the door to the street.

Thwang! Something flew past his ear. "Holy shit," he gasped, still running as if his life depended on it, which it did. "She's shooting at us." He made a quick left, his maneuver taking them into a row of tanks that momentarily shielded them but took them further away from the outer door.

"No shit, Sherlock," Candace answered.

They kept running. Behind them, Gabe could hear the slap of running feet as Tiffany and Julian gave chase. He threw a look over his shoulder just in time to see Tiffany lift her gun and fire again.

Bang! The bullet bounced off the side of a machine within inches of Gabe's ear. "Crap!"

"Hurry" Candace panted, her legs pumping twice as fast as his since she was shorter, and apparently more scared.

He hung another left and darted around the side of another big black machine. "I'm hurrying. But where?" They wound back and forth between all the massive machinery, trying to stay out of sight, and out of reach of the bullets, but eventually they would run out of places to run. His legs had begun to burn, and he gasped for air, as did Candace.

They rounded another corner, when suddenly Candace stopped, jerking him to a halt. "Here." She pulled him through a small opening between two ten-foot-tall vats.

"They'll see us here," Gabe whispered.

"No. See." She pointed to a ladder on the side of the vat.

In the distance, he could still hear Tiffany and Julian yelling at each other and as he listened, the voices came closer.

She pointed toward the ceiling. "See," she said again.

He lifted his head, following the length of narrow metal ladder attached to the side of the tank to where it ended at the top. "What is this?" he asked, still whispering.

"Liquid chocolate. What we call chocolate liquor," she whispered back. She rapped on the side of the tank several times then smiled. "Almost empty. Follow me."

The voices drew near, now seemingly feet away. Wondering if this was a good idea but willing to try anything at this point, Gabe followed. At the top, Candace quickly turned a lever and a round hatch slide open. She threw a leg over the side and dropped down into the tank. He clambered up and over. Evidently there was also a ladder on the inside of the tank, but no one had told him about it and the next thing he knew he was drowning.

In chocolate.

* * * *

"Come on, Candy, answer the phone," Wendy muttered as she paced back and forth, but Candace didn't pick up, and the call went to voice mail.

Wendy left a message, hoping it would do some good but suspecting it wouldn't.

What should she do? This was one of those times when she wished her daughter was here to help but, unfortunately, she wasn't because she was the one in trouble. Not knowing what else to do, she tried again to call Candy...

No, not Candy. If her daughter survived this, Wendy would never call her Candy again. She would call her Candace, or Miss McCready, or even Lassie if that was what her daughter wanted as long as she came home alive.

She redialed. No one answered the phone this time either. What should she do? Maybe the better question was, what would her daughter do?

She wouldn't stand around here, thumb up her you-know-what, waiting for disaster to happen. She would spring into action, like a little blond dynamo, arms swinging, loaded for bear, as the saying goes. She'd go to the source of the trouble. Her daughter was awesome, so Wendy needed to be too. Decision made, Wendy grabbed her purse, ran to the door, and yanked it open.

"Aaaaack!" A broad black obstacle blocked her path. "Oh my goodness." Her heart jumped in her chest as she stared at the obstacle, groping for his name. Remembering names was unfortunately not her thing. For that matter, remembering faces wasn't her thing either. "Uh... Hi...uh who..."

"Dolan," the obstacle said wryly, not looking amused. "Sergeant Dolan."

The fear and the tension winding her up suddenly disappeared. "Oh, thank God." She grabbed his hand and yanked him over to the elevator. The door opened as soon as she hit the button, and she pulled him inside.

"Whoa, wait a minute. What's going on?" He pulled his hand out of her grasp then hit the button stopping the elevator. It jerked to a halt. Crossing his arms over his chest, he leveled a stony look at her. "What are you doing?" he asked.

Wendy spun around and started the elevator again. It dropped a few feet before he hit STOP again and it jerked to a halt. "Where's your daughter? I need to speak with her."

"Oooooooh," Wendy screamed and stomped her foot. "We need to go. Candace is in trouble. I mean she's not here, and they're going to kill her. They have guns and evil thoughts, and they hate her and... They want something in Fred's office, but I don't know what it is, and—"

Dolan clapped his hand over her mouth but at the same time, he punched the start button. "Okay. Slowly. Tell me what's going on."

By the time they reached the lobby she had spilled the whole thing, including her negligence in not listening to the bug until it was too late and the fact that she felt horribly guilty about it but really, there wasn't time to feel guilty, so she tried to make sense when she related the story. It wasn't easy.

He nodded, looking even stonier as he hustled her out to the street and shoved her into a black sedan.

"Buckle up," he said. Grabbing a red revolving light sitting on his dashboard, he reached out the window and affixed it to the roof of his car. It whirred and shrieked as they sped across town. By the time they hit 59th Street he was already on the phone with a bunch of guys, marshalling his forces, and Wendy was reduced to feeling as if she was going to have a panic attack instead of a full-on heart spasm.

* * * *

"Damn it. Where the fuck are they?" Tiffany groused in a low voice as she prowled through the aisle alongside the long expanse of conveyer belts. Every so often, she reached a corner blocked by a large machine where she would hesitate a moment before jumping around the corner, gun in hand as if she expected to find Candace and Gabe lurking there. So far, they weren't.

Julian looked over his shoulder uneasily. "I dunno, but this wasn't supposed to happen this way. You said once you got the code to his office door from the owner of the cleaning company, it wouldn't be a problem, right? The stuff was supposed to be in Fred's drawer so we could just sneak in and outta here with no one the wiser. That way we wasn't going to need no one else and now this whole thing has turned to shit. I think we oughta just pack it in and get outta here."

Tiffany swung around. "No fucking way. I'm not giving up."

"But Babe..."

"No buts, you moron. Those contracts are mine. That money is mine. Fred owes it to me after stiffing me like he did."

Julian thought for a moment, wondering how she arrived at that conclusion since, really, if they belonged to anyone, they belonged to Candace. He and Tiffany were just stealing them, which was okay since that's what they did but, unlike Tiffany, he believed in being honest about his criminal behavior. Unfortunately, he was dumb enough to say so. "Well, actually no. I mean, Fred is the one who put up the money for the contracts so Candace—"

He didn't get any further because Tiffany conked him over the head with her gun. He dropped to the concrete floor.

Damn. That hurt! He could sense Tiffany standing over him, but he played dead, or rather unconscious, since he wasn't in any hurry to get conked again, and while he lay there playing dead, he began to seriously have second thoughts about this stupid plan of Tiffany's. Fuck, he didn't even understand it. Futures contracts? What the hell. Now that he thought about it, he decided he was just going to stay on the floor a while longer, or at least until Tiffany left, and then he was getting out of here while the getting was good.

She continued to stand there but he kept his mouth shut, and his eyes closed, even when she muttered a few curse words at him and gave him a solid kick in the ribs for good measure. He was okay with that because then she left. Once she was gone, he jumped to his feet and skedaddled.

He didn't get far.

The bullet hit him before he heard the bang, but he definitely heard Tiffany's voice when she stood over him and said, "You know, Julian, if I didn't love you so much, I'd kill you."

"I love you too, Babe," he mumbled and then fell into a deep dark hole of unconsciousness.

* * * *

Candace pressed her ear to the side of the tank, listening for Tiffany and Julian, but all was silent. Either they gave up and moved elsewhere in their quest to find her and Gabe, or they got smart enough to stay quiet, hoping Candace and Gabe would be fooled into making some kind of noise. If it was just Julian out there with a gun and evil intent, Candace would feel pretty comfortable, but this was Tiffany they were talking about, and, in spite of the insipid charade, Tiffany was a lot smarter than she appeared, as well as relentless. If Candace were taking bets, she'd stake everything she owned—which wasn't much these days—that Tiffany still skulked around the tanks, just waiting for her chance to pounce.

Suddenly they heard the sound of a gunshot. "Damn, she's shooting again." In the dim light shining through the open hatch, she could barely see Gabe, but she could feel him standing close to her, his breath warm in her ear. She groped for his hand.

"You know if they find us in this tank, it will be like shooting ducks in a barrel."

Did he need to remind her? She was already scared shitless. Once upon a time, actually not too long ago, she had thought being on the back of Gabe's motorcycle was the ultimate in scary, but now she realized she hadn't really experienced true fear. Her breath scraped in and out of her chest in erratic bursts as she thought about dying. She didn't want to die. She was still young. She hadn't done all the things she wanted to do. She wanted to learn how to ski. Maybe learn to play the organ, like her mom wanted, or the guitar, which sounded easier, and she wanted to visit Rome someday, and Paris, the city of love.

And, she suddenly realized, she wanted to have children. "I don't want to die."

The liquid chocolate swirled around her as he moved closer. His front pressed up against her back and arms surrounded her. Warm lips touched her neck. "We're not going to die," he whispered.

Easy for him to say. "How do you know? She's never going to give up. She's like a damned virus. There's no cure."

He snorted with surpassed laughter. His tongue touched her check and he licked. "Mmm. Tasty."

Regardless of the danger they were in, a hot shaft of desire shot through her. She turned to face him and looped her arms around his neck. Lifting a hand, she searched for his lips and once she located them, rose on her toes and kissed him. If she was going to die, she wanted one last taste of him, even if the taste was more chocolate than Gabe. "Yum."

The next thing she knew, Gabe hoisted her up in his arms and his lips were all over her. This is what she wanted. She wrapped her legs around his waist and held on and she could feel his maleness even through the layers of fabric separating them.

"We're not going to die," he said again, and for those few moments she believed him because his arms represented security and strength and protection although the hand creeping down her back and reaching under her skirt to stroke her ass represented something all-together different.

His tongue probed hers. It tasted of chocolate, but not ready-for-the-consumer chocolate. This was raw chocolate liquor that needed sugar, and milk, and, obviously their secret ingredients from *The Recipe*, which was why, as much as she loved to continue to taste him, the taste reminded her they needed to get their asses out of the chocolate and do something.

"How do you know we won't die?"

"I won't let it happen. I have too much to lose." He nuzzled her neck, sending a shiver up her spine.

Aww. "Yeah. About that." She cleared her throat. "I just need to tell you…I mean, I want you to know… I don't hate you."

She heard him chuckle.

"I know."

"How do you know?"

"I know you. You wouldn't sleep with me if you hated me. You're the most honest person I know. You drive me crazy, but you're not sneaky."

Okay, now she felt embarrassed because in the beginning, she did have ulterior motives. "Well…" She stopped. Probably best not to go there. "Can I ask you a question?" She needed to ask because there this small kernel of doubt that still existed. She hated that she doubted but her doubt existed because so much was left unsaid between them. She needed to get it out in the open.

"Sure. Ask away." His breath ruffled her hair as he spoke. It ruffled her heart, and her mind and her body too.

She took a deep breath. "Why don't you want Contessa?"

There was a long pause before he answered. "This really bothers you, doesn't it?"

"Yes, it does. I don't understand it."

Another long pause. She was glad he paused because it meant he took her question seriously and thought about it. Finally, "I love Contessa but to me it's like adopting an eighteen-year-old. The job is done. There's nothing of me in it. It's full-grown, the course set, and nothing I do will change that fact, except maybe for the negative. Now Sweet Remembrances? That's my baby. I gave birth to it. I planned and schemed and dreamed it. I've coddled and nurtured and made it what it is. I love it, and I'm looking forward to making it as successful a company as Contessa."

His sincerity was evident in every word he uttered. He didn't want Contessa, but it was his anyway, and it broke her heart, because it was entirely possible she loved him. What she felt certainly wasn't a crush, and it wasn't infatuation, like when she was eighteen. It felt like love, like the real thing where people got married and bought a house and had kids and everything. This was real, and forever, and no way did she want to give this up because of fake Tiffany.

The problem was this... this... thing with the business would always stand in the way. Love was out there waiting for her to grab, but how long would love last in the face of her desire to have Contessa and her resentment that it wasn't hers?

A weak, "Okay," was the best she could manage.

He kept silent for a minute. Then, "There's something else."

"No, that's okay. I get it. You're on your way to big things. Even if you don't want it, you're going to take over the candy world, but maybe I can—'

He clapped his hand over her mouth. "I'm going to sell you the company."

She yanked his hand away. "No, you— Wait. What?" *What did he just say?*

"I said, I'm going to sell you the company."

That's what she thought he said, but she didn't believe it. It must be a con. "You can't do that."

"Why not?"

Why not? Hmmm. Good question. She thought for a minute. "First of all, I can't afford it."

He chuckled. "I'll give you a good price."

Hah! She knew it. It was totally a con. She knew exactly how it would go: she would give him her money, then he would up the ante and when she couldn't cough up the extra dough, he would renege. Just let him try. He'd never get a dime. Not even a penny. Not that she had more than a few thousand in the bank right now, and the prospect for future thousands was slim as well.

She shook her head, squashing her doubt, because she knew that her suspicions were wrong. Gabe wouldn't cheat her. Just to prove it, she said, "Okay, you want to sell me the company, I'll give you ten bucks."

Groping in the darkness, he grabbed her hand. He shook it. "Deal."

What! Blood rushed to her head then suddenly left it, leaving her dizzy. She grabbed his arm to keep from falling over. "No way! You are so full of it."

He grinned. "No. Seriously. It's a deal. I'll sell you Contessa for ten dollars.

"What! You can't do that."

"Okay, maybe not ten dollars, but cheap, really cheap."

She could hear in his voice that Gabe truly meant it. The problem was it was probably illegal. Still, her heart yearned toward the solution Gabe offered.

She sighed. "I don't think it's legal."

Gabe pulled her into a hug and rested his chin on top of her head. "No, it's legal but it's a little tricky. I can't just sell you a company worth hundreds of millions of dollars for ten bucks or so. The IRS will consider it a gift and I'll get taxed out the wazoo. We'll have the lawyers figure out some kind of contract."

Her heart broke all over again. He teased her, taunted her with her heart's desire... well, actually Gabe was her heart's desire since it became clear she loved him with all her heart, but she also realized that, unless they could resolve this issue of who owned Contessa, she couldn't have Gabe either. The thought of having neither left her feeling dead inside. "Well, thanks, but no thanks."

"Look, it'll be a ninety-nine-year contract. You'll pay me a nominal amount each year."

She inhaled deeply. The rich scent of chocolate filled her nostrils, reminding her all over again what was at stake. "What about when the ninety-nine years is up?"

He laughed. "What do you care? We'll both be dead."

Right. She mulled it over. "What's a nominal amount?"

"I don't know." He thought for a moment. "There's a lot to consider tax-wise. Why don't we visit the attorneys, work out a plan?"

Every part of her yearned toward his offering. Her heart pounding in her chest, she nodded, even though he couldn't see it. After all, what did she have to lose?

Although maybe the better question was, what did she have to gain?

The answer was simple. Everything.

Suddenly everything made sense. All the ups, the downs, the anger, the crazy happiness, all added up to love. She loved Gabe. And the doubts? There were none. It wasn't the crush she'd had when she was eighteen. Nor was it the nostalgic memory of a love enhanced by time and a bad memory.

This was *I want to be with you the rest of my life. I want to wake up next to you every morning, morning breath or not. I want to celebrate with you in the good times and comfort you through the bad times* love. She wanted to tell him right now, but now was not the time. Right now, they had bigger problems.

Standing on her tiptoes, she wrapped her arms around his chocolate-covered neck, and gave him a slow, sweet, tongue-laden kiss.

"That's to seal the deal," she whispered. "Now, how do we escape?"

22 Love Can Conquer All But a Gun Does It Better.

His heart gave a giant leap, threatening to explode out of his chest. Damn, what was she doing to him? His heart raced, and his mouth went dry, and his brain grew so fuzzy he could barely think. He'd never felt like this before.

Okay, so he felt great because he made her happy. Big deal. It wasn't as if he did something great. All he did was find a solution to what they both wanted. Yet this amazing emotion filled him up. If their lives weren't in danger, he would bay at the moon in exhilaration.

Why? Why did he feel this way?

Words like love and forever hovered on the tip of his tongue but he discarded them because even the idea of being in love made his heart pound and sweat break out on his forehead.

He scrolled through his thoughts again, and once again that word, *love,* presented itself but this time it didn't flit away. It stayed. It lingered and dug itself deeper into his mind and into his heart, leaving behind a sense of rightness, of completeness.

What the hell? Was he in love? He listened to the uneven tenor of Candace's breathing, felt her tremble under his hands, and his heart pounded with fear for her. The idea of someone hurting her scared the crap out of him. She didn't deserve this. She deserved everlasting love, and a ring on her finger, and the two-point three kids. Wait, wasn't that now one point-six kids? Whatever, she deserved it all. His kids. His ring. His love. Crap, he *was* in love! Even better; he loved her, which was a very different thing from being in love. It was deeper, more intense, it was forever. It was just more.

He opened his mouth to tell her all this but what came out was, "I have a plan."

"Right," she said. She didn't sound confident in his abilities which sucked. Granted, Tiffany had a gun, and he didn't, plus she had Julian—useless as he was—and he didn't, but he had a plan, and they didn't. Actually, Tiffany did have a plan, it just wasn't one constructed out of terror. People would be shocked at how creative someone like Gabe could get when motivated by terror, especially when the terror he felt wasn't for himself but for Candace.

"I saw there's a catwalk along the ceiling, right?"

"Right." She still didn't sound convinced.

"If I can get up on the catwalk, I can distract them which will give you time to escape and call the cops."

"They'll shoot you." Her voice was flat.

No point in telling her, in addition to dogs, he was afraid of heights, never mind that he wasn't crazy about the idea of bullet holes in his body. She depended on him, as the bigger, stronger person, to save them.

"They'll have to shoot at me through the grids of the catwalk and the grids are pretty solid. The odds are astronomical that a bullet would get through all those tiny openings. Anyway, I don't plan on standing still long enough for them to get a good shot."

"I don't like your plan."

Oh, shit. "Okay, have you got a better one?"

"No. I just don't want you going out there by yourself." She paused.

He winced because he knew what would come next.

"I'll go with you," she said.

Yep, that was it. "No."

"Yes."

"No."

"Yes!"

Their argument was conducted in whispers, but it was still an argument. "No," he tried one more time although he knew at this point he'd been defeated.

She jabbed him on his upper arm. "Ow!" he protested. Quietly. "All right, fine. Go ahead, get shot. See if I care." Yet he did care, a lot, and to prove it, he grabbed her, hiked her up so her lips were reachable, and gave her a long, slow kiss, pouring into it all the rampant, contradictory, hot, burning emotion that filled him. God, he wanted her in every possible way. Because, yes, he could finally admit he loved her.

With a sigh, she finally slid her lips away from his. "You don't mean that," she said. Her hand strayed to his chest, and her fingers stroked his collar bone.

"No, I don't."

"So I'm coming with you, right?"

"Candace. No. Please."

Another sigh. He knew he needed to say the right thing. After a minute, it came to him. "Look, if, while I'm trying to escape, I have to watch out for you, it will distract me, and I could get caught." He knew it was dirty pool, but he didn't care. If he thought it would do any good, he would order her to stay but he knew it would have just the opposite effect. Although, he had never *really* tried ordering her. "Whether you like it or not, you're staying here," he said in a tone offering no compromise.

She growled. "This is a partnership," she said. "Not a master/slave relationship where you tell me what to do and I meekly obey."

Crap. When you looked at it that way, she had a point. Still... "Please. It would kill me if you got hurt."

She huffed. "Fine. I'll stay here. Just don't think it's because I'm obeying you." She said the words, but she didn't sound convincing.

"Promise me," he said in a demanding voice because he didn't trust her. "Fine."

"I said I'd stay, and I will."

He grabbed her hands and checked her fingers to make sure they weren't crossed, making her promise null and void. They weren't. "Okay. Good."

Feeling around in the darkness, he located the ladder and quietly climbed up to the top. He carefully poked his head out of the opening and looked around. Nothing. "Looks good," he whispered, and climbed out of the hole. He got to his feet, crouching so he made a low profile while he scanned the floor below him for movement. The next thing he knew, Candace was next to him. She looked at him, rolled her eyes, and shrugged.

"Sorry," she mouthed, which irked him as he knew that she knew he couldn't argue with her now they were out in the open as Tiffany and Julian would hear them.

"I just couldn't get over the master/slave thing. Like I said, this is a partnership, including taking equal risk," she whispered then pointed at the overhead catwalk. "Can you reach it?"

He surrendered and admitted that if he was going to spend the rest of his life with Candace, which it appeared he was, he would have to admit he wouldn't be able to control her. She had her own thoughts, her own desires, and her own way of doing things, and the sooner he admitted it, the happier both of them would be. Leaning forward, he planted a hard kiss on her lips.

They both took a moment to scrape off as much of the liquid chocolate as they could so it didn't drip down to the floor and give them away.

He pulled himself up onto the metal platform and pulled Candace up beside him. Moving carefully, they traversed the length of the narrow walkway until they reached a ladder they could climb down. He looked around, checking out the space below then scanned the enormous space filled with machinery. The door to the street was about twenty feet away. Nothing stirred. "It looks clear. Let's go."

They quickly, and quietly, slid down the ladder, then tip-toed along a narrow aisle. Ahead, they could see the tall door leading to the outside, freedom and safety.

Still in front, Gabe rounded a corner, and stopped so short Candace ran into his back.

"What...? Geez, Gabe!"

"Look." He pointed, a sinking feeling constricting his chest as he stared at the slack face of the limp, leisure-suit clad body sprawled out on the concrete floor.

Candace poked her head around him and gawked at the still body at his feet. "Is that blood?" she whispered, pointing at the dark circle covering the light blue velour zip-up jacket.

Gabe nodded. He felt as horrified as Candace looked. Julian was a creep, never mind a terrible dresser, but he didn't deserve to get shot, although some people would consider still wearing a leisure suit in the Twenty-First century a criminal offense.

Candace reached out a hand to grab Gabe's. He was happy to hold her hand as well since seeing dead people wasn't exactly high on his bucket list. "Is he dead?" she asked, echoing his fear.

Suddenly one of Julian's eyes popped open. "I ain't dead," he whispered as the other eye opened so he could look wildly around.

"No, but you're going to be any second now, you stupid ass," a voice said behind them.

They turned. Unsurprisingly, it was Tiffany. And her gun.

* * * *

"Give it up, Tiffany," Candace said with a sigh. "I'm not going to give you the combination for the safe and I'm not going to give you the contracts."

Bang! The tip of Candace's running shoe disappeared.

"Holy shit, you bitch!" Candace yelped.

"Are you crazy?" Gabe swore.

Tiffany laughed. "No, just greedy." She glanced down at Julian who still lay on the floor staring up at Tiffany with terror on his face. "Come on, you little prick. Get your lazy ass up off the floor and help me."

Julian shook his head. Candace grimaced. Either Julian had grown a pair, or he was stupid. Candace voted for stupid.

When Julian didn't move, Tiffany kicked him in the side. "Get up!"

"Nuh uh." He shook his head again.

Bang! The gun went off again. Julian screamed and grabbed his thigh.

Candace gasped. Without thinking, she lunged forward, but Gabe's arm tightened around her shoulders, holding her back. "Don't," he whispered in her ear. "She's out of control."

He was right, Tiffany was "'round the bend," even willing to kill her own lover in pursuit of money.

"Oh, gee. I'm so sorry," Tiffany said in a saccharine voice as she stared down at Julian. "Did I hurt you." She nudged him with the toe of her shoe.

Julian howled. "You gotta help me. I'm bleeding to death. I need a doctor."

"Tsk, tsk," Tiffany said, her voice full of regret as she stared down at Julian. "Maybe later, when I'm not so busy." Her eyes rose and Candace felt a frisson of fear ripple down her spine as Tiffany's fingers tightened on the trigger of the gun.

"Okay. Enough bullshit. We're going to Fred's office and you're going to open that frickin' safe and give me those contracts."

Candace threw a look at Gabe. His lips were tight with fury, but worry wrinkled his brow, and his dark brown eyes held fear. Candace darted a look toward the outer door, silently asking if they should run.

He gave a slight shake of his head.

Okay, then maybe they could just stall.

Tiffany's gun poked her in the back.

All righty, so no stalling.

"Tiffany," Gabe said, his voice tight with tension. "You don't want to do this."

Candace swung her head around to stare at Gabe in astonishment. Obviously, Tiffany did want to do this. Didn't he see the gun in her hand and the evil gleam in her eyes?

She gave him a poke in the side.

Tiffany laughed. "Oh, my God, you are so naïve. Of course, I want to do this," she said, verbalizing Candace's thought. "I want to be rich, and this is the only way."

"You'll go to prison."

"Only if I'm caught," was her response. "And I don't plan on getting caught."

Gabe's hand tightened on Candace's because the implication was obvious. She wouldn't get caught because Gabe and Candace wouldn't be around to make sure it happened. They would just be another unsolved New York City murder; that was, if their bodies were even found.

Tiffany waved the gun at them. "Go," she ordered.

Out of options, they went.

It was the walk of doom. With the sun now set and just a few overhead lights on, dark shadows loomed over them as she and Gabe slowly walked the length of the factory until they reached the stairs taking them to the executive suite level. The smell of chocolate and cleaning fluid seemed heightened by her fear. As they approached the staircase, Candace slowed. Apparently, she was going to stall after all. Once they reached the executive floor, they would be shit-out-of-luck. There would be no place to run, no place to hide, so it was now or never.

"Why are you stopping!"

This was so unfair. She hadn't even been able to tell Gabe she loved him. If she was ever going to tell him, now was the time to speak up. It was time for something else too.

Candace turned to face Gabe. She took his hands in hers. He gazed down at her, his brow wrinkled in puzzlement. "What?" he whispered.

Tiffany jabbed the gun in her ribs. "Move, damn it."

Candace looked over her shoulder and glared. "In a minute. I have something I need to say to Gabe first."

"Oh, for cryin' out loud." Tiffany rolled her eyes. "What? What do you need to say?"

Gazing into Gabe's eyes, Candace said, "Gabe, I love you."

He inhaled sharply, and his face softened. "God, Candace, I love you too."

Behind her, Tiffany snorted and muttered, "Jesus Christ, I'm going to be sick."

"Stuff it, Tiffany," Candace muttered out of the side of her mouth.

This earned another snort but nothing more.

Candace gritted her teeth but was determined to get the rest out. After all, their lives depended on it. "I'm sorry I didn't tell you before."

Gabe opened his mouth as if to say something, but Candace put her finger across his mouth, stopping him. He frowned.

"And I'd tell you how much I want to spend my life with you..." She stared intently up at him. "But..." She licked her lip. Blinked. Rolled her eyes back in her head then looked straight at him again, trying to inject her thoughts into her gaze. She took a deep, stuttering breath.

"But... Oh... Oh... I..."

His eyes narrowed. "Are you okay? You don't look good," he said slowly.

"No..." she started then stopped. Lifting a hand to her brow, she moaned. "I feel..." She peeked at him between her fingers then moaned again.

"Oh, poor baby" he responded then his fingers slowly uncurled from around her arms.

And Candace let herself go limp. Just long enough for Gabe to leap forward and grab Tiffany's arm.

Bang!

Gabe yelled and grabbed his arm. "Geez," he gasped out. "You shot me." He made another grab at the gun, but Tiffany smacked him in the face with it. He reeled backwards and fell. Tiffany swung back around, her arm lifting to aim at Candace, but Candace was ready for her. She straightened from her pseudo-faint and swung at Tiffany's stomach. Unfortunately, her fist glanced off Tiffany's arm, but at least it spoiled her aim. The shot flew up, hitting one of the metal catwalks.

The other woman screeched. "I'm going to kill you, you bitch." She brought her gun up to eye-level.

"You can certainly try, Ms. Tempest," a voice said from behind Candace. "But I don't recommend it."

Candace swung around. Five men in blue were lined up behind her nemesis, Sergeant Dolan, guns leveled at Tiffany.

Behind him was her mother, her eyes big as quarters. "Sorry we took so long. I got busy and forgot to check the bug."

What else was new?

23 And Then There Were None—
Okay, Actually, There Were Three

They were all there, all except for Tiffany and Julian, who were in jail where they deserved to be. The little Korean guy who had delivered Fred's pizzas for fifteen years wasn't there either, but there was no reason for him to be even though he inherited money, but everyone else was; Vanessa and her grotty twins, plus her boyfriend Arthur Middleton, who'd insisted on being with them, saying he didn't trust the cops. Go figure. Susan sat on the loveseat, looking bored as she filed her fingernails. Murray and Junior finally showed up, better late than never, and immediately squatted on the remaining comfortable couch in the apartment leaving everyone else to either stand or sit on the straight-backed dining room chairs they hauled into the living room. Even Anthony, the super, came since he was Julian's cousin and he had helped fill in a lot of the missing pieces of Tiffany's plot that she refused to talk about.

The standees were Wendy, Gabe and Candace, and half a dozen police officers. Oh, and Floyd, who lurked in the background, his eyes darting around the room as if he couldn't wait to escape. How she and Wendy ended up standing, since this was their home, Candace still couldn't figure out, but she couldn't say she minded as it gave her the opportunity to lean against Gabe while he put his arm around her. It also allowed her to keep everyone else in the room in view.

Of course, Sergeant Dolan stood, having called the meeting.

It was a real Agatha Christie moment.

Taking his place in front of the room, Dolan cleared his throat. Everyone snapped to attention, similar to what they had done two weeks ago when Fred's goodies were going to be distributed, only this time no one looked at all excited about the outcome.

"I've asked you all to be here to talk about who killed Fred Jones."

A flurry of conversation filled the air, the gist of which was, "We thought Tiffany killed Fred."

Yeah, Candace had thought so too, despite the showgirl's denial, until Dolan told Candace differently after Tiffany and Julian were arrested. But today Dolan would announce the real culprits, and they would get what was coming to them. Candace couldn't wait.

Their (un)friendly neighborhood detective paced slowly around the room. "This was an unusual case." Stopping, he opened a small notepad he held. He flipped through several pages, checking out his notes, muttering a few *"hmmms"* as he read. Finally, he looked up. "Interesting case. Lots of twists and turns and contradictory information so it took us a while to determine how he was killed."

The man should be an actor; he had great timing because after a long, pregnant pause, it forced Junior—the sacrificial toad—to finally croak, "Yeah, okay, so what's the deal?"

Knowing the answer, Candace just chewed on a thumbnail, which still tasted like chocolate, so it was okay to gnaw on it, or at least that was what she told herself as she attempted to nibble it down to a nub. Until Gabe gently took her hand and lifted it to his mouth. He kissed her knuckles and smiled, then they both turned to watch the drama unfold.

"Yeah, we all know he was shot," Murray added.

Dolan nodded. "Yes, and we even found the gun that shot him." He pulled a baggie from inside his coat and held it out for everyone to see the small revolver inside. He turned and leveled a steely stare on Lance. "Recognize this?"

Lance shook his head back and forth. "Nuh uh. Not my gun," he said as the shaking got faster and faster.

"Really? It had your fingerprints on it. So it must be your gun, which means you're the one who shot Fred Jones."

Lance's eyes bulged until they approached Murray's toad territory. "No! I didn't! It wasn't me." His gaze darted wildly around the room then landed on Lucy, sitting across from him on one of the sofas. "It was her! She shot Fred!" he yelled, pointing a finger. "Then she threw the gun at me, and I caught it. That's why my fingerprints are on the gun."

Lucy jumped up and lunged at Lance. "Shut the fuck up, you moron." She whacked him over the head. Lance threw his arms up to protect himself as Lucy continued to wallop her twin. Dolan grabbed Lucy, hauling her off her brother, holding her while she snarled and swung her fists vainly in her rage. "I'm going to kill you," she screamed.

"What?" Lance yelled back. "Like you killed Fred? It was your stupid idea. I told you it was a dumb idea." He turned to face the detective. "I thought all we were gonna do was get those letters Mom kept going on and on about." He pointed at his sister. "She said all we were going to do was find the book where Mom hid them. 'It'll be easy,' she said, but she didn't even look for the book. She went right to the safe. She kept talking about how there had to be valuable shit inside. Only she couldn't get into the safe because she didn't have the key. So she started getting mad." He tugged at the ring on his upper lip, a look of panic on his face. "Next thing I know, she's got a gun in her hand, and she shoots the lock out."

Candace blinked. She couldn't believe the deluge of words coming out of Lance's mouth. No wonder Lucy finished all his sentences. Everything Lance said was either incriminating or incredibly stupid. But the deluge didn't stop there. Once the bottle was uncorked, Lance was going to spill everything.

"And she calls me a moron," he continued. "Everybody knows you don't bring a gun to a burglary. It's just asking for trouble, but she did, and she didn't tell me. How was I to know she would bring a gun and be dumb enough to actually shoot it?" He turned to Vanessa. "Like, I'm sorry, but you just kept bugging us and we couldn't take it anymore."

"Lance!" Vanessa gasped. "Yes, I wanted my letters back, but I never said for you to rob the safe." She turned and jabbed an accusatory finger at Lucy. "And I certainly didn't tell you to shoot Fred!"

Lucy wilted. "I didn't mean to," she whispered. A mascara-blackened tear trailed down her cheek. "It was an accident. I was trying to get into the safe and I was getting frustrated so I just shot the stupid lock off but when

I opened the safe, there was nothing in there except that stupid red box but when I opened the box there was nothing in it either."

"Nothing? Are you sure?" Candace jumped in, hoping against hope.

"Nothing! Not a damned thing. And I was so pissed, then I turned around and there was Fred sitting in his recliner, kinda just staring at me, and it scared the crap out of me and I jumped and my finger just pulled the trigger." She burst into tears. "It was an accident."

All this over a bunch of letters? "What the hell was in those letters, Vanessa?" Candace asked. Whatever they contained, it better reveal something pretty spectacular or she would to be so disappointed.

Vanessa turned white, then red. Covering her face with her hands, she moaned. "Oh, please. I don't want to talk about it."

Walking over to stand in front of her, Dolan ordered, "You need to tell us what was in those letters. It might be material evidence."

"It's not. I promise it's not," she wailed. Turning to her boyfriend, Arthur, she buried her head in his shoulder. "Make them stop."

Candace exchanged a look with Gabe. Good God. It seemed the Stiff wasn't so stiff any longer, in fact she had folded like ten-day-old celery.

Arthur wrapped his arms around Vanessa. "Vanessa, you need to tell them."

"No! You'll hate me."

"Vanessa..." Arthur grabbed her shoulders and shook her gently.

"Oh, all right," Vanessa answered.

"No! Don't do it, Vanessa."

Everyone turned to stare at Anthony. Eyes darting wildly around the room, his shoulders rose defensively until his head almost disappeared, like a turtle into its shell. A sickly smile appeared. "Uh..."

"I'm sorry, Anthony. It seems I must." Turning, she walked stiffly to the bookcase and scanned the shelves. "Well, unless someone moved them, they must still be where I hid them." She pulled down a book and opened it. Inside was a thin bundle of letters. Taking it out, she handed it to Dolan then turned to Lucy. "You didn't even look," she accused.

Dolan opened the letters and perused them. "Good grief," he muttered under his breath. His gaze went back and forth between Vanessa and Anthony.

Anthony turned red. Vanessa wilted even further. Arthur's jaw tightened. "Vanessa," he said, disappointment rife in his voice.

"I told you!" she responded and burst into noisy sobs.

Candace shared another look with Gabe. He looked as gob smacked as she felt. Who'da thought?

"Vanessa, I don't understand, if the letters were that big a deal, why you didn't take them with you when you left Fred," Candace asked.

"You know I left after Fred and I had a fight, and then I simply forgot about them but then I started dating Arthur and I suddenly remembered and I was just mortified that someone might read them and tell Arthur and I knew that would be disastrous." She sent a pleading look in his direction.

There was a long silence during which everyone stared awkwardly at each other, no one wanting to be the first to speak.

Finally Dolan broke the silence. "Okay. Moving on." He waved over one of the uniformed officers, keeping one hand clamped on Lucy's shoulder so she wouldn't run. "You're both under arrest," he told the twins.

The officer approached and pulled out handcuffs, then snapped them on.

Lance squawked. Lucy whimpered then burst into tears.

"Take them both downtown and book them," Dolan instructed the officer.

"Murder one?" he asked.

Dolan shook his head with a sigh. "Not murder. As amazing as it seems, they didn't actually kill the victim."

That elicited a gasp and a flurry of questions from the others in the room.

"Then why are you arresting them?" Vanessa asked.

Dolan ran a hand over his face, looking tired and depressed. "I don't know. I'll think of something. Desecration of a corpse. Attempted burglary. I'm sure there's other things we can charge them with, but I'll have to think about it."

After a brief struggle and major weeping and handwringing on the part of Vanessa, two officers led the twins out, with Vanessa and Arthur trailing in their wake. Anthony, the super, slunk out after them with a guilty look on his face. No one protested his departure.

Another long silence descended except a muttered, "What a coupla dopes," from Junior. Like he could afford to talk.

Candace shared a look with her mother, who looked back at her and rolled her eyes. At least now they knew why the twins kept showing up. Sort of. But she knew this wasn't the end of it by a long shot (geez, terrible choice of words) but they were all instructed to stay silent, and as hard as it was to do, she would.

Susan raised her hand. "I don't understand. Lucy did shoot Fred, right?"

"Dumb as the two of them are," Dolan answered Susan, "I'd love to book them for murder however, they didn't kill Fred Jones since he was already dead when Lucy shot him."

"What!" Murray struggled to get out of his chair, not an easy task given his bulk. "What do you mean he was already dead?" Murray demanded. "From what?"

"Well, this is where it got interesting. We almost wrote it up as death by gunshot but then the coroner found the Petechial hemorrhaging."

"Huh? Pet-what?" Junior asked.

"Petechial hemorrhaging. It's tiny broken capillaries in the whites of the eyes which occurs from lack of oxygen, i.e., when someone is suffocated. If he'd died from a gunshot, he wouldn't have Petechial hemorrhaging."

Murray sat down abruptly. "So someone strangled him?"

"Not strangled. Suffocated. Probably with a pillow."

Susan made a face. "Are you telling me Fred let someone sneak up on him with a pillow? I don't believe it. He wouldn't be so stupid but even if he was, he'd fight back. So you need to explain to me how that happened."

"Glad to," Dolan said, and smiled a sinister smile.

Great, they were finally getting to the important part, Candace thought, leaning forward eagerly, not wanting to miss anything. She was dying to blurt out what she knew but Gabe grabbed her knee and squeezed to shut her up. She transferred her attention to Dolan as the detective paced the short width of the living room, back and forth, back and forth. Any more pacing on the part of the detective and she was going to need a chiropractor for her neck.

"As to the how, an analysis of the contents of his stomach proved he ingested an almost lethal dose of benzodiazepine pills, specifically Valium, along with a fair amount of alcohol."

"Huh?" again from Junior.

"Sedatives. That, combined with the martini in his system, was almost enough to kill him. Once he was unconscious, it was easy for the murderer to finish him off with a pillow."

Another silence followed Dolan's statement then two sets of bulgy toad eyes, and Susan's more normal ones, turned to stare malevolently at Candace and Wendy.

"Hey. Not me. I was at the spa," Wendy said. "Getting my massage and having my nails done. All day." She held her hands out so everyone could see the pale rose polish on each nail. "Anyway, I don't drink, and I don't know how to make a martini. Ask Candace." She threw a glance at Candace.

Candace nodded then raised her hands in front of herself. "Don't look at me. I was also out. Otherwise I would have seen Lucy and Lance come in."

Dolan held a hand up, indicating he had the floor. "The doorman said Mister Jones called down at twelve-thirty about a package he was expecting. According to the same doorman, he sounded fine at that time. At two o'clock, Floyd Daniels was seen leaving the building. Ten minutes later Lance and Lucy entered and went upstairs where they subsequently shot an already dead Fred Jones.

"Now this is when it starts to get interesting. With the amount of drugs in his system," Dolan continued, "Mister Jones would have been unconscious within a half hour of drinking the martini, which we believe was laced with the sedative. So, by our estimates, it means he was probably given that drink sometime between the time he spoke to the doorman—twelve-thirty—and two o'clock when Lance and Lucy arrived. So, the culprit must be someone with access to him in that short timeframe and was trusted enough to serve him a drink.

As one, everyone in the room turned to stare at Floyd. His eyes widened. "Eep!" he squeaked as he shook his head in denial, but it didn't stop him from backpedaling toward the door leading to the closest escape route. An escape route quickly cut off by two uniformed officers blocking the door.

"No!" he protested as they grabbed his arms. "I'm innocent. I didn't do it."

"No?" Dolan responded. He turned and walked down the hall to Floyd's bedroom. Since the investigation seemed to have changed locales, the uniformed cops dragged a protesting Floyd along as well and pushed him up against a wall once inside the bedroom.

Dolan waved the other detective toward the attached bathroom. "Franklin, I'll let you do the honors," he said.

With a nod, the other detective, tall, slender, and friendly looking, with his round cheeks and round glasses, pulled out a pair of latex gloves and snapped them on. "Wouldn't want to leave any doubts about whatever we find." He opened the dresser drawers and rifled through them. Finding nothing, he moved over to the nightstand. Still nothing. After a moment, he yanked the sheets off the bed, then pulled the mattress onto the floor. Sitting on top of the box springs was a pill bottle.

"Hah," Franklin said, and lifted an amber-colored plastic prescription bottle. He held it out for everyone to read the printed label on the front. Everyone surged forward, craning their necks so they could read the small type.

"Valium," Susan said, her face grim.

Floyd pointed a shaky hand at the evidence. "That's not mine," he yelled. "Someone planted it."

Dolan heaved a big sigh and shared a look with Gabe. "The world is full of nothing but innocent people, and it seems like I get all of them." Without touching the small bottle, he pointed at the name typed on the bottle. "Floyd Daniels. Take one three times daily. When we get it to the lab, I'll bet it has your fingerprints on the bottle."

Floyd blinked. His mouth puckered as if he were going to cry, and he heaved a big sigh. "He told me he was going to change his will and fire me," he said. "I'm too old to be looking for another job. I had to do something."

"But you're not too old to go to prison for murder," Gabe said, his voice heavy with anger. What, he was supposed to feel sorry for the bastard? Not a chance.

"A trial will decide," Dolan said then turned to the uniformed officer holding Floyd's arm. "Take him downtown and book him. We'll sort this out later."

"Wait!" Candace yelled.

Gabe jumped. "Geez, what now?"

The officer stopped.

"Floyd, what about *The Recipe*?" she asked, her throat tight with tension. "Do you know where it is?"

Floyd sneered. "No, but if I did, I certainly wouldn't tell you."

Candace sagged. Gabe pulled her to his side, offering what support he could. She looked up at him and felt a tear trickle down her cheek. With a grimace of sympathy, he wiped it way with his thumb.

It was quiet for a few minutes then Wendy shrugged. "Good heavens. The butler did it." She glanced at Candace. "Don't you dare say a word."

Candace just blinked, left with nothing to say.

"And on that note," Susan said. "I guess it's time to wrap this up. It's my night to play bridge and I've got a lot of things to do before everyone arrives."

Gabe groaned. "Good God, Mom, is that all you can say? That's pretty heartless."

"Listen, young man, Fred was our bridge alternate so he would understand I need to find a fourth for tonight. It's not easy to find good bridge players, and for your information, we canceled the last two Wednesdays in his honor so I'm not completely heartless." With that pronouncement, she grabbed her purse and left.

In the void created by the absence of her dynamic personality, the remaining non-suspects fidgeted awkwardly. Finally, Murray cleared his throat. "Guess we should leave too. Nothing more to do here and I have a meeting with my photographer and my editor to select the pictures for my next book and I need time to pick out a dress and apply my makeup." He grabbed Junior's arm and they followed Susan out the door.

Dolan shared a look with Candace and Gabe. "I won't ask." Shaking his head, he shoved the small notepad he carried into the breast pocket of his suit coat. "This has to be the weirdest case I've ever conducted, and I'd bet money it's going to get weirder before it's done, but I'll keep you informed." With a nod, he left. The remaining cops followed.

Now that their crowd was reduced to a mere three, the silence was deafening. It all felt sort of unfinished.

Determined to find the silver lining in this pile of shit, Candace said, "Well, at least you can use your soaking tub again, Mom."

Wendy blinked. "Why would I do that? I never used it before."

Closing her eyes, Candace dropped her head into her hands. "Oh, Mom."

Wendy lifted her chin enough she could look down her nose at Candace. "I think I'll go take a *shower*," she said pointedly, and left.

Gabe put his arms around Candace and pulled her close. His chin rested on Candace's head as he rocked her.

"I was hoping one of them had *The Recipe*," she mumbled into his chest.

"I know. I'm sorry it didn't work out like you wanted."

"Hey, y'all," a voice blared from behind them.

Candace jumped. She turned to find Fred's fifth, and last, wife by the door, guitar case in hand as she kicked off her cowboy boots.

Candace's mouth dropped. "Hillary, what are you doing here?"

Ex-wife number five dropped her overnight bag. "Well, I was hopin' y'all would put me up for a few days. Did I get here in time for Fred's funeral?"

"No, we cremated him four days ago," Gabe told her after clearing his throat.

"Who're you?" Hillary asked, giving Gabe the once over, then she gave him a twice over, a gleam of interest in her eyes.

He reached out a hand, which she shook. "I'm Fred's son, Gabe." He put his arm around Candace's waist, hoping she took the hint. "And Candace's fiancé."

Her eyes widened. "Oh, right, I see that now. Yer dad showed me pitchers of you. Well, geez, I'm real sorry about what happened. I was hopin' I'd make it in time, but we only had the studio for a week so my producer wouldn't let me leave until this mornin'." She gave Candace a look of sympathy. "I'm sorry, girl. I liked the old buzzard even though he divorced me. So tell me what's going on."

Candace rubbed the back of her neck. "Sit," she said to Hillary.

Between the two of them, they filled the country western singer in on everything since the day Fred was murdered. Candace finished with, "And after all that, we never found *The Recipe* and without it, Contessa is doomed."

Hillary stood. Hands thrust on hips, she looked at Candace with disgust. "Well, shoot, girl, is that all?"

$\mathcal{E}p$ Forever and Ever, Amen
Randy Travis - 1987

Candace peered through the crack between the wide double doors and surveyed the crowd of people. Lots of people she hadn't seen in a while, some she didn't know, some she didn't even like, but what could she do, right?

Even though the reason for the gathering was different, it was weird how much today's crowd resembled the one held at the Sweet Tooth a few months ago. Murray came along with his son Junior, and low and behold, Junior actually brought a girlfriend, a girl named Dani who bore no resemblance to a frog whatsoever. Susan Jones came, once again breaking her rule of never coming to New York City except in October and at Christmas. She made up for her sin by wearing six pounds of diamonds and a fur wrap even though it was early September. The little Korean pizza guy came, for once leaving behind his delivery bicycle. Even the ravens, Mott and Mott decided to show up.

Obviously missing, but not missed, were Tiffany, Julian, and the Goth twins. They all had another event they needed to attend, preparing for their respective trials. However, Candace gave Vanessa props. Despite Lance and Lucy's incarceration, she and her beau, Arthur Middleton, who seemed to have put Vanessa's affair behind them, decided to attend. Vanessa didn't say much when she entered, but it said a lot that she came.

Candace took a deep breath, her heart clenching in her chest as she thought about everything that happened in the last few months. It could have been such a disaster but somehow, they pulled it out of the fire, in part because of her twangy friend, Hillary.

Glancing from the corner of her eye, Candace nodded at the petite country western singer, who looked totally appropriate for Nashville in her fringed skirt, fancy western shirt, and her cowboy boots. But New York City? Not so much. Hillary grinned and gave her a wink. Candace smiled back. After what Hillary did for them, Candace was willing to forgive any fashion faux pas Fred's last wife might commit. It gave Candace the shivers to think what might have happened if not for the day Hillary returned.

"*Well, geez, girl, is that all,*" Hillary had said in a dismissive tone, like losing a recipe worth millions was equivalent to losing one of the fake jewels on her bedazzled shirt.

Having dismissed Candace's distress, she marched into the TV room, scanned the wide expanse of bookshelves surrounding Fred's state-of-the-art eighty-five-inch television and eventually pulled out a narrow plastic CD case. Opening it, she held it out.

"Is this what y'all are lookin' for?" she had asked.

Sitting inside on top of a silver CD disk was a three-by-five card, yellowed and tattered, with *The Recipe* written on it in Fred's sloppy, back-sloping handwriting.

After Candace was done having heart failure and was able to catch her breath with Gabe's help (it only took two minutes of him pounding on her back for it to happen) she asked Hillary how she knew where to find *The Recipe.*

"Well, shit, girl. I ain't one to hold a grudge, you know, and even though we got divorced, we still were friends. That week, I had to make a quick trip to New York to get publicity photos done, so I didn't mind when he asked me to stop in and sign some papers. When I got here, he was foolin' around with that ol' tape machine of his, cursin' and swearin' up a storm 'cause the damned thing was eatin' up the tapes." She grinned. "Dumb ass. I told him he needed to save whatever he was trying to record digitally on the cloud but the idjit didn't trust anything he couldn't see or touch, so we decided on a CD."

Gabe shook his head, a reminiscent smile on his face. "My father was great at what he did for a living, but technology was not his thing."

"Don't I know it," Hillary returned. "I started my career in production, and I know all about taping and recordin', so I went out and bought him all this shit here." She pointed up at a shelf holding several pieces of video equipment including a camera. "I tried to show him how to use it, but it was like tryin' to teach a kindergartner how to build a spaceship, so I taped him while he did his thing, then we burned it into this here CD. Since this card was part of his will, he pulled it out and showed it to me then stashed it back in the same CD case. I think he wasn't payin' attention to what he was doin' as he was kinda busy kissin' me."

She frowned. "But now I think on it, you might want to watch that stuff we taped. Hang on." She turned the TV on and slid the CD into a slot in a machine under the television.

"Okay, you greedy bastards," Fred said from the television, looking larger than life and twice as cunning as when he was alive, but quite a few years older than the last video.

The new but not improved Fred chuckled. "Thought I'd start out the same as last time even though I've got some changes to make." He went on to list some of the changes, mostly to some charities he wanted to benefit as well as leaving money to employees who were new at Contessa since the last will.

"Also," he grumbled. "I guess I've gotta give something to that brother of mine. Looks like he finally got his act together and is earning a decent living, not that there's anything decent about writing porn." Eye roll. "Lastly, I'm NOT leaving anything to that bloodsucking lying cheat Floyd Daniels. He's lucky I don't have him arrested." He sighed. "But I guess I can't fire him. He's too old to get another job."

Candace and Gabe shared a look. So Floyd's main reason for killing Fred didn't actually exist. What a bummer, both for Floyd and for Fred.

There were a few more bequests, then Fred got to the main reason for the new will; yes, he was leaving Contessa to Gabe, but it was his dearest hope Candace and Gabe would end up together. Thanks to Candace's big mouth, he was aware of their little fling when they were young, but time had passed, they weren't kids anymore, and now it was time to get serious. If they married, Candace would get half of Contessa to co-own with Gabe.

There was more, but as far as Candace was concerned, she didn't need to hear anything else.

Wendy nudged her arm. "Candace," she said, making Candace startle as she came back to the present. "Are you ready?"

Candace shook out the skirt of her dress. She loved her dress, not just because it was gorgeous, but because it was the type of dress she never thought she'd wear. She just wished she had a little more cleavage to fill it out.

The massive double doors opened, music swelled, and everyone stood.

Hillary clicked the heels of her cowboy boots together for luck then stepped through the doors. Candace followed, Wendy at her side as they walked slowly toward Gabe who was standing next to his best man at the end of the long aisle, looking like a million bucks in his fancy tux and shiny shoes and his gorgeous hair all slicked back off his face for a change.

Looking like the man she loved, the man she was going to share a future with, share children with, share a long-held dream with.

Forever and ever, amen.

About the Author

KATY BERRITT started writing, a historical with herself as the heroine, when she was nine years old. Since there were no word processors then, all she got for her efforts was forty hand-written pages and a blister on her middle finger.

Working in the financial industry, a field not known for its sense of humor, she loves writing stories with a humorous slant that feature not-so-perfect heroes, quirky heroines and bizarre relatives.

Katy lives in New York City, a city rich in history, eccentric residents and fantastic neighborhoods, a treasure trove to draw upon when writing.

FACEBOOK - katyberrittauthor
INSTAGRAM - www.instagram.com/katyberrittauthor
WEBSITE - www. Katyberritt.com
EMAIL ADDRESS - katyberritt@gmail.com

Note from the Author

Word-of-mouth is crucial for any author to succeed. If you enjoyed *The Candy Capers*, please leave a review online—anywhere you are able. Even if it's just a sentence or two. It would make all the difference and would be very much appreciated.

Thanks!
KATY BERRITT

We hope you enjoyed reading this title from:

www.blackrosewriting.com

Subscribe to our mailing list – *The Rosevine* – and receive **FREE** books, daily deals, and stay current with news about upcoming releases and our hottest authors.
Scan the QR code below to sign up.

Already a subscriber? Please accept a sincere thank you for being a fan of Black Rose Writing authors.

View other Black Rose Writing titles at
www.blackrosewriting.com/books and use promo code
PRINT to receive a **20% discount** when purchasing.

www.ingramcontent.com/pod-product-compliance
Lightning Source LLC
Chambersburg PA
CBHW010733100726
47899CB00009B/3027

* 9 7 8 1 6 8 4 3 3 9 4 7 1 *